MW01148144

THE LEADERSHIP CRISIS

THE LEADERSHIP CRISIS

HOW AMERICA LOST THE MIDDLE EAST TO ISLAMIC EXTREMISTS

A NOVEL INSPIRED BY TRUE EVENTS FROM 1973 TO 1981

BY A. PATRICK & W.B. KING

The Leadership Crisis
How America Lost the Middle East to Islamic Extremists—A novel inspired by
true events from 1973 to 1981

Cover Photo Sources:
Washington International
Karl Schumarker
The History Guy

Graphic designer (cover art): Farrah Hussain

iUniverse books may be ordered through booksellers or by contacting:

iUniverse
1663 Liberty Drive
Bloomington, IN 47403
www.iuniverse.com
1-800-Authors (1-800-288-4677)

ISBN: 978-1-4759-7332-7 (sc)
ISBN: 978-1-4759-7333-4 (hc)
ISBN: 978-1-4759-7334-1 (e)

Library of Congress Control Number: 2013901376

Printed in the United States of America

iUniverse rev. date: 11/18/2014

Acknowledgements

This book is dedicated to the innocent lives lost, the families and loved ones separated from one another and all those who were impacted socially and economically due to the sequences of events recounted in these pages. The "untold truths" examined herein are significantly tragic historical events that have forever impacted world politics, especially in relation to the United States and the Middle East. The purpose of this book is to teach forthcoming generations that these unfortunate events and policies of the past should not be repeated.

From outline to fruition, this project benefited from countless supporters. In no particular order, A. Patrick and W.B. King wish to offer special thanks to the following people who helped make this book a reality: John and Nancy King, Laura Moulder (and John, Brianne, Jack, Aidan), Joe King (and Julie, Barrett, Ben), J.D. King, Reilly, Valerie Coleman Morris, Chris Coleman, John Kelly, Chris Nierman, Ed Caraballo, Farrah Hussain, Shaun and Lorena Toub, Laura Kwartler as well as many other dear friends, family members and colleagues!

The authors of this book will donate a portion of the proceeds to charities and non-for-profit organizations supporting education and medical aid to children impacted by war in the Middle East and the United States.

SECTION ONE

"There is nothing new in this world
except the history you don't know."

~ President Harry S. Truman

Chapter 1

Though she tried with a scraper, Diane Babel couldn't chip free the ice that adhered to her windshield like glue. It was a rough topography not easily traversed. She had forgotten her gloves. Her fingers were numb. It was early morning and the sun wasn't expected.

She was running late for class. Frustrated, she sat in the car as it slowly warmed. She passed her hand over the end of the dashboard where it met the sloped windshield; the forced air was cold but slightly warmer than outside. She rubbed her hands together, flexed the collar of her green tweed coat and slouched so her ears were covered. She sighed, waving her fingers through her chilled, smoky breath. Her hand fell to the radio dial, and soon the frigid air was filled with talk radio. It was eight a.m., news hour.

"The Egyptian uprising continues to offer hope and inspire its people. Some analysts say the Tunisian uprising has set off a domino effect that has reached Egypt and won't stop until it has penetrated other Arab nations." The announcer's voice was English and sounded distant but crisp.

Nearly a world away, Diane listened with her well-trained reporter's ears to background cheers and sneers, louder than the humming, occasionally sputtering engine of her 2001 brown Subaru wagon. She closed her eyes and pictured red desert winds sweeping through crowds of confused, albeit energized people. She envisioned the streets teeming with protestors and recalled seeing signs they carried on the previous night's news: "Mubarak Leave Egypt Now!" The crudely drawn sign depicted the leader's profile with a hand pointing toward an "exit" sign.

The ice began to thaw. She turned on the windshield wipers, but the mass moved only slightly across the glass. Like the deep winter, time passed slowly.

"We welcome Shahid Hafez, a political analyst reporting from Cairo," the news host said.

"The people have spoken loud and clear. Any normal person should get the message," said Hafez. His voice was direct, and while he spoke with an English accent, Diane heard hints of Farsi in his delivery. "And this message is not only for President Hosni Mubarak, but also for other leaders in the region. The time for change is now!"

Diane hit the wipers again. With a slow-moving force, the blades pushed the sheet of ice in one motion off the windshield, causing the sheet to crash into pieces as it hit the ground. The air in the car was finally warming, so she unzipped her jacket and adjusted the rearview mirror. Wisps of gray hair fell past her olive cheeks. She slowly ran the side of her index finger under her tired eye. Briefly the wrinkles disappeared, only to return as soon as she placed one hand on the steering wheel and shifted the gear into drive.

Realizing she couldn't see behind her, Diane hit the defrost button. On such cold winter mornings, she was never sure if the ice would clear. That was among the reasons she always preferred to look forward.

As she drove, the news reports from the Middle East caused trepidation. She rolled past a stop sign, skidding on a patch of black ice.

"Will this time be different?" she said aloud, switching off the radio.

Twenty minutes later, she arrived at Bates University and watched as bundled students hustled to class. Frigid winter air enveloped the small Maine town, leaving its residents hoping for the change a far-off spring would bring.

She had taught journalism and political science for twenty-six years, starting in 1985. An award-winning journalist, she knew how to follow leads, but she also knew all too well the consequences of becoming part of the tale. Now she had tenure, a life more ordinary but less intrepid.

"Sorry I'm late. The winter won again this morning," Diane said as she entered her classroom.

Her hair was curly and thick, appearing uncombed but somehow together. Her glasses often fell to the end of her nose, forcing her to constantly push them up toward her hazel eyes. Other times, she would suck on one of the stems or rest them in her hair like an egg in a bird nest.

She dropped her bags on the desk. *No God but God: The Origins, Evolution and Future of Islam* by Reza Aslan fell to the floor with a thud. She picked it up and looked across the room as nearly thirty students sat idle. Thin wires fell from nearly all their ears. Laptops were open, casting a dim blue light on their future.

"So . . . what do we think about Egypt?" Diane said. Her voice took on a smooth but authoritative tone. She mimed pulling out headphones, and the students began entering the moment. She walked over to one student and picked up his iPhone, powered it down, smiled and placed it on his desk.

"It's about expression and freedom, not just religion and power," Atisha, an African-American girl with shiny skin and curious, wide brown eyes, said aloud. Her posture was near perfect. A purple wool scarf covered her neck and fell behind her back. "That's what those people want. I'm tired of it just being a Muslim argument."

Three desks to her right, Franklin brushed his dirty blond bangs to the left. He had high cheek bones and an angular face populated with patches of stubble, a weak attempt at a beard. His eyes were the color of the sea surrounding the Greek islands.

"I agree these people have been caged, but you can't expect 5,000 years of rule—the way people are conditioned to live and think—to be changed overnight." Franklin looked down when he spoke. "This is the same problem with Iraq and Afghanistan . . . we expect to inject democracy and just have it accepted."

Diane fished through her bag. She enjoyed this advanced political science class. These seniors were soon off to the real world. Most of the students were aspiring journalists and politicians, and she thought maybe some would become talking heads or policy wonks, though she feared the greater portion would likely turn out like Keith Olbermann or Bill O'Reilly, fighting for headlines while being cheered by respective sheep-like masses. News—purported or otherwise—was simply fuel to them, a way to pontificate to a questionable end. And the people behind the scenes, mostly corporate brass, were slave-driven casualties of a news cycle that catered to moments rather than movements. She didn't think any of her students would become a head of state, but she hoped at least a few might be able to foster meaningful change, a goal she'd held herself when she was their age.

"Democracy has a cost, a high value. In the beginning, it often requires riots, death and overthrowing dictatorships," Diane said, looking up from her bag. She took off her glasses, placed the stem in her mouth, stood and grimaced. "What makes you believe the people of Egypt will succeed, Atisha?"

"Because of everything you've told us about the 1970s and the hostage crisis in Iran. I mean, Ms. Babel, you were one of the—"

Diane waved her hand across the class, as if trying to cast a spell. She rubbed her wrists when she responded as if they had just been untied. "Yes, America was taken hostage then. Your point is?" Diane questioned sharply.

"It's a pattern. Look, we have a Middle East uprising in Tunisia, Egypt, and it seems like it is spreading throughout the region. We'll soon be facing another energy crisis and another helpless president," Atisha said. Her voice grated on some of her classmates who rolled their eyes and others who moaned under their breath.

One student said, "Obama is doing okay." He was of Middle Eastern origin, Diane surmised.

Atisha shook her hand. "It's like the same era with the same errors. If we isolate where we went wrong in the past, we can stop this crisis, the uprisings and the spread of terrorism."

Franklin raised his hand.

No one else was debating, so Diane gestured to him and then Atisha. "I can always count on you two," Diane said as she walked between the aisles of desks. "The rest of you, I hope you are reading, listening and understanding the enormity of these events—not what it means to your grade or what job you might get next year, but to the future of the country and to the world."

Diane motioned back to Franklin. "Go ahead."

"It's not that easy, Atisha. And don't forget that after those 1970s uprisings, everyone—including the Shah of Iran—thought it was going to be change and progressive enlightenment, but the Shah was ousted and replaced by Ayatollah Khomeini. A few years later, Muslim extremists killed Egypt's Anwar Sadat in broad daylight. They opened fired on him and his people. That's also change but not the change I want to believe in."

Atisha shook her head. "Don't regenerate that tired old Obama slander to me. What we think is enlightened thought and what *they* do is so different. We are not operating under the same definition. And just because a small minority killed Sadat doesn't mean that reflected the will of the Muslim people as a whole!" Diane reached into her bag grabbing a water bottle. She walked over to the windowsill, where a robust bamboo plant sat fighting for distant sunlight. She poured water over the rocky soil. "I once believed these crises could be averted through effective communication," Diane said. "I covered these leaders—Sadat, the Shah, Carter, Saddam—all of them. I still believe that in their own way, they all *wanted* to avoid the next crisis, but competing interests made it impossible. Oil, money, religion and power—what has changed?" Diane took a sip of water, the plastic bottle crackled in her hand. "There were terrorist attacks before, of course, but when Sadat was killed, the method marked a new way, a new order for Islamic extremism. During the next twenty years, the world experienced devastating attacks, the *USS Cole* bombing, and most notably, September 11. The movement continues."

The class nodded, though not in unison. The majority of students feigned interest. They would rather be chatting on Facebook or Tweeting, Diane thought as she caught some sneaking text messages. Notes, funny or private, were no longer passed between students but electronically through the air.

She walked to her desk and took out an iPad. With her index finger, she moved across the screen left to right, until she landed on a news story she had saved. Diane read aloud from the January 29, 2011 headline: "Egypt's Anger Spills into the Streets for the Fifth Day." She glanced up to make sure her students were paying attention and continued, "The Associated Press reports that police have opened fire on a massive crowd of protesters in downtown Cairo, killing at least one demonstrator. Thousands of protesters are trying to storm the Interior Ministry located in the heart of the city . . . the usually bustling Tahrir Square located in the heart of Cairo is a war zone with the headquarters of Mubarak's ruling National Democratic Party torched and plumes of smoke still billowing from it."

After reading, Diane placed the iPad on her desk. "I don't want you to tell me what you think about what I just read. Keep your eyes and ears on the news. I want a 400 word piece on the Egyptian uprising on my desk by the end of the week. Here is the catch, you can only source Twitter and Facebook updates."

A few students lightly applauded. Diane shushed them with a smirk.

As their fractured noises filled the room with chatter, moving desks and chairs, Diane approached Atisha and Franklin. "Can you join me in my office now?"

"Sure," said Atisha. A modest smile appeared on her otherwise placid face.

"Can I help you with your bags?" Franklin asked.

"That would be great," Diane said, handing him a bagful of books.

As they hurriedly walked across the cold quad, dormant ivy clung to the walls. They entered a building named Bouton. It was three stories tall and nondescript less the entrance which was highlighted by the engraving, "*Sine labore nihil.*"

"Do you know what that means?" Diane questioned as they approached.

"I Googled it once," said Atisha.

"And?" Diane questioned. Her words were chilled by the cold air.

"Something like . . . nothing without work.'"

"Right," said Diane as she opened the door and ushered them inside.

As they walked toward the elevator, Franklin stared at Atisha's face. Her skin seemed smooth but not yet touched by a man that cared. He wondered what type of life she would lead after graduation. He caught a glimpse of his refection in a pane of glass in the doorway and wondered the same of himself.

Diane's office was decorated with career highlights, including awards, news clippings and pictures taken with celebrities and dignitaries, including two framed photos with President Jimmy Carter and the Shah of Iran. One picture was sans Diane. It was a state dinner at the White House on November 11, 1977, where the Shah of Iran and his wife, the Shahbanou, presented Jimmy Carter and Rosalynn Carter with a tapestry of George Washington.

"This is a cool picture," Franklin said, pointing.

"One of my favorite George Washington quotes is 'Experience teaches us that it is much easier to prevent an enemy from posting themselves than it is to dislodge them after they have got possession,'" Diane said.

It was Atisha and Franklin's first invitation to her office, and they understood it was an honor. Atisha walked around the room, which was filled with books and papers. Plants, full of life, sat on the windowsill, juxtaposing the cold winter winds that bellowed on the other side of the window.

Franklin sat in a worn cherry leather chair that exuded both age and character. He settled in comfortably and looked to his left noticing a book that sat on an end table: *How Carter Got it Wrong: The Years Leading up to the Iran Hostage Crisis* by Jack Quaid, former Assistant Press Secretary to President Jimmy Carter. "Were you interviewed for this book?" Franklin questioned.

"No. My husband—or more accurately, my *ex*-husband—wrote it," Diane said as she watered her plants. "It was a bestseller when it came out in the early 1990s."

"Wow! Press secretary to the President? That's some job. I guess he is not a fan of President Carter then?" Franklin offered.

"He was at one point, as many people were," Diane said, "and he was only the *assistant* press secretary."

"Were you a fan?" Franklin asked.

"Politics and politicians are all based on ego. For the most part, it's just a dirty game. Mr. Quaid experienced that full well, but you read the book, Franklin, and tell me what you think. Go ahead and take that copy. I have others," Diane offered, walking closer to him.

"I think our political system still has merit despite the flaws, but I will read this book with interest. Thanks, Professor Babel," Franklin said leafing through the pages.

"What was it really like?" Atisha asked, pointing to a framed news clipping of the Iran hostage crisis. The headline read: "Fifty-Two Americans. 444 Days. Free."

Diane sighed. "I was let go early on with other women and those of color. You should talk to the others who endured for the duration, not me. My producer at the time, Bart Duran, was one of those men. You should Google him." She walked over to her desk and sifted through the mail. A brown nameplate with a worn brass frame read in fading white letters: "Diane Babel." Her name was nearly lost in a sea of papers, folders and books.

"A few years ago, while Carter was in Chiang Mai Thailand, building houses for Habitat for Humanity, he said one proposed option was a military strike on Iran, but he chose to stick with negotiations to prevent bloodshed and bring the hostages home safely," Diane said. "He thought if he attacked, he would end up killing the hostages and some 20,000 Iranians."

"In the end, he handled it all wrong, and President Reagan received the credit for freeing the hostages," Franklin said, his new book face down on his lap. A picture of Jack Quaid filled the top section. He wore a blue blazer and white button-down shirt, but no tie. Franklin noticed Jack's piercing blue eyes and short salt-and-pepper hair, parted to the left side. Feigning embracement for perhaps talking out of turn, he opened the book.

Diane noticed Franklin silently mouthing the words from the dedication page: "For my brother John . . . and my son Elias."

"You should read what it says on the back cover," Diane said in an icy tone.

Franklin nodded and flipped the book over again. There were a number of blurbs under Jack's picture, including one from Vice President Walter Mondale. Franklin read aloud: "The first book that provides insider context to the pivotal years and months leading up to the Iran hostage crisis."

"So, why did you invite us here? I mean, it's nice to be here and all but . . . well, I'm just curious," Atisha said directly.

"Take a look around this room. These images and awards . . . all of it is a direct result of taking chances and trying to affect change. But all these years later, I am here with you on this cold winter day, simply looking at fading memories."

"You've accomplished so much," Franklin said.

"Maybe," Diane offered.

"Just keep an open mind and consider all opportunities that come your way." She spoke to them as if an end-of-class bell was about to ring.

Atisha and Franklin looked at each other, puzzled. Diane sat in her chair and swiveled around. Her back was to the students. She pressed play on her stereo. Soon the room was filled with Bob Dylan's song *"Hurricane"*:

> *Pistol shots ring out in the barroom night.*
> *Enter Patty Valentine from the upper hall.*
> *She sees the bartender in a pool of blood,*
> *Cries out, "My God, they killed them all!"*
> *Here comes the story of the Hurricane*

From behind, Atisha and Franklin studied Diane as her head swayed to the music. They saw someone new. This wasn't their professor. This was the woman that traveled the world, won awards, hobnobbed with politicians, celebrities and the like. She'd fought the good fight but didn't always win.

Atisha signaled to Franklin, who tightly nestled his new book between his arm and torso. They both nodded and headed toward the door.

"We are going to go now," Franklin said, trying to compete with Dylan's nasally overtones.

Diane turned around. "Enjoy the book and remember what I told you. Keep your options open."

Atisha and Franklin closed the door behind them. As they walked down the hall, the music slowly faded.

"That was sort of . . . bizarre," Atisha said.

"Did you see all those pictures of the hostages and the framed news clippings?" Franklin whispered with his new book in hand.

"Yeah, she doesn't seem to talk about *it* that much," Atisha said in a hushed tone. "I mean, there are pictures of her with Elton John and then one with Saddam Hussein, what a strange mix. I'm surprised she never wrote a book about her experiences—*that*, I would read."

Moments later, Diane was again alone but had two more classes to teach. The university tower bell bellowed deeply, like a call to prayer, drowning out "Hurricane." Another afternoon had arrived. The cold chill of morning had yet to fully vacate. She rubbed her hands together quickly and walked across her office to a hot plate and prepared water for tea.

She thought about Atisha. She saw herself in her young, hopeful and strident face. *It is this energy that serves youth well,* she thought. She opened her laptop and began writing an e-mail to her old college professor, who was now retired, living in Washington DC and nearing eighty:

Professor Stanley,

Hope this note finds you well. As per your request, I have identified two students of interest. They remind me a lot of Jack and me at that age—bright and full of vim and vigor. They could be good candidates for recruitment. If Richard Harden were still alive, I think he would agree. If the agency wants a recommendation, I am happy to provide one on their behalf. They may turn down the CIA's offer (should they get one) like we did and pursue journalism and politics, but it's worth a shot.

Best Regards,
Diane

After Diane hit send on the e-mail and waited for her tea to steep, she picked up a book that she had long been meaning to start. There were always books to be read, and time never seemed to provide enough bounty. This book was entitled: *Sword of Islam: Muslim Extremism from the Arab Conquests to the Attack on America,* by John F. Murphy Jr., an author who had recently visited the campus. He wrote: "This book is not an indictment of Islam, one of the three beautiful religions which bloomed in this desert land. It is an indictment of those who took from Islam only its most uncompromising tenets, forgetting the message of love that accompanies them. Extremism is a part of all three religions born of this land," he wrote. "If modern Muslims have their extremism in terrorism, Christianity had its during the Crusades, and the Hebrews in the killing of all those who opposed them when they made their march to the Promised Land. Yet I have chosen to write about Islamic extremism because it represents the most clear and present danger today."

She placed the book down and reached into her pocketbook to retrieve her phone. She read a few text messages and noticed an alert for voicemail. It was from her ex-husband and current lover, Jack Quaid.

His voice sent her happily spinning into a time warp. Whenever she heard his deep cadence and uncanny ability to annunciate the right words at the right time, she felt younger, vibrant and more vigilant. "I would love to see your smiling face and bring some of those chocolates," Jack said. He coughed as if fighting for oxygen before hanging up.

Diane was snapped back to reality as the tea kettle screamed.

Chapter 2

After her last class, while walking toward her car, Diane wondered if her words meant anything to Franklin and Atisha. Her ideals, once tethered by steel cables, now seemed to be held together by frayed rope. The life she sought to live, the change she once saw in herself, was only half-realized, but still she had hope. Every few years, students the likes of Franklin and Atisha buoyed her spirits—the promise of the change that could come. It was in this role as educator and mentor that she now felt the most fulfilled.

The late afternoon was a bit warmer, just above freezing. She sat in the car and let it idle and warm. She took out her iPhone and typed a text to Jack: "Be there soon." She turned the radio on and tuned in to Rush Limbaugh.

"Now, we're told that what's going on in Egypt is all political. And that's silly. It would be the same thing as being told that riots in this country are purely about policy, when they aren't. If you go back over the history of riots in this country, it has always been about economic matters, one way or another," Limbaugh's voice was characteristically booming and unapologetically certain.

As she drove through the campus, her eyes were averted to a student playing Frisbee with a black and white Labrador mix. There was so much snow and ice on the ground that they were slipping and sliding. There was peacefulness to their abandon.

Rush boomed. "Now, the riots and revolutionary activity burning down Tunisia. You've heard about that, right? You haven't? Well, yeah, it's happening in Tunisia too, folks. If you read foreign media on the Internet, I'm sure you've heard about the riots in Tunisia . . . and in Yemen. You've heard about the riots in Yemen, right? You haven't? Well, read the foreign media, and you'll read about the riots in Yemen and Tunisia . . . and now Egypt." He cleared his throat without losing his rhythm. "Egypt is third to the party here. Jordan—that's exactly right, Jordan, King Abdullah, big ally of the United States, as is Egypt, by the way. That's what's kind of scary about this. But anyway, there's unrest throughout the Middle East."

Diane turned the dial low and muttered, "Is that news—unrest in the Middle East?' C'mon, Rush."

She hit the blinker and turned right. She knew the street well, and every tree and bush that lined the upscale neighborhood was accounted for in her memory. She'd taken many long walks up and down this road. Year after year she watched as the trees grew toward the sky while she and Jack bandied about, almost always helplessly possessed by a strange, tangible love.

Before arriving at the driveway, she stopped at a telephone pole. It was marred and bruised; a distant sting pricked her heart. She turned the radio off and slowly drove up to 13 Jacob Way. The color of the house hadn't changed in over twenty years. Diane had picked out lime green with off-white trim, and now it showed signs of wear. The paint job, though, had held up better than their marriage. Jack never liked the color, but he was forgiving; he chose more tactical battles.

Diane was growing tired of her Merrill hiking boots, but they were the only footwear that kept her feet warm. As she nearly slipped on the walkway, she wondered what was worse: old leather boots cracked and creased from time or the high heels she'd once worn to events like the Correspondents' Dinner during President Jimmy Carter's tenure. It had been too long since she had *occasion* to wear heels, she thought while steadying her balance.

Diane arrived at the double oak front doors. She pondered whether to ring the bell or use her key. After all these years, she was still slightly unsure of herself when it came to Jack. She slid the key into the lock, and the bolt clicked free. The house smelled like Lysol. The entry hallway was long, nearly thirty feet. On either side were pictures—plenty of them. She stopped and lightly brushed her fingers over a picture of a teenager. He wore a big smile and sat atop a blue and white motorcycle with a big red bow tied around the handlebars.

"I thought I heard something."

Diane's spell was broken by Rosie, who stood at the end of the hall, smiling, with open arms. "Come give me a hug."

Rosie was a quick-witted Jamaican who loved to cook for Jack, even though that wasn't part of her job; she preferred preparing Cuban food.

Her favorite was *ropa vieja* ("old clothes"), a wonderful beef stew of sorts. She said Diane and Jack were like old clothes that were mismatched but somehow went well together.

Diane embraced Rosie and whispered in her ear, "How is he today?"

"Ask only the questions you want honest answers to," Rosie said. Her white uniform juxtaposed the darkness of her skin. When she smiled, her face lit up; it had often been a beacon of hope and solace during hard times.

"How are you today?" Diane returned with a smile.

"Oh, child, I'm tired of dealing with Mr. Jack." Her hearty laugh began loud and trailed off. "Go see him."

Diane took a deep breath and proceeded further down the hall yielding to the left as she approached the master bedroom. She knew what floorboards creaked in the old home; and while the floor didn't squeal, the door did as she sheepishly pushed it open.

"I remember how you used to burst into a room, ready to take it over," Jack said in a weak voice.

He had an IV dripping clear liquid—a saline solution—into his right arm. The drops slowly formed into beads and then dropped like clockwork, though no one wanted to keep that sort of time. A hospital gurney replaced the king-sized bed they'd once shared nightly. He was balding and gaunt. His complexion was yellowish, but his steel-blue eyes somehow danced amidst the decay that was taking over his body. It was that spirit Diane was always drawn to.

"Now you push the door open like you are afraid of what you might see." Jack coughed, bringing a handkerchief to his mouth. He tried to clear his throat.

"I thought you might be sleeping," Diane said as she walked hesitantly into the bedroom. The wallpaper border that framed the walls as they met the ceiling was waved and peeling. She walked over to the window and drew the curtains further back, but the winter sun was falling toward night again.

"Bullshit. I heard you talking to Rosie," Jack said. "And I bet you forgot the chocolate."

"Oh no! You're right. My mind is just always somewhere else. I'm sorry. I'll go now and get it."

"Don't worry. I haven't been able to keep anything down all day. Just stay here," Jack said. He picked up the remote control. It took effort and energy for him to point it at the television that was muted. *Fox News* was on. He turned up the volume.

"Republicans, 81 percent, and those who consider themselves part of the Tea Party movement, 82 percent, are among the most likely to describe the Egyptian events as worrisome," a blonde female news reporter said. "Democrats, 26 percent, and independents, 23 percent, are more than twice as likely as Republicans, 9 percent, to see the events in Egypt as inspiring."

Jack began a series of long, deep coughs. He spit phlegm speckled with blood into a handkerchief. He reached for a glass of water on the table but grimaced as his torso turned and fell back into the bed.

Diane rushed to his side. She grabbed the water and leaned his head forward; Jack slowly sipped. Rosie entered the doorway and smiled with a motherly glow. With her eyes she said, *"It is going to be okay."*

Diane looked down at the iPhone she had bought for Jack. Her text messages were unread.

Jack composed himself. "All these news stations are getting it wrong. I've been flipping through all week." his voice grew stronger when talking about politics. "We might have disagreed back then on some issues, me with Carter, you tackling the Middle East, but all this shit could have been avoided. That goddamn hostage crisis!" He began coughing. "The thing is, we never learn from our mistakes . . . different politicians but the same old mistakes. We spend billions and stick our noses all too often in the wrong places."

"You have to rest and try and calm down," Diane said and stood up placing the glass of water on the table.

"Rest for what? There is plenty of rest in front of me. So, have you been listening to Limbaugh like I asked?"

"Yes," Diane said softly. "Just now actually in the car . . . he makes his case, but I often take issue with it."

"He should be on primetime television with his message," Jack said. He pointed to the dresser where all his medications stood idle like chess pawns. There were more than twenty prescription bottles.

Diane knew the one he wanted, the one for pain. She pressed her hand firmly on top of the cap and turned. "These two students of mine—I think I mentioned them before, Atisha and Franklin? Anyway, we had this discussion today. You know, all the kids, my students, are curious about what's happening over there. Some pay more attention to their phones than me. These two, though, they are like us, or at least what we once were."

Diane handed two white, oblong pills to Jack. Again, she brought the water to his mouth. When he swallowed, he closed his eyes and winced. Without the brilliant blue of his eyes dressing his face, he looked like a man who had only months to live. Half the wrinkles he wore were from a life well lived, while the others were from his cancer. Diane could no longer differentiate.

Jack cleared his throat. "I often wonder how much of a difference we really made. I wanted to do more. You did more. There is a cancer in the Middle East, like in this here body. Carter screwed things up, and then Reagan came in and got the credit. But for what?" Jack muttered under his breath, as if talking to himself. "That's why I stopped working for politicians. There was more of a chance changing policy through lobbying."

"Well, we might have disagreed, and still do on some things, but Jack, you made a difference . . . to me," Diane said, taking his hand in hers. *Fox News* was muted again and the television cast a bluish hue on the off-white walls.

Their son was conceived in this bedroom, a reality that caused Diane to fight back tears on a daily basis. She knew the same room would soon take the other true love of her life.

Diane took a deep breath and sighed. "He was so young. Why did he need a motorcycle? We would have bought him a car," Diane said. Tears made her vision blurry as she looked at Jack.

"If only that telephone pole wasn't there. He . . . Elias . . . was a great guy. He had your wanderlust, Diane."

They had this remorseful conversation before, but with more frequency in recent months. The passage of time hadn't healed this wound. It had been four years since *the accident*. Diane walked over to Jack's bed. She leaned down and kissed his lips. They were dried and cracked only moistened by her falling tears.

"I cry sometimes before you come, so there are no tears left for you to see," Jack conceded. He brushed Diane's hair from her warm, vibrant left cheek. "What was it, September 1972?" Jack asked, mustering a warm smile.

Their conversations about Elias always led to how they met. As they grew older, and Jack more sick, it was these memories that provided safe haven.

"I think we first talked, or argued, that October. It was one of our political courses, something about Vietnam," Diane returned.

"I would have never thought that I would marry you ten years later, only to divorce ten years after that," Diane said with a laugh. She never laughed loud or often, and when she did, it surprised her.

Laughter came easier to Jack. He chuckled and began coughing again. "And then ten years later, we start dating again . . . and here we are."

Diane looked down at her purse. Her phone indicated an e-mail had been received. She assumed it was Professor Stanley but she ignored it. "After Elias's accident, the only place I didn't feel alone was with you."

"We feel the same," Jack said, "but you should give up that condo already and move in here where you belong. I miss Sammy too."

"I would have brought him today, but I came from campus. It's too cold out there for that old dog."

"He's not the only old one," Jack said.

"Hey now! We're the same age," Diane said with a tart grin.

"So, these students of yours, they *have* something?" Jack questioned.

"Maybe," Diane returned, "but people thought *we* had something too. I gave one of them your book and sent an e-mail to Professor Stanley—you know, just to see if the agency is looking for recruits."

"Stanley, huh? I can't believe that old bastard is still alive. We could have stopped what eventually became al-Qaeda. I really think we were close, but what are these kids going to stop?" Jack slowly leaned up in the bed, and a little color returned to his face. "How many more times can we see people around the world shouting, 'Death to America!' or see them burning our flag. We are good people, we have big hearts, and we care and we believe in freedom and liberty, but we are always viewed as aggressors or occupiers not liberators."

Diane only half-agreed changing the subject. "Every time I see that picture of Elias in the hall, my heart breaks. He was so young—just nineteen," Diane said, her tone uncharacteristically bitter. "That was our own personal September 11, Jack. Then I see all these young students, especially the ones who hold promise, and that gives me hope."

Rosie came into the room again. She sensed tension but was accustomed to strain and grief. She walked through it as if she was a beekeeper surrounded by smoke. "Mr. Jack, now you lie back down on that bed! All the way now," she coached. Then she picked up a clean bed pan. "Now no fuss or back talk, lift up." She slid the cold steel under the sheets and under Jack's frail body. "Maybe tomorrow we will try and use the bathroom again," Rosie said with a big smile. "Now you call me when you're ready." She then turned and walked toward Diane. With her back to Jack, she reached into her pocket. "Here. This will make him happy," Rosie said and then left the room.

Diane looked through the cellophane bag and spotted his favorite brand of chocolates.

"I don't even have to go," Jack said. "Pull this thing out from under me."

Diane did as she was asked. The cold steel sent a shiver down her legs and arms, and goose flesh spread over her body like March winds across an Illinois prairie field. "I've been listening to all the talking heads—Olbermann, Matthews, O'Reilly—and they should all know better. They lived through the 1970s, but they might not have been paying attention to the Middle East like we were," Diane said. "Matthews maybe. Remember when he was writing for Carter? He was so eager and just a nice guy, but his political leanings were too clear and that is still his problem, all their problems. They see what's happening in the Middle East today through whatever lens makes them feel most comfortable, or their bosses. Whatever makes their viewers happy . . . advertising?" Diane said as she dropped the bed pan on the floor; it rang out like an obstinate singing bowl.

Rosie rushed into the room, summoned by the clatter, and looked to the floor.

"He didn't have to go," Diane said.

Rosie gave a half-smile and sighed. "All right, Mr. Jack. In that case, you let me know when you *do* need to go."

Diane walked over to the bed and dropped the chocolate on his chest.

"I thought you forgot," he said with a big smile.

"I thought you couldn't eat," she said.

"I didn't want you to feel bad," Jack said. His fingers were weak and no longer nimble, so Diane helped him untie the bag. He fished out a square of dark chocolate, placed it on his tongue, closed his eyes and smiled.

"Can you get the Maker's Mark from behind the dresser," Jack said.

"Uh, whiskey and chocolate?"

"It's bourbon, and I need it."

Diane looked toward the door. Once she was sure Rosie was not in sight, she took a small plastic cup, leaned down, found the bottle and poured one shot in the cup. She walked over to Jack, sat beside him, leaned his head up and poured the booze down his throat.

"It just makes me feel so warm," Jack said as he slid back into the bed.

Diane's eyes fell to a picture she had seen many times before which had always arrested her. She sat in a red Mustang convertible, riding slowly in a tickertape parade in New York City. Crowds of people were in the streets, cheering, smiling and waving American flags. Bart Duran, her old producer with the brilliant red hair, sat to her side, smiling.

"I remember that day like it was yesterday," said Jack. "I know that sounds cliché, but it's so fresh in my mind. You were so strong, so beautiful."

"The *real* hostages deserved that parade," Diane said as she picked up the picture and walked toward the television. She read the ticker on the bottom of the screen: "*Anderson Cooper and his crew were attacked by Hosni Mubarak supporters in Egypt . . .*" She flipped the television off.

She looked at Jack and didn't see a sick man; rather, she saw the man he used to be, the former assistant press secretary to President Carter. She walked over to a desk he had worked at until a few months earlier, when the pain had finally forced him into bed.

Above the desk were pictures from a celebrated career. Jack went on to found a political public relations firm in Washington DC. He kept an apartment in Washington and traveled back and forth after he and Diane were married in 1985. His clients included Governor George Pataki, Mayor Rudolf Giuliani and Senator Jessie Helms. His political leanings moved to the right after the Iran hostage crisis, when Carter was handily beaten by Ronald Reagan for the highest seat in the nation.

Diane looked across to the picture of her at the parade. She was younger and vibrant, yet amidst the celebration, she saw in her demeanor a loss. She looked back to Jack. With a little bourbon, painkillers and chocolate in his system, he looked content, if only for a moment. His eyes were closed, though, and she knew soon it would be a permanent way of being for him.

As she had done for countless days and nights over the last year, she let her mind wander past her days at Bates University, before her divorce, her son's death, and before the balance of her life trapped her.

She walked across the room and took notice of a composition book on Jack's nightstand. His eyes were still closed. She opened it to find notes and scribbles:

"We had problems with Iran then and handled it the wrong way. Now we have problems with Iran again. We had problems with Afghanistan back then and got it all wrong. We supported the Afghanis against the Soviet Union while funding the anti-American/West war lords. CIA Chief William Casey and the *Soldier of Fortune* readers attracted by the Reagan administration like Congressman Charlie Wilson and Oliver North supported the Afghanis against the Soviets directly with heaps of cash. Then weapons filtered through Pakistan at first, then directly, and in a matching program with Saudi Arabia. All this did was strengthen the burgeoning Egyptian-influenced anti-Western sentiment and pro-Jihadist agenda taking hold in the universities attended by the sons of warlords and future fighters.

Today, the problem is worse. We had problems with Israel and the Arabs and did not handle it right, so we still have a big mess on our hands. We had an oil crisis back then, and we did not invest in alternative energy; now we are fighting a war over oil again . . ."

As Diane read, she looked over at Jack, who was drifting. His thoughts ate at him like the cancer did.

The evening had arrived, a winter darkness. She walked to the bedroom window and could see her reflection in the glass. A tear fell. "How did it all go so wrong?" she muttered, and then she heard the bed rustle.

"Did you say something?"

"Sleep for a while. Sleep, Jack," Diane said as she pressed her cheek against the cold bedroom window. "I miss my old life," Diane said, her breath fogging the window.

Chapter 3

It was November 1973, and the wind on the streets of Yemen blew Diane's brunette hair into a tailspin; thick and stringy, it looked like a disheveled bin in a yarn store. She carefully brushed her coarse locks to the left side of her face so as not to show too much skin. She stared into the rearview mirror of the camouflaged Land Rover that had bullet holes in the back left fender. It was parked outside her hotel, the Hadda Tower, and the mirrors were thick with dust. She tried to clean it by wetting her fingers, but the smudged pancake dust further distorted the reflection of her otherwise piercing hazel eyes.

As she waited for her chaperon, guide and source, Mr. Richard Harden, she wrapped a black-and-white checkered scarf tightly around her head, even though it was more than eighty degrees. On Richard's suggestion, she wore a *caucasus*, a traditional man's coat made from felt and karakul. She checked her camera for film and took out a small notebook. She leaned out the window slightly and looked to the sky. It was a brilliant blue, the shade of Jack's eyes, a classmate back in DC, as well as an occasional lover.

Diane had landed a three-week journalism internship. When she accepted, Diane had no idea where she would be going or with whom exactly. Her mentor, Professor Stanley, placed her in line with his old military buddy Richard Harden, a high-raking CIA operative. Harden was always on the lookout for soon-to-be-graduate recruits. Despite Diane's reluctance to join the Agency, since she truly yearned to work as a journalist, she happily agreed to accompany Richard on the adventure, as long as she could serve as a journalist in training.

Back in the States, the oil crisis hit a fever pitch when the members of Organization of Arab Petroleum Exporting Countries (OAPEC), along with Egypt, Syria and Tunisia, launched an oil embargo against the U.S., in part for their support of Israel. The Shah of Iran called for the end of longstanding oil contracts with Great Britain and other countries. Within a month, the oil price per barrel jumped from three to twelve dollars, and long lines became the norm at gas stations. This resulted in fuel rationing and even a reduction in the speed limit across the U.S. Conservation wasn't a common approach for most Americans, but new campaigns began, touting taglines such as "Don't Be Fuelish . . ."

Now, in the faraway land of Yemen, Diane watched as a man with dark, leathery skin slowly rode a camel towing what looked like a calf attached to a long rope. His only expression was a big smile, and his eyes were dark and sand swept; she wrote in her pad that those eyes held secrets from years traveling the vast desert. The man rode along a makeshift fence crudely constructed from discarded sticks and brush.

Diane's skin was dark too by way of her father's North African ancestry, a Moroccan. The combination of her mother's fair Russian-Jewish looks made her appear exotic, uniquely different. In that region, she was often taken for being from North Afghanistan, and she'd twice been asked about it by inquisitive strangers.

Diane fell in love with Yemen, known for its coffee and honey. She was especially fond of Qamariya, a symbol of the city's distinct architecture. With her favorite Canon camera, she took many pictures of the decorative, multicolored stained-glass windows that adorn Yemen's buildings, architectural beauties situated at the feet of majestic mountain ranges.

Diane was intrigued by Yemen's history and had studied it before her arrival. Prior to Islam, the country was ruled by Bilqis, the Queen of Sheba, mentioned in both the Bible and Quran. After Islam, Queen Arwa bint Ahmed Al-Sulaihi ruled for fifty-five years, until 1138. Despite its rich, forward-thinking history, she knew it remained a man's world.

She was now far from the city in the mountains of Zafar, following Richard Harden. Salt-and-pepper hair framed his tan face. He wore shiny aviator glasses, and when he smiled, Diane felt as if she'd somehow missed the joke.

Diane was slender and on the tall side, nearly five-eight. Richard stood at about six feet. He had strong hands and often chewed tobacco or smoked cigars. He wore a khaki uniform with a bush jacket that made him look more like a safari leader than a decorated U.S. soldier who'd fought in both the Korean and Vietnam Wars. While the latter was still going on, and after a few drinks, Richard would often mumble to anyone who asked, "This one is a lost cause."

Diane had met Richard for the first time at the airport in Washington DC and knew little about him. He didn't have much of a bedside manner. Though she tried to pry like any good journalist would, he wasn't an open book. She was learning as she went along. "You're on a need-to-know basis," Richard often said when she queried about this or that. When she asked about the bullet holes in the car, Richard plainly said, "They are from the guns of people who want to see America defeated."

For one week, Richard showed Diane Yemen's sites, local food and cultural flavors. They met with some dignitaries, but it was more of a dog-and-pony show than anything else. While interesting, it was nothing more than "fluff" to Diane. Richard said, "Just get the lay of the land," and that was exactly what Diane did. She did what she was told. "You are just an observer," he often reiterated.

The one thing he made clear was the importance of Diane understanding the "black gold" roots, an oil deal that dated back to the 1800s. Like a good student, Diane studied the packet of information Richard had provided to help her "understand" what was "really at stake." When she asked about his relationship with Professor Stanley, Richard only said they were "good old friends."

One night over dinner, Richard provided Diane with a lesson no stateside classroom could equate. After they ate kabob and rice, they sat in the back of an otherwise empty restaurant. Occasionally Richard would signal a waiter to bring more tea. The lighting was dim, and Richard appeared all-knowing to Diane, who for the most part sat and listened.

"What we know as British Petroleum, BP, dates back decades and decades. It wasn't until the early twentieth century, when wealthy entrepreneur William Knox D'Arcy, under the full encouragement of the British government, began looking for oil in Iran. This guy D'Arcy was crafty and struck up a concession agreement with the then-dissolute Iranian monarchy, some of whom he bribed with promises of great fortune," Richard said, lighting a cigar. His eye brows were thick and dark. Shadows from candles danced across his face. "Under the contract, D'Arcy would own whatever oil he discovered in Iran and pay the government a measly 16 percent of any profits. But the thing of it was, D'Arcy never allowed any Iranian to review his accounting methods, so they never really knew what 16 percent represented," Richard said with a half smile tapping his cigar into the ashtray.

"Jeez," Diane said, blowing her bangs off her forehead.

"His first big oil strike was in 1908, and he became the sole owner of the entire ocean of oil lying beneath Iran's soil. Imagine that! No one else was allowed to drill for, refine, extract or sell it. Back then, in oh say 1911, Winston Churchill was the First Lord of the Admiralty and famously said of the discovery, 'Fortune brought us a prize from a fairyland beyond our wildest dreams.'"

"The Iranians didn't try and fight it or get control?" Diane offered.

"They were locked by the contract. Two years later, the British government bought that contract and formed the Anglo-Persian Oil Company, which later became BP. Next, the world's biggest oil refinery was built at the port of Abadan on the Persian Gulf. From the 1920s to the 1940s, Britain's standard of living was supported by oil from Iran. British cars, trucks and buses ran on cheap Iranian oil. Factories throughout Britain were fueled by Iranian oil. The Royal Navy, which tried to project British power all over the world, ran its ships with that same oil," Richard said, signaling for more tea. Then his voice lowered as he leaned closer to Diane. "It wasn't until after World War II that the winds of nationalism and anti-colonialism blew through the developing world and the Iranians started to grow any sort of backbone. They wanted their oil back, and in April of 1951, Parliament voted Mohammad Mossadegh in as prime minister. He was their champion of nationalism. Days later, they unanimously approved his bill, nationalizing the oil company. Mossadegh promised his people that oil profits would be used to develop Iran, not enrich Britain."

"What type of guy was he?" Diane said.

A waiter dressed all in white filled her tea cup, then Richard's. He smiled and slowly backed away from the table, a sign of respect.

Richard paused before speaking. "He was tough, well educated, and had been around the block serving in multiple positions in different governmental agencies from taxation to elected office. He wasn't asking for the moon from BP. He simply wanted a 50/50 profit share," Richard said, dropping three cubes of sugar in his small cup of tea.

"Seems reasonable to me," Diane said.

Richard stirred his tea with his index finger and rolled his eyes. "You have to understand though that the old adage that the sun rose and set on the British Empire was true in many respects, and this oil company was the most lucrative British enterprise anywhere on the planet. To the Brits, nationalization seemed absurdly contrary to the unwritten rules of *their* world. So, early in this confrontation, the directors of the Anglo-Iranian Oil Company and their partners in Britain's government settled on a strategy. There would be no mediation, no compromise, and no acceptance of nationalization in any form."

"I have never heard this story before, at least not like this. Now the Shah of Iran's recent OPEC speech makes more sense, ending those oil contracts. No wonder they're raising oil prices," Diane said, bewildered.

"Yes, exactly . . . or at least in part," Richard said, tapping the table as if giving her a high-five. "We'll get to that soon, but it's important to know the whole story. See, the Brits took a series of steps to push Mossadegh off his nationalist path. They withdrew their technicians from Abadan, blockaded the port, cut off exports of vital goods to Iran, froze the country's hard-currency accounts in British banks and tried to win anti-Iran resolutions from the U.N. and the World Court. This campaign only intensified Iranian determination."

"All of this over oil and power," Diane said, shaking her head.

Richard, uncharacteristically enthused and excited, had to measure his voice. "Finally, the British turned to Washington and asked for a favor, basically saying, 'Please overthrow this madman for us so we can have our oil company back.' President Eisenhower, encouraged by Secretary of State John Foster Dulles, a lifelong defender of transnational corporate power, agreed to send the CIA to depose Mossadegh. The operation took less than a month in the summer of 1953. It was the first time the CIA had ever overthrown a government. They called it Operation AJAX."

"That I heard about, and learned that you . . ." Diane said. Richard cut her off.

"Yes, I was involved in that operation. In fact, AJAX was one of my first. It seemed like a remarkably successful covert operation. The West had deposed a leader it didn't like and replaced him with someone who would perform as directed, which was Mohammad Reza Shah Pahlavi, the Shah. The goal was achieved, in that Mossadegh's government was thwarted, but so was democracy. AJAX returned Mohammad Reza Pahlavi to his Peacock Throne. All this added to a growing hatred among certain Islamic factions—Islamic extremists. These militants see the West as evil and are looking to fight back."

"Islamic extremists?" Diane questioned.

"You will understand soon enough. Listen, you might think this is just some fluffy recruiting mission. You know, I show you the excitement of far-off lands and all the bells and whistles, but Diane, what is equally important in the CIA or the White House or whatever road you choose is understanding the truth. More importantly, if you are going to be a journalist, your mission must always be to report the facts."

"I think the latter, journalism, really is my calling. It's flattering to even be considered for the CIA. I know my dad would be proud but I have this desire." Diane paused and took a sip of tea, overwhelmed by the moment. She looked around the room nervously before making eye contact again with Richard. "I want to learn the truth and share it with others, regardless of the consequences." She brushed hair from her eyes. "The one thing I'm still trying to figure out, though, is why we are in Yemen."

"The same reason D'Arcy went to Iran. Yemen has one of the largest untapped oil fields in the world. We are here to protect its interest, including that of the Shah," Richard said, his face distorted by the now dim candlelight. "Tomorrow you will learn whether you want to write feature stories about international food and culture or investigate the underbelly of world politics." Now he wasn't smiling. "Time to turn in. We have a big day tomorrow," Richard said, signaling for the check.

The following morning, Diane waited outside the hotel doors for Richard. The street bizarre was in full motion. She took a picture of a man selling plastic bottles filled with honey. There was no label just a word written in red marker: Doa'ni. The man smiled at Diane and motioned for her to come over to him. As she approached the honey salesman, she felt a tap on her shoulder.

"I said you should wait in the lobby," Richard said gruffly.

"Sorry," Diane said, stunned. She hurried to catch up as he was already steps ahead of her.

Richard had hired a driver, the owner of the Land Rover. With the early morning temperature on the rise, they drove out of town and toward the mountains, where they eventually arrived at a makeshift military base. Armored trucks were moving about. When the vehicle came to a dusty skid, Richard jumped out and looked into the cabin. "C'mon," he prompted.

Diane slid across the seat and into the thick desert air. She was startled when, almost in an instant, they were surrounded by a handful of soldiers.

"Don't worry," Richard said to Diane. "We are being hosted by the Shah of Iran's Royal Guard, American allies. Plus, some of these boys are our own."

Diane took out her camera and began snapping pictures, her journalistic instincts kicking into full gear.

A large man with a more colorful uniform than the others put his hand in front of the camera. "No!" he said angrily.

"Just take some notes if you like," Richard said quietly to Diane. He then walked to the center of the men, like a quarterback entering a huddle. "I got the call. I'm here. What the hell are we doing here, boys? I only see fucking sand and desert snakes. Can somebody tell me just what the hell is going on?"

Diane hadn't seen this side of Richard yet. He was in command. She looked around suspiciously.

A man in his early thirties, clearly American, wearing fatigues came through the dusty circle. He was smoking a cigarette and had a Band-aid under his left eye. His hair was jet black and cut short, and atop it, he wore a beret. "Hello sir," he said. "My name is John Anton. It's an honor to meet you. I have heard great things about you, and—"

Richard cut him off with a dismissive wave of the hand. He reached into his pouch and stuffed his mouth full of tobacco. "Thanks for the kind words, but if I wanted something sweet, I'd have me a lollipop. Now, tell me what the hell is going on here."

"Sir, we're here fighting a group of . . . well, we call them Islamic radicals."

Richard shot a knowing glance at Diane.

John Anton went on, "These are tough—forgive me, sir—bastards, and they're known to have ties to Islamic extremists," John said.

"Who exactly are these people'? I've dealt with extremists before," Richard said.

Diane covertly held her camera to the side and sneaked shots as the men listened to Richard. She found John attractive, but she didn't make eye contact.

"We're here to help and support the Shah's Royal Guard and their allies fighting these Islamic extremists who are trying to overthrow the Omni's Kingdom," John said. "They've been attacking in a militia, terrorist style and are gaining position. They live and breathe in the mountains and caves and attack us mostly at night. They are ruthless, sir. They behead our soldiers and have radical ideologies to the point of blowing themselves up. They *want* to be martyrs."

Diane wrote the word "martyr" in her pad and underlined it.

John motioned to his left. "This is General Shirazi from the Shah's Royal Guard. He's in charge of this base."

General Shirazi was older than Richard, likely around sixty. His right pinky was missing, as were a handful of teeth. He had a salty black beard that ran three inches past his chin. His uniform had even more color than the other ranking officer, which juxtaposed the redness of the desert sands that wisped and blew hard. He extended his hand to Richard.

Diane was busy scribbling in her notebook. Her nails were bitten and her cuticles chewed. With her traditional garb and scarf, she almost appeared to be a man, which was Richard's intention.

"These are the roots of Islamic extremists from Yemen and Saudi Arabia, but they don't represent Islam. I am Muslim myself, but I do not approve of their radical, extreme point of views," General Shirazi said.

Diane found his English surprisingly rhythmic and soothing.

"As you can see, we have joined forces with our neighbors, mostly Muslims. We are allies in trying to stop them from growing, for we all see this as a cancer in the Persian Gulf region. That's why we need more support from your government to stop it from spreading. His majesty, the Shah of Iran, prepaid for several jet fighters and one A-WAX when he met your President Nixon's men. We're promised to receive them, but as of yet, no one has made good on that promise. Unless we have your support to fight these Islamic radicals, they are going to gain ground on us," General Shirazi said, noticing Diane leaning toward him.

"Pardon me, General, but are you saying the U.S. government is aware of this situation and is not supporting you?" Diane questioned nervously.

Richard removed his sunglasses and rubbed his eyes.

"Who is this person?" the general snapped, none too happy with the interrogation by a stranger.

Richard stared at Diane with the power of a second sun. "She is here to observe."

Diane sheepishly stepped back.

John wiped his brow with the back of his hand and interjected as the sands blew harder, "Let's not get into pointing fingers. Frankly, we don't have the time for it. Bottom line, the support is very limited, and as General Shirazi alluded, unless we increase support on the ground here, we're going to face a bigger issue a few years from now."

Richard briefly paused. All eyes were on him, as if he had the jet fighters in his back pocket, ready to hand over.

"I guess what I'm hearing is that these particular Islamic extremists are not a fly-by-night militant group and are here to stay? Is that right, son?" Richard asked, and Diane knew he already knew the answer.

"Unless we defeat them now, they're here . . . to stay," General Shirazi interjected.

"I know about the promise and the arrangement, but we are fighting a war in Vietnam and let's face it, we have our limitations," Richard said. He turned and spat into the wind. "Now, I need to bring back actionable intelligence. These Arabs, no offense—have been running, and in some cases ruining, these region for centuries. A few jets are not going to stop that."

John unbuttoned his vest and pulled out five-by-eight black and white pictures. Two men were tied to chairs headless. There bloody heads were placed on their laps. He handed the disturbing photo to Richard. "One was an American, CIA and the other, Iranian," John said solemnly. "Sir, *this* is the future. We are dealing with a new kind of monster."

Diane tried to get a better look at the picture, but Richard quickly folded it and placed it in his jacket.

"Is that . . . was that an *American* soldier? Was his family notified?" Diane said, her voice shrill.

"Not now. You may need to step away from this," Richard whispered to Diane.

"No!" Her quick response surprised Diane more than Richard.

He dragged her by the arm and pulled her aside, and Diane caught John looking at her as Richard spoke in a hushed, deliberate tone. "This isn't the college newspaper, sweetheart. This is not the shit to tell your friends when you're stoned and bashing Nixon over Vietnam back in DC. This is the underbelly. It gets dirty. There are no rules here. Now that poor solider died and his parents will likely never know why, but I do." Richard put his thumb and index finger into the shape of a C and brought it to his mouth slowly, while never taking his eyes off Diane. He pulled out a soaking wad of tobacco and threw it to the ground in one clean stroke. "The Shah's men might just get their jets now because of this situation." He looked back at the soldiers, some thirty yards in the distance pretending not to watch. "This is how it works. It's not all about oil and gas prices. When these guys say 'extremists,' they are talking about a twisted vision of Allah or God or whatever, and that shit doesn't have a price other than death." Richard leaned close to Diane's ear. "You've seen a few things now. It's time to figure out what kind of writer you want to be, because this isn't the story. It goes far deeper. Only when you know the answers can you report. Otherwise, more heads will be found in more laps, and that won't be nice to think about late at night when you're drunk on wanderlust."

"I didn't . . . they didn't tell me it was going to be like this," Diane said.

"Who? Professor Stanley? If he did would you have come?" Richard offered.

"As a member of the military, don't you have an obligation to tell the truth?" Diane questioned.

"There are many relationships with the U.S. military. Mine is not normal and is none of your concern. You were selected for a reason. You have graduate school ahead of you and more experiences. In time, you will be in position to tell these stories, but that time is not now." Richard looked around at the base. It was dismal, an unworthy oasis. "Be a reporter and write some good things about this trip. Buy some honey and coffee, but don't write what you saw today. Don't share this with your friends or your family. Go back and study, watch the news and see what *they* get wrong. Your time will either come or it won't. I'll keep my eyes on you. If you play your cards right, you'll have a platform to tell it how you see it—one day." With that, Richard walked off, leaving Diane spinning in the wind.

She removed her scarf, and her hair blew in every direction. She fought it back and looked to the mountains, wondering if the Islamic extremists who had decapitated those men were hiding in the shadows of some deep, dark cave, watching her—watching all of them. A chill ran down her spine.

Her trip would end in two days, and she would be back in the States, heading off for winter break. As the sun beat down on her face and the sands blew around her in that desert, she couldn't even recall the feeling of a winter chill. She looked at the blue sky and thought about Jack and figured he was just another boy. She also wondered what made her special in Richard's eyes.

She took out her camera, extended her arms as far as they would go and pointed the lens at herself, barely managing a smile. She clicked off a few shots, took out her notebook, looked back to the mountains and wrote "wanderlust" as dust filled the pages.

Chapter 4

As per the requirements of her internship, Diane had submitted writings that were exactly what Richard called "fluffy bullshit." She received an A for her efforts. Though she didn't hear from him again, she knew Richard was right; there were nights when friends asked about her adventure. She wanted to describe the headless bodies, and on a few boastful occasions she almost did, but something always held her back. Instead, she talked about Yemen's honey, coffee and architecture.

Secretly she wrote about her transformative experiences in her journal, just like she'd done when she was a gawky, brace-faced pre-teen living in New York City. Her father was the assistant to the United States Ambassador to Morocco, and her mother taught political science at Brooklyn College. She was an only child, but never felt alone in the world.

Diane figured her father would know more than she did about world politics, but still she believed in the promise, the words Richard had spoken that day in the dusty desert. Often she would look at the picture she'd taken of herself in Yemen. It was out of focus, and her wild hair blew in the wind, covering most of her face, but in that moment more than any other, she knew she was alive and close to an untold truth.

She entitled her secret essay "America's Next War: Islam and the Middle East." Diane followed international news as Richard had instructed, and she also studied Islam. She bought a copy of the Quran from a used bookstore; it didn't seem like it had ever been read. Being half-Jewish and half-Christian, she never quite knew where she stood spiritually, as her parents did not practice their respective faiths. Diane read the following Quran passage often: "Had the People of the Book (Jews and Christians) accepted the Faith (Islam), it would surely have been better for them. Some are true believers, but most are evil-doers." She knew the decapitated soldiers burned into her conscience were considered evil. What she didn't know was why.

She studied the Quran more; like the Bible, she thought maybe it could be used to express any point of view. Nevertheless, certain passages troubled her: "Believers, take neither the Jews nor the Christians for your friends. They are friends with one another. Whoever of you seeks their friendship shall become one of their number. God does not guide the wrong-doers."

The one person she trusted against all intuition and better judgment was Jack, the boy with the brilliant blue eyes. Roughly a year after returning from Yemen, on a vulnerable fall night, she smoked pot with Jack. He was a political science major, too, but his concentration was communications with a bend toward governmental public relations. They often disagreed about the Vietnam War. Jack's younger brother, James, had enlisted against his wishes and sustained a severe head injury, condemning him to a veteran's hospital for life. James barely recognized Jack whenever he had the chance to visit, and that was heartbreaking for Jack.

Though Diane and Jack argued, they did share an undeniable passion. He was the closest Diane had ever come to having a boyfriend. Most people thought of her as a bookish loner, but that one night, stoned without inhibition, while tempted, she didn't show Jack her writing. Rather, she began talking about Qamariya, Yemen architecture. She spoke about the unique-tasting honey and the coffee, which she declared, "the best ever!" She knew he wanted more information.

"Well, we're still getting hit at those gas pumps," Jack said, breaking from a kiss. His face reflected the glowing candlelight that lit the room. Beads hung from doorways, and tapestries lined the walls of Diane's apartment. A Grateful Dead concert poster from the Robert F. Kennedy stadium, complete with a dancing skeleton holding red roses, hung on the far wall.

"What about the oil, Diane?" Jack said, exhaling a cloud of smoke from a wooden pipe.

"We think it's about oil, but it's not."

"Then what is it about?"

"Religion," Diane said. She kneel-walked over to the record player, unsheathed a record and held it between her palms. She blew off some dust and gently laid it on the turntable. She slowly moved the needle and placed it down. "I just love Cat Stevens's voice," Diane said.

They sat in silence and listened to "The Hurt":

You say you want to learn to laugh 'cause music makes you cry,
but the tears you shed are only in your eye,
so you turn to any phony mouth with a tale to tell,
but he's just a hoaxer, don't you know, selling peace and religion
between his jokes and his karma chewing gum.

Diane kneel-walked back toward Jack and somewhat awkwardly rested her head in his lap. She looked at him, those blue eyes and his Cheshire smile putting her in a trance-like state. She closed her eyes and drifted away, listening to the music.

That was the last time Diane saw Jack for a while. After graduating from George Washington University in 1974, they fell out of touch.

Diane went to New York for a few weeks. When she returned, a mutual friend told her that Jack had taken a job as a campaign manager for an unknown Republican congressman hopeful in Virginia. "A Republican?" Diane muttered under her breath.

Diane accepted a cub reporter job with a weekly newspaper in the suburbs of Washington DC. Regional politics and the occasional features were her normal assignments. She also began freelance on-air reporting for a local television station. Diane encountered some interesting characters, as all journalists do, but still, she couldn't erase the images from the deserts of Yemen; the horrible picture of those decapitated soldiers haunted her, always lingering in the back of her mind.

While covering one story that required hard-hitting investigation into a controversial congressional redistricting issue, Diane discovered that in the previous local election, over 1,000 votes had supposedly been cast by the deceased. The story made national news, and Diane was awarded runner-up for Rookie Reporter of the Year in 1974.

The following week, her editor handed her an unopened envelope. His sandy hair was balding. A bit paunchy and in his mid-fifties, his fingers were stained yellow from chain-smoking. "This came for you, kid, he said. It's got a Washington DC address."

Diane went to her desk, situated in a bright, open newsroom without windows. Typewriters clicked and clacked and phones rang while she opened the letter:

Diane:

It's nice to see that my instincts were right about you. Keep up the good work. It wouldn't hurt to return to graduate school. You'll be a big fish in that pond soon enough. Be sure to say hi to Professor Stanley for me.

Richard Harden

Before long, Diane again took Richard's advice and returned to George Washington University to pursue a master's degree in political science. Back on campus, she recalled hapless days in the pursuit of book knowledge. She had graduated with a 3.8 grade point average and high praise from most of her professors. She had been Valedictorian at graduation from Stuyvesant High School in New York City. Her parents were proud that day and expected the same from her college experience. When she failed to hit the mark, only her mother attended the graduation; her father was "traveling on business."

Diane kept busy with newspaper reporting while attending school, missing class on occasion. With the upcoming bicentennial, she covered a few events, including April 1, 1975, when the American Freedom Train was launched in Wilmington, Delaware, to start its 21-month, 25,388-mile tour of the 48 contiguous states. Then, on April 18, 1975, she covered President Gerald Ford's trip to Boston to light a third lantern at the historic Old North Church, something he said "symbolized America's third century." The following day, she followed the President as he delivered a major speech commemorating the 200th anniversary of the Battles of Lexington and Concord in Massachusetts, the sites where the military aspect of the American Revolution against British colonial rule had begun.

While Ford wasn't an "elected" President and caught his share of grief from the press and jests from *Saturday Night Live*, Diane had a soft spot for him, even though she never interviewed him one on one. She dreamt about such opportunities: interviewing presidents and heads of state. Those were the dreams that scattered through her mind like clouds across a blue sky.

It was July 4, 1976, and Jack Quaid had serendipitously returned to graduate school at the same time, although Diane barely saw him. He had just broken up with a jealous girlfriend and was more open to conversation.

The final class of the summer session also marked the last class before a late summer graduation. She knew Jack would be in her class, an intensive six-week course taught by Professor Christopher Stanley.

On the first day, Diane watched as Jack walked into class with a slightly more mature air to his gait. He donned pork chop sideburns, blue jeans, a white t-shirt with a leather vest. As he took his seat, he locked eyes with her, and she felt a flutter within.

"Okay, guys and girls, whether we like it or not, wars no longer exist overseas. What Vietnam showed us is that war can take place in our living rooms—live, twenty-four hours a day, seven days a week," said Professor Stanley. His gray hair was pulled back into a wispy ponytail. After he spoke, he had a nervous habit of tapping his teeth and squinting, as if he was trying to see how his words landed on the ears of his students. When he wasn't doing that, he was smoking a cigarette. Standing roughly five-ten, he often walked with a cane; a two-headed serpent adorned the handle. "Now, all this Nixon Watergate business took the real truth from the headlines," said Professor Stanley. He slowly walked behind his desk and pointed to an image of General Nguyen Knock Loam, executing a Vietcong prisoner in Saigon. On either side of the blackboard, signs celebrating the Bicentennial were vibrant with red, white and blue.

Diane, hidden behind a wall of dark bangs, addressed the professor. "It's our duty as journalists to show people the truth," she said. Again, her mind flashed to the Yemen desert, to the pictures of the headless bodies. She could still smell the desert sands.

Jack, cool and confident, fired a retort at Diane from across the room. "War is not meant to be seen by those who don't fight it."

The twenty or so classmates seated around them began to crane their necks back and forth between debaters.

"It's our duty as journalists to educate people on current events, not breed a new generation of violent youths via oversaturation of violence on TV," Diane said.

"We *are* this so-called new generation. Do you want to kill right now?" Jack said.

Professor Stanley lit a cigarette and interjected.

"Well, I can see this issue inspires spirited debate . . . and on the first day of class! This is a good sign."

"Excuse me, Professor, but may I wrap up my opinion?" Diane said.

"Briefly."

"We need to expose ourselves to the world. We must not be blind to injustice, for our ignorance—not our intelligence—will be our downfall as a civilization. Knowledge is power, and the more people who have it, the more powerful our generation can be. When the next war or conflict—or whatever the suits and brass want to call it—goes down, we must all pledge to show every frame of truth we can capture," Diane said, looking at Jack, who rolled his eyes.

The professor cleared his throat. "Okay, it's clear you have enthusiasm, Diane. I know you were all discouraged that you have class today, on the Fourth of July and the Bicentennial of our nation, but that's exactly why I hold this class in the summer. I am looking for commitment. At the end of this summer semester next month, and upon your graduation, I will be offering an important position to the person who finishes top in my class. The title will be bestowed anonymously upon the reception of your degree. Wrapped in your diploma will be a message. Tell no one, for this assignment is top secret."

Murmurs and banter filled the room.

A sheepish girl with cropped black hair and a yellow summer dress leaned forward in her seat and whispered in Diane's right ear, "Top secret. Wow! I hope I get it. Well, you too, but you know I hope I do really. I'm mean you got that cool internship and the rest of us—"

Diane rotated her head to the right and whispered out of the side of her mouth, "Best of luck, Jasmine." She next looked at Jack who was whispering with a few guys seemingly about the same thing. She could see Jack waiving off their words and pointing to them as to say, "No, you're going to get the special prize."

Diane furrowed her brow looked back at Professor Stanley and thought about Richard's promise. She wondered if this was a piece to the puzzle they started in Yemen.

"Now settle. Maybe I should have told you individually, seems I caused a stir," Professor Stanley said with a wise smirk. "Go forth and celebrate the freedom this great land offers," he exclaimed. He tapped his cane three times and saluted the class like a dutiful solider.

As the class disbanded and dispersed, Jack walked over to Diane. "Well, you are sure looking well," he said, noticing how her blue jeans hugged her hips perfectly. The thought of the prize hovered around them but they resisted the obvious.

"I took up running, and am sort of addicted now," Diane returned.

"It's working for you."

"So . . . Virginia? Campaign manager?" Diane said with a smirk. "We never really talked about that."

"He lost. *We* lost. I thought he had a chance, but I have set new goals."

"Such as?"

"The White House."

"President?"

"No! Of course not," Jack said, laughing, as if it were the most absurd notion. "Although any one can do better than Nixon."

"Then what?"

"Press and communications. Someone has to wrangle the real truth from you reporters," Jack said with a grin.

"My job will be to tell the American people the truth, not what they hear from the White House," Diane said.

"Anyway, are you going to that party tonight?" Jack said. "I need a date, you know." He smiled again.

"I don't know . . . maybe," Diane returned. "Anyway, for now, I have to get to the library." She walked off, holding her books close to her chest, and smiled.

Later that evening, with Washington DC as the backdrop, a group of students gathered for a Bicentennial party. Patriotic banners and lights were hanging off every house, apartment and street corner lamp.

Diane sat in her apartment and read *The Washington Post.* When asked about the celebration, President Nixon said, "The 1976 Bicentennial is not going to be invented in Washington, printed in triplicate by the Government Printing Office [and] mailed to you by the United States Postal Service."

A born and bred Democrat, she abandoned the notion that either party had it right. "Nixon," she said with a sigh, "thanks for nothing."

As the night rolled on, she thought about Jack, his leather vest and pork chop sideburns. The party was only a few blocks away, and she realized she wouldn't be able to study in the noisy chaos of the fireworks and all the cheers.

She went to her closet and pulled out a denim skirt and white blouse. It was too hot and sticky for panties and a bra. While she didn't accentuate it, her body curved just right. She looked at herself in the mirror. She tapped under her chin and touched the bluish-gray bags under her eyes and smiled. Her teeth were nearly perfect, except for one that was snagged slightly on the top right. Her thick, coarse hair had a few faint, reddish highlights. Her skin tone was similar in hue to how she took her coffee: just a little milk. She rarely wore makeup, but applied some old red lipstick she found in her bathroom drawer. She grabbed her old Army surplus bag and headed out the door.

As she ascended the apartment on M Street, she heard the noise of the party grow louder. Classmates passing her on the stairs were surprised to see her. "Hey! It's cool you made it, Diane!"

She walked into the dimly lit room and found people packed wall-to-wall. Someone passed by and slapped a beer in her hand. She looked across the room to French doors that led to an expansive balcony.

Jack, a whiskey on the rocks in hand, was surrounded by a group of his friends, some of whom Diane recognized from class. They were engaged, hanging on his every word.

"So then she said, 'I was blindfolded. I thought that *was* your nose!'" Jack said, laughing aloud, and the group erupted in laughter. Moments later, Jack saw Diane leaning against the balcony. He walked over and joined her.

"So maybe, just maybe I'm sorry about class today," Diane said.

"You have nothing to apologize for," Jack said. He noticed her wedge high heels and how good they made her legs look.

"C'mon, Jack. I kicked your ass. Don't you remember our little debate?"

"Kicked my ass? If you call whining and spitting out recycled hyperbole winning, then let me be the first to concede," Jack said with a smirk.

"Bitterness is a bitch wrapped in self-doubt. Didn't you say that all the time as an undergrad?" Diane mocked.

"The thing that pisses me off the most about you is that you have so much potential and you're going to waste it on idealism," Jack said. He watched as Diane leaned against the railing; he could tell she wasn't wearing a bra.

"Not when I receive Professor Stanley's secret position," Diane said with a smile. Fireworks blasted off behind them, but they didn't look away from each other. Diane was caught staring at Jack's brass belt buckle, which bore the initials "JQ."

"That confirms my point," Jack said. He sipped his whiskey.

"My apologies if I have grander aspirations. If you could step off your soapbox for once, you might see we're the same height," Diane said, leaning closer to him and looking up.

"Even if we are the same *height*, we are always looking at things from a different angle," he returned, leaning closer.

"Yeah, you're always the conservative one."

Jack recoiled slightly. "Hardly. I'm just . . . sensible."

"A sensible Republican? Did Nixon teach you that?"

"I'm independent . . . and you're right. Nixon blew it," Jack said, giving her a piercing, seductive look.

Diane held up her beer bottle as more fireworks filled the skies with the nation's colors. People were screaming in the streets below and chanting, "Red, white and blue!"

"Cheers to America," Diane said, clinking Jack's glass.

"Cheers indeed," Jack said.

"So, what does a girl have to do around here to get another beer?" Diane asked, leaning closer to Jack.

Chapter 5

The festivities were over. The sun had risen again. The nation was another year older but adrift in many ways. The Washington DC summer heat was unrelenting. The humidity started early and ended late. With no air conditioning, the windows in Diane's apartment were always open. A long, wobbling, droning car horn lifted from the street and caused a stir.

Diane, hung over from drinks the night before, felt underneath the sheets for her body, it was all skin. She took a deep breath, kept her eyes closed and felt to the left-hand side of the bed; a warm, sweaty lump barely moved. The street noise soon quieted, but her head ached. She took another deep breath and rolled over. "Hey," Diane whispered, then cleared her throat. "Pass me that water from the end table."

"Hey there," Jack said, rubbing one eye with his palm and yawning. He smacked his lips and stuck his tongue out. "I could use a drink too."

"Did we . . . ?" Diane said, reaching for the glass.

Jack looked under the sheets at his bare body. "I think we did."

Diane's studio was a no-frills apartment, complete with water-stained ceilings and a refrigerator that sounded like a freight train every time it kicked on. There were trappings of a journalistic tomboy scattered about. Empty coffee cups, a few beer bottles, and a week-old pizza box populated her small kitchen counter. She burned incense often, and the stale smell of lilac and vanilla wafted about the room. Aside from a Smith-Corona Galaxie 12 beige typewriter that sat on her makeshift desk/coffee table surrounded by papers, there was a sculpture of a monkey holding a skull in his hand, pondering while sitting on top of a stack of books. The book directly under his bum said "Darwin" on its spine.

"The guys aren't gonna believe this," Diane said.

"Excuse me?" Jack sat up in bed and lit a cigarette.

"I hate it when you smoke," Diane snapped.

"You had a few last night."

"Whatever. So I did."

"So what do you mean, they won't believe this? We were kissing at the party last night!"

"That is the last time I go out drinking with you," Diane said, crinkling her nose.

Even though it was hot, Diane wrapped a blanket around her naked body and sat on the edge of the bed. The shades were pulled down almost all the way, but through the few inches of exposed glass, she could see that the world was again turning.

"Hey, we were safe. I mean, there's nothing to worry about. You know, we blew off some steam." Jack said. He edged his way over to her side of the bed, three feet from the couch and five feet from the kitchen sink. There were only two doors: the entrance and the bathroom. It was quaint.

"I don't even remember. That's sad. I mean, it's been a while and all, and then I do, and I'm too drunk to really remember," Diane said, shaking her head. "I should listen to my father. He never smokes or drinks."

"Well, you were . . . good," Jack said, with some hesitation. He wasn't as confident in the bedroom as he was in the classroom.

"Anything would be better than your hand, right?" Diane said and poked him in his cheek lightly. "Now put out that cigarette. I'll cook us something."

"You're going to cook?" Jack said, raising his right eyebrow.

"I know a few things."

Diane stood up, and with her back to Jack, stretched and dropped the blanket. As she slightly turned to the left, for a moment, Jack saw her natural beauty: a curvy silhouette. She had a guitar pick-shaped birthmark above her tailbone, like faded red wine against her olive skin. Her hair was in a bushy ponytail. She slipped on a long white t-shirt. As she walked around the bed, she tripped on Jack's underwear, boxers depicting the stars and stripes of the American flag.

"I told you I don't remember last night. If I had to take these off you, I'm not sure how far we would have gone," Diane said, smiling. She threw the boxers at Jack's head as he snubbed his cigarette.

"Hey! Red, white and blue, baby!"

Jack watched as she crossed the room. He liked how free she was. She never wore a bra but never felt the need to burn one either. Her apartment was littered with books, stacked all over the room, covering most of the available floor space. He let out a great big yawn, put on his patriotic boxers, and walked over to a stack of books. He picked up a book of quotations from famous philosophers and politicians and opened to a page of one of his heroes, Winston Churchill. He read to himself, "Men occasionally stumble over the truth, but most of them pick themselves up and hurry off as if nothing happened."

Jack looked at Diane as she threw the pizza box in the garbage and piled cups and dishes high in the sink.

She turned the water on. "How about some eggs?" she said over her shoulder.

"Yeah, fine. Great," Jack said, flipping through the pages. "I love this book of yours," Jack said.

Diane turned. "Oh yeah, that one. It's good. Read me a quote."

Jack flipped the pages again. "Oh, here's a good one from Gandhi. It says, 'Those who say religion has nothing to do with politics do not know what religion is.'" Jack put the book down.

"That's one of my favorites," Diane said.

"Yeah, it makes sense." Jack walked closer to her. As she washed dishes, he wanted to grab her by the hips and pull her close and whisper something, anything. But sober, he couldn't muster the gumption. "So, last night you said a few things—you know . . . after we were done."

"I did?" Diane said, holding a frying pan. She walked to the refrigerator to get eggs and milk. She placed the eggs down and opened the milk container. She smelled it, crinkled her nose and shook her head slightly.

"You said something about Yemen and the desert," Jack said. He walked over to a blurry picture of Diane that was taped to the wall. He examined it carefully.

"That's me, in Yemen," Diane said.

"Hmm. That's interesting. It doesn't really look like you," Jack said.

"I changed on that day."

"What do you mean you *changed*?"

"In that very moment, I grew up in many ways," Diane said as she whisked the eggs.

"Last night, you mentioned that you saw things over there," Jack said. He walked closer to her. "What things?"

"I wish I could tell you. I guess a part of me wants to, but I promised," Diane said, stirring the eggs over a flame. "I guess there are certain truths that take a while to come to the surface."

Jack walked back and picked up the book. "Let me see if I can find a quote about truth," he said and began flipping through the pages.

Diane looked up from cooking the eggs and noticed he was licking his finger when he turned the page. It would have bothered her to see anyone else doing that, as it was a pet peeve of hers, but with Jack, she didn't mind. While he could have used a few laps around the track to tighten up, she liked that he was a bit hairy and unkempt. He was turning into a man, and of course those blue eyes.

"If you want your dreams to come true, don't sleep," Jack read. "That's a good one for you, Diane."

"Who said that?" Diane asked as she plated the eggs.

"It's a Yiddish proverb," Jack responded.

"I guess I should know that," Diane said. "Come over and eat before they get cold."

Jack nodded and walked over to her. He never noticed her motherly side, but there it was for him to see. Her guard was down, and there weren't any politics to argue about. For the first time, he saw a beautiful girl, even if a little lost and a little lonely.

"You know what truth quote I like?" Diane said.

"What?"

"If you tell the truth, you don't have to remember anything."

"Who said that?" Jack asked and nodded.

"Mark Twain."

"Cool."

"We can eat at the couch if you want, or sometimes I just stand," Diane said.

"Let's do the couch," Jack said.

They walked over with plates of steaming scrambled eggs. Diane moved some papers to the floor, and Jack tossed a couple of purple pillows from the gray sofa before sitting down. A few feet away, the bed was still unmade and likely warm from the night before.

"Not bad," he said as chewed his first bite.

"Thanks," Diane said. "I'm really not a cook. This is about it for me."

"Hey, it's food and tastes good." Jack pointed to the sculpture sitting on the table. "Darwin, huh?"

"You know, I just like that this monkey is thinking," Diane said.

They both laughed and finished their eggs.

Diane reached for a newspaper on the carpeted floor. "I was reading about the Brazilian government and their bio-ethanol program. These guys learned from the oil crisis a few years ago, while we didn't. I mean, last year they launched the National Alcohol Program financed by the government to phase out automobile fuels derived from fossil fuels, like gasoline and oil. Instead, they're favoring ethanol produced from sugarcane," Diane said, shaking her head.

"I agree we have to do something about the dependency on oil. It's like Gandhi said about the connection between religion and politics. In the Middle East, there seems to be no line, and that's who we depend on."

"Well, next month, we're on our way. Graduate school over," Diane said. "We have to create change somehow. Any way I can, I will."

"Yeah, I wonder where we'll end up. It's one thing to argue about politics in class with you, but soon, Washington DC, the world becomes our classroom. It's time for fight or flight. I just see changing policy as the answer."

"Policy is one thing, but there are truths to be uncovered first, Jack. We know so little," Diane said before she threw the newspaper down. "Someone's going to get that secret special assignment from the professor. It sounds like cloak-and-dagger stuff," Diane said. She sat Indian style on the couch and reached for an incense burner on the coffee table, then lit a stick.

"I bet you'll get it. He seems to like you," Jack said. "And *my cigarettes* bother you," he said with a smile, waving the thick smoke from his face.

"He likes both of us because we're coming at change from different angles," she said, "and this is the good kind of smoke, by the way . . . calming."

Diane got up and walked over to the windows near the bed. She pulled the shades down quickly. They flung up, snapping into place.

The late morning sun filled the room, and Jack shielded his eyes, mimicking a vampire. "The sun! Not the sun!" he joked in a bad Transylvanian accent. "My head hurts. My skin! Oh, please stop the pain. I will agree to your bio-ethanol program now if you'll only shield the sun!"

Diane rolled her stoic hazel eyes and looked out over the busy streets. She heard a baby crying from a passing stroller. She watched as the mother gently picked the baby up. She couldn't tell if it was a boy or girl, but the baby was tightly swaddled and secure. The mother looked younger than

Diane, and she kissed her baby repeatedly. While Diane couldn't hear her, she watched the mother mouth the word "Hush."

Diane turned away. The room smelled of cooked eggs and vanilla. She looked back at Jack and saw him looking at her. His thick, dark hair was dirty, a little greasy and pulled back. He seemed as comfortable as a hung-over person could be, sitting there in his patriotic boxers. He had a bulbous nose and a small space between his two front teeth; he smiled often, and she always noticed the space. Sometimes she hated arguing with him because she secretly wanted him to grin. She liked his differences, but so did many others.

Diane pulled the curtains down, and the room was twilight again. She walked over to the radio and flipped it on. Led Zeppelin's "Kashmir" filled the room. Diane closed her eyes. "This reminds me of Yemen," she said.

Jack watched as she swayed and danced. They listened as the drums pounded, the melodies soared and vocals ascended:

> *All I see turns to brown, as the sun burns the ground,*
> *and my eyes fill with sand, as I scan this wasted land,*
> *tryin' to find, tryin' to find where I've been.*

Diane slowly opened her eyes, realizing she'd been lost for minutes. She smiled at Jack. She walked over to the nightstand. The music continued to envelop the room. She took a sip of water, placed the glass down and took off her shirt in one fluid motion, as if she'd practiced for the moment. She stood and stared at Jack. "Aren't you thirsty too?" she said.

Jack hurried over, tripping on a leg of the coffee table. They fell onto the bed in a passionate embrace. The music played on.

Diane kissed Jack deeply and held him tight. She knew he'd soon be gone again, on to another campaign or dreaming big at the White House. She pulled his hair slightly and lightly scratched his back. She stopped and kissed him on the nose, then looked into his blue eyes; they were welcoming, warm and friendly. He simply smiled. She wanted to put her index finger between the space in his front teeth but resisted.

Diane looked down at his boxers and saluted Jack as if re-creating a spoofed outtake from *Hogan's Heroes*. "This time, I'm going to remember," Diane said.

Chapter 6

A few weeks had passed. A secret love had developed, but in public, during class, few if any knew of the relationship that was stewing between Jack and Diane. A seasoned, discerning eye, like that of Professor Stanley, however, knew differently.

The end of that July in 1976, the Son of Sam struck for the first time. Newspaper reports said he pulled a gun from a paper bag, killed one woman and seriously wounded a man. Residents of all of New York's boroughs and beyond were panic stricken; they were being terrorized.

"So what do we think of this character, the 44-Caliber Killer?" Professor Stanley questioned the class, throwing down *The Washington Post* on his desk. The summer heat was nearing its height, and the attention spans of the soon-to-be graduates swayed. Two fans at either end of the classroom provided more noises and squeaks than airflow.

"They are telling girls up in New York with long brown hair to cut it or dye it blonde," Diane said. "I just got back from New York, visiting my folks. It's crazy up there. Everyone is in crisis—a real panic."

"So you think it's okay to be forced to give up your rights, to just do what you're told just to be safe?" Jack challenged from across the room.

Diane looked over at Jack. His brilliant blue eyes showed signs of wear. They'd spent the previous night together, drinking red wine and making love. She'd left him sleeping in the early morning hours, but before leaving the apartment, she'd watched as he quietly slept, unhindered by the cares and troubles of the world.

"I fit the demographic, so yes, I thought about it," Diane said, "but then I thought if I give in to this pressure, the chance of it happening to me, then what else might I cave to in the future?" She ran her fingers through her long brown ponytail. She then clasped her hair in her hand and brought the tail tight across her throat.

"If I was living in New York and I were you, I might cut my hair or dye it," Jack said.

Professor Stanley walked over to the window, paused and sat on the sill, facing the class. He sucked on the stem of his glasses and rubbed his eyes. He always lifted his cane when making a point. "There have always been mad men—and some women too," he said now walking between the rows of chairs. "Old blowhards like me around the country and the world try and figure out their motivation. Who knows what is driving this latest murderer?"

"I heard a dog's been telling him to do it," Jack said.

The class laughed.

"No, it's true," he defended. "I read it."

"In a few weeks, you will all be set loose on society, armed with a graduate degree from this fine university," Professor Stanley said, standing next to one of the fans, trying to cool down. "You will be the writers and the thinkers shaping the general public's view. Maybe journalists or communication specialists, or maybe some of you will even go on to the FBI or the CIA. What's most important is delivering the right message."

"You haven't mentioned our final," Diane said.

"My observations of you, along with the essays you have handed in, will result in your final grade. This is your last class before you receive that diploma in your hot little hands. There are no grades out in the real world," he said, pointing to the window. "You will be judged on your merits and your mind. Work hard, I say, and the rest will come to you."

"Were you serious about that special assignment?" asked a student in a tie-dyed t-shirt from the back row.

"Are you serious about this class and your future?" Professor Stanley countered.

"I am," Jack interjected.

"Me too," the student replied with less gusto.

"Yes, my dears. One prize awaits one special person," Professor Stanley said. "Okay, now, quick as you can, class is over."

*   *   *

A week had passed. It was a Friday, and Diane had met her parents at the Willard Hotel. They arrived in town for the graduation ceremony the next day, and she was happy her father made it.

"You could have stayed with me," Diane said as she hugged her mother in the lobby.

"It's easier this way, and . . . well, your father made up his mind," said Diane's mother Carol. Diane had her mother's nose that beveled to a point at the tip and her same thick hair, though Carol's now showed streaks of gray.

"Your sunglasses! You look like Jackie O," Diane said.

"Oh please! You know, I saw her not long ago, walking along Central Park West. She was a vision, a real beauty," Carol said. Her blouse was multicolored and fit snugly to her body. Her tan skirt ran to her knees. "Simply gorgeous, that woman is."

"Where is Dad?" Diane questioned.

"He had to take a call, something about a visa for his assistant. It's always something, you know, honey," Carol said, motioning to a couch in the lobby, and they both sat down. "So tell me, are you ready for what comes next?"

"I want to travel and report—you know, just get into the details of it," Diane said.

"It?" Carol questioned.

"Remember when you and Dad marched with Martin Luther King from Selma to Montgomery in '65?"

"Yes, of course."

"Well, that's the sort of 'it' I'm after," Diane said.

"You know how badly beaten your father was. Change can be tough," Carol said, shaking her head. "Sometimes I worry for you."

"Every time I look at his left eye, I think about the police baton that struck his head repeatedly. I also remember that he didn't stop marching," Diane said and then bit her middle fingernail nervously.

"We just dressed his wounds and kept moving forward . . . and stop biting your nails," Carol said lightly tapping Diane's hand. "Oh look! Here he is now," Carol said, pointing toward the elevator.

Hassan Ziati stood just over six feet. He was slender, with sharp, angular facial features. He had full, thick, coarse hair that was graying at the temples. His brown tailored suit was offset by a blue, metallic tie. While he became a U.S. citizen in 1959, he was fearful of his Moroccan lineage, particularity that of his Muslim father that impregnated his Christian mother and only stuck around for three years. Ziati was his given surname, but for his only daughter Diane; he wanted to break his father's legacy. It was decided that she would use Carol's family name, Babel.

"Dad!" Diane yelled across the lobby.

He walked over with a smile that brightened his dark complexion. He often wore brown tinted prescription sunglasses to hide his damaged eye.

"You're sure I can't convince you to work with me at the United Nations?" Hassan said in a slight English accent. "I'm so very proud of you, my daughter."

"We've had this discussion before. I want to be a journalist, on the air, breaking hard news," Diane said, brushing lint off his shoulder and straightening his tie. "And I'm proud of you . . . for making it here today."

"Well, I have to leave right after the ceremony tomorrow on a flight to London, but of course I would not miss this . . . my little girl."

"There is a nice spot down the street to eat, and then I'm meeting up with some friends—you know, just a little celebration," Diane said.

"Is this Jack going to be there?" Carol said.

"Jack?" Hassan questioned.

"Mom, he's just a friend."

"All I'm saying is that you were quick to change the subject of that horrid Son of Sam killer last time you visited. It seemed you much rather wanted to talk about this *Jack* and your heated classroom debates," Carol said. "You know, your dad and I used to debate about politics," she said, smiling at Hassan. "Remember the Bay of Pigs?"

"How could I forget?" Hassan asked, smiling.

"Oh how we loved Kennedy, but I hated his handling of it. Your dad thought otherwise. One night, when all the weight of war and the world hung on our shoulders, we went to this little club in the Village. Maybe it was the Gaslight. In any case, there he was, Bob Dylan. We really didn't know much about him at the time. It was an off night, sort of slow, and he was playing this song . . ."

Carol looked around the lobby. There was a grand piano unoccupied, and she walked over to it.

"Your mother," Hassan said, shaking his head.

Carol sat at the piano and tapped the chords to "A Hard Rain Is Going to Fall." She lightly sang:

Oh, what did you see, my blue-eyed son?
And what did you see, my darling young one?

Their voices weren't terribly good, but they evoked character and passion. As the verses rolled on, a tear fell past the rim of Hassan's glasses. He sat on the bench next to Carol and joined on the chorus: *"And it's a hard, it's a hard, it's a hard, and it's a hard, it's a hard rain's a-gonna fall."*

Porters and bellhops looked on with curiosity. A young, golden-haired woman sitting on an adjacent brown leather couch with a drawn face broke into a sheepish smile. Diane looked around and smiled too. She walked behind her parents and placed her hands on their shoulders. She could feel the reverberations of the notes cycle through their bodies. When the next chorus came around, Diane joined with their voices: *"And it's a hard, it's a hard, it's a hard, and it's a hard, it's a hard rain's a-gonna fall."*

By the last verse, a small group watched from a few feet away. As Carol hit the last note on the piano, some people clapped and then slowly went about their day.

"When we heard that song on that desperate night, we realized that no matter what we were up against, if nothing else, we had each other." Carol grabbed Hassan's hand and smiled. "Now, let's eat. You look too thin, Diane."

*   *   *

The following morning, Diane awoke to an alarm. She knocked it off the nightstand in a failed attempt to turn it off; it broke, sending shards of glass across the floor.

"You are such a heavy sleeper," Jack said. He was standing across the room, holding Diane's cap and gown.

"How long have you been here?" Diane asked, rubbing her eyes.

"Not long. You're so weird, not letting me stay here when your parents are in town," Jack said. He pointed to the floor. "Put on some slippers or shoes before you walk around." He walked over to the bed and laid the gown down, then leaned in and gave her a kiss.

"Did you already have a cigarette today? I thought you were quitting," Diane said and crinkled her nose. "Those things will kill you one day."

"What can I say? I'm nervous. Aren't you?"

"About graduation?" Diane queried as she stepped into a pair of sandals.

"About the prize . . . from Stanley," Jack said.

"Well, your grades are a bit better than mine. You'll probably get it. Seems like a boys' club anyway. And remember what we agreed. We wait until we're back in our seats and open the diploma at the same time, not onstage or sneak it when walking back, Jack," Diane said, closing the bathroom door.

Jack walked over to her coffee table and smelled a vase of sunflowers. The attached note read, "Congratulations! The world is now yours. Love you always, Mom and Dad."

The ceremony commenced at one p.m. The temperature neared ninety degrees, and the air was thick. Jack and Diane arrived separately, Diane with her parents and Jack alone. His father had died four years earlier from pancreatic cancer, and his mother had then remarried and moved to Hawaii; she claimed the trip would be "too much" for her. His brother James was not well enough to attend.

Bob Woodward gave the commencement speech, a journalist's journalist. When he addressed the crowd, he did so knowing that his reporting, along with Carl Bernstein's, had brought down the most important man in the country, the President of the United States.

Sweat beaded on Diane's forehead, but she couldn't take her eyes off the podium. To Woodward's left sat Professor Stanley.

Woodward said, "In January 1973, at age twenty-nine, Carl Bernstein and I had written the major Watergate story, saying there was a criminal conspiracy in the Nixon White House and that the highest-level people were involved. *The Washington Post* backed us, and quite frankly, most people, including our colleagues at *The Washington Post* did not believe what we had written.

"Katharine Graham, the owner and publisher of *The Washington Post*, invited me for lunch in her dining room. So I went up and met with her. As I said, she backed what we did. I walked into the room, and she had this look on her face of, *What have you boys been doing with my newspaper?* People have wondered, *How can you get a look like that on your face?* If you'd been there, you would have realized what it was.

"Then we sat down and she started questioning me about Watergate and Nixon and his people and what it was about. I was blown away with what she knew. She was so conversant with the material. But she had a management style that I would later describe as mind-on, hands-off. Intellectually, we were totally engaged in what we were doing, but her hands were not on, telling us how to do it—not ever."

Diane looked for her parents and then for Jack. The speech became distant as she again thought about her diploma and what might else be included. Applause erupted when his speech ended. Diane fanned herself with her program and wished she could disrobe from the black cloak that surrounded her.

The diplomas were handed out by department. There were only seventeen students in Jack and Diane's class. As her name was called, Diane could hear her parents cheering her name. Her father had a distinctive whistle that sounded like a royal trumpet.

As she ascended the stairs, she looked at Mr. Woodward and mouthed, "Thank you." He nodded. She next walked to Professor Stanley. The noise of the cheering crowd insulated her thoughts.

As she was given her diploma, Professor Stanley whispered in her ear "Always do your best work . . . always."

The diploma was in a bi-fold red leather book, and it felt heavy in her hands. She wanted to open it right there onstage and see if she was, in fact, the chosen one, but she couldn't—not until Jack had his in his own hands. Again she heard the trumpet whistle and was briefly distracted long enough to keep walking and resist the urge to look. Other classmates ahead of her had already looked, and no one seemed to have cause for special celebration. She looked at Jasmine, the only other possible contender than Jack. Her face was transparent like a scoreboard underscoring a home team loss.

Jack will win, she thought to herself.

As she sat back in her seat, she watched as Jack received his diploma, he was second to last. Professor Stanley whispered in his ear too, and Jack proudly raised it in the air. He caught Diane's eyes and mocked opening the diploma; she returned a stern look. He smirked and walked back to his seat. Professor Stanley watched stoically.

The diploma sat in Diane's lap like a hot stone, burning her with anticipation. As the president of the university gave his closing remarks, she knew caps would soon decorate the sky briefly before falling back to Earth.

When Diane heard the president say, "I wish you, the graduate class of this year, 1976, progress, servitude and Godspeed," she figured the speech was over and opened the diploma. A small piece of white paper stuck out from behind the degree. She pulled it out slowly. Her classmates to either side craned their necks, but Jack was too far away to see.

The note read: "WASHINGTON MONUMENT. NOON. TOMORROW."

She quickly tucked it away without notice. Diane lost herself in the moment and threw her cap into the air and yelled, "Yes!" but the President's speech wasn't yet done. With that, her classmates followed.

The begrudged president stopped mid-sentence, threw up his arms and exclaimed, "Congratulations!"

Diane's faced turned red. The whistle trumpeter was in full swing. She slipped the note into her pocket. Caps fell from the sky all around. She bent down to pick up a cap when she heard Jack call from behind, "What got into you? Did you—"

"I'm so embarrassed. It must be the heat," Diane said.

"But did you . . . uh, you know. Did you *win*?" Jack said.

"No, not me. You?" Diane said.

"I didn't win," Jack said.

Chapter 7

"How many times do I have to say it, Jack?" Diane screamed into the phone. "I didn't win. Listen, I need some space. This just . . . it isn't working for me!" She slammed the phone down and stared at the white piece of paper that seemingly held more weight than her diploma. Having accepted the position, she assumed this would be the first of a long string of necessary lies.

She'd been unable to sleep the night before and had failed to meet Jack at a graduation party on K Street. It was now nearly ten in the morning, and minutes ticked slowly toward her noon meeting. Diane walked over and looked at the picture she'd taken of herself in Yemen a few years earlier. She walked to the bathroom mirror and noticed that she'd aged a bit; there were a few new wrinkles around her eyes and deeper, darker circles from too many sleepless nights.

The flowers her parents had given her were already wilting from the summer heat. Feeling nervous, she flipped on the television. A reporter was interviewing Bruce Jenner, who had just won the gold medal in the decathlon during the summer Olympic Games that had recently concluded in Montreal. Diane was impressed to learn that he'd set a new world record, scoring 8,634 points.

The reporter asked, "Last month, no one knew your name. Now everyone knows the name Bruce Jenner. How does it feel to win on such a grand scale?"

Jenner had thick, feathered-back, dirty blond hair and wore his medal with pride. His tank top featured three letters, "USA," and his smile was ear to ear. "I learned that the only way you are going to get anywhere in life is to work hard at it. Whether you're a musician, a writer, an athlete or a businessman, there is no getting around it. If you do, you'll win. If you don't, you won't."

Diane flipped the TV off and walked over to a stack of books. She grabbed a notebook and a few pens and threw it into a leather bag she'd used when on assignment in Yemen. Often she would smell it, close her eyes and see whirling sands. She also saw the dead men in the photograph, as if the beheaded images had been silk-screened on her memory. She often wondered why she'd never heard of Muslim extremism in the States. It wasn't a topic that was readily covered in the news. *The only thing Americans seem to care about is the price of gasoline,* she thought.

She recalled her mother's concern for her future but was resolute, knowing that a tough road ahead was to be expected. Diane, or Di, as her mom would sometimes call her, wanted to call Jack and apologize and tell him the truth, but she couldn't. She was preparing to be alone.

She picked up one of her favorite books, *Black Like Me,* by journalist John Howard Griffin. In 1959, he left behind a white, privileged, Southern lifestyle and, under a doctor's care, changed the color of his skin, darkening it so as to appear black. He then spent six weeks traveling through the Deep South and chronicled in his journal about how poorly he was treated. Diane had received the book as a sixteenth birthday gift from her father, and she'd dog-eared her favorite parts, revisiting them often.

She opened to Page 12 and read: "The completeness of this transformation appalled me. It was unlike anything I had imagined. I became two men, the observing one and the one who panicked, who felt Negroid even to the depths of my entrails. I felt the beginnings of great loneliness, not because I was a Negro, but because the man I had been, the self I knew, was hidden in the flesh of another."

Diane closed the book and fought back a tear. Her heart raced. She threw the book in her bag, grabbed the hidden diploma note off the coffee table and walked toward the door. As she opened the front door, she looked across the hall and saw a daily newspaper on the ground. The headline read: "After More Bombings and Death, 10,000 Protestant and Catholic Women Demonstrate for Peace in Northern Ireland."

Diane let out a heavy sigh and moved forward. Once off the bus, she walked to the reflecting pool leading up to the Washington Monument. She looked over her shoulder occasionally, wondering if she was being watched or followed. She looked for Professor Stanley and for Jack, but the mall was busy with tourists snapping pictures, dog-walkers and joggers. Everything seemed to be as it should.

From a distance, the monument was so much more than the phallic joke it had become among Diane's women's rights friends. She knew, much like the White House, that it represented America. And it would be here that a new chapter in her life would begin.

She walked on the right side of the reflecting pool. With every step, her heart beat faster. She stopped and bent down and looked at her reflection. She ran her hand through the tepid water and watched as her reflection distorted. She took a series of deep breaths, stood up and walked closer and closer, realizing she couldn't recall ever being that close to the monument.

She again looked around but saw nothing out of the ordinary. Diane walked to the far side of the monument and came to a door. A sign read: "Closed for renovations." She looked around again and knocked.

Within moments, the door opened. A group of Japanese tourists, oblivious, snapped away, taking pictures of the monument.

A man, over six-six, wore sunglasses and a brown beard that was tight to his face. A white wire fell from his ear, and he spoke in a low voice, "Diane Babel?"

"Yes," she said, fishing for her wallet. "Do you need identification?"

"The note. Just show me the note."

Diane produced the little piece of white paper, worn from her handling.

The man's cologne was strong and barely covered his odor from the heat of the day. He took the note and looked at it closely, then pointed down the hall. Diane, confused but excited, made her way down the marble hallway. It was cool but stuffy, and she saw a figure standing at the end of it. She walked closer; every step echoed. She looked behind her, but the guard was gone.

"Ms. Babel, I'm glad to see you could make it," a man's voice said, though it was still hard for Diane to see his face, "and you are right on time."

"Of course," she said, walking faster, at a speed to match her beating heart. When she was close enough to see his face, she stepped back. "Mr. Harden? It's you!"

"It's been some time since Yemen," he said. He looked taller and more rugged than Diane remembered, and he was dressed in a sports jacket and blue jeans. "I've asked about you several times, but Professor Stanley was always . . . aloof," Diane said. "Thanks for your note. You know, when I won the award, it really meant a lot to me and pushed me toward graduate school."

"Well, you deserve it, as well as our support. Listen. Stanley told me you were asking for me. I've been *observing* you. You didn't actually finish first in the class."

"What? How do you know?"

"It's my business to know. That honor belongs to Jack Quaid."

"Jack? I don't get it. Then why am I here?"

"I know how difficult it is being a reporter, but you're a woman, Jewish and half-black to boot. Those are some serious odds. I can get you a position at Intrepid Television News (ITN) as a correspondent," Richard said and lit a cigar. He looked both ways and exhaled. "Jack will do all right. He has a future too."

"I'm flattered, and I certainly appreciate your effort. I get the woman part and the black part, of course, but what's the deal about being Jewish? I mean, look at Hollywood," Diane said. She rested her leather bag on the ground and tried not to be bothered by the smoke.

"That brings me to my point. I'm sure you're wondering what this is all about."

"Of course."

"How much do you know about me, Diane?"

"Well . . . the desert, Yemen . . . I was an intern, and . . . well, you probably know as much as you think I know."

"And that's just the way I like it. I'm a man who finds deep comfort in privacy. I've always wanted to remain more or less anonymous. However, you Diane, have different aspirations. You have that spark in your eye, Diane. You want to be a household name."

"I only want to tell the truth."

"Exactly, and that's the power I'm going to give you. I've seen a lot of things that I've been powerless to prevent. Knowledge is a heavy burden. I know people. I spent thirty years of my life working as a secret operative for the CIA and NSA and have formed an alliance of some of the greatest intelligence units ever assembled. We're ready to go public with our information related to the Middle East. You, Diane, could be our voice."

"What are you saying?" Diane exhaled. "This is a lot to take it."

"Listen, I've been hired, at least on paper, as a military political consultant and have the rank to hire any journalist I see fit for the on-camera position. It's not a primetime network, but—and no offense, of course—no network in the world is going to take a risk of putting a half-Jewish, black, post-graduate student in front their camera. But you have an interesting look. I don't see Jewish or black. Rather, I see you as universal. We watched you on the local stations while you were going to grad school. You look good on camera. You look the part. I also read a couple of your freelance articles, and I want you in on the ground floor."

"That's just . . . it's incredible." Diane took out her notebook and began scribbling notes.

"I'm sure you're overwhelmed. I can explain more later, but for now—"

Diane cut him off. "When do I begin?"

Richard motioned down the hall. "Do me a favor and read what that plaque says, Diane."

Diane looked at the words.

"Read it aloud," Richard said. "I want to hear George Washington's words coming from *your* lips."

Diane cleared her throat. "Um, okay. I have no lust after power but wish with as much fervency as any man upon this wide, extended continent for an opportunity of turning the sword into a plowshare."

"He wrote that in 1776, 200 years ago, almost to the day. What does it mean to you?"

"That knowledge is power," Diane said.

"Yes, and do you remember how I told you to *observe* in Yemen?" Richard said.

"Yes, when I misspoke in front of the general," Diane conceded.

"Exactly! Now is the time to turn the sword into a plowshare, and this position I'm offering has the ability to serve our collective interests . . . and those of the nation." Richard dropped the cigar and snubbed it with his black boots; Diane noticed a bulge on his left ankle and figured it was a gun.

"It's nearly twelve thirty," the guard's voice bellowed down the hall.

Richard looked at his watch. "Is your passport in order?"

"Yes. I've traveled a lot because of my parents . . . well, my dad."

"Yes. We know all about your family. We have a record of it. We know about your father, and he will likely not be supportive of ITN due to its connections to questionable investors overseas," Richard said. "Will that be a problem for you?"

"Who are these investors?" Diane questioned.

"Interested parties from Iran, Soviets, and some guys I know from England. Their names aren't important. They are on the right side of things these days, but they do have a questionable past," Richard said.

"Soviets? Are they communists?" Diane asked.

"They were."

"And now?"

"Now they enjoy a shared mission of turning profit while telling the real news things that CBS and NBC won't tell the American people—or the world, for that matter. There is a *world* out there, Diane, and most Americans only see what the media wants them to see, and when I say the *media*, I'm including the White House."

Diane shook her head and looked to the ground. After seeing Richard's scuffed boots, she wondered why she'd opted for dress shoes. "So I will have free reign to report?" Diane said.

"We set the assignments, but yes, you are free to report as you will. Of course you will have a producer, Bart Duran, but we all have a shared mission," Richard said. "But no one must know of our connection, at least to ITN. Never mention my name to Bart—or to anyone else, for that matter."

"How will we communicate?" Diane asked.

"We will meet frequently in and around this city. I will send word to you through various means. My conversations will help you to set the tone, and in many cases, bring you up to speed, because you have a lot to learn if you plan on teaching the American public the truth."

"So what do I tell my parents? My friends?" Diane said.

"You applied for a job and were hired as a reporter. It makes perfect sense, and they'll buy it," Richard said, looking down the hall.

"Well, to be honest, I don't think many people know about ITN. If I wasn't in the business, I don't think I'd be aware of it."

"Fair enough. It's only a year old, but we just signed a deal with PBS, so we are securing weekly airtime. That's where people in the U.S. will find you." Richard handed Diane a pile of paperwork. "Read through these materials to find answers to most of your questions. You'll have to fill out some forms and provide information—you know, administrative protocol. Your annual salary will be $15,000, and all expenses will be paid. Be prepared to be on the road more than at home."

"In regard to the money—"

Richard cut her off. "The terms are not negotiable."

"Okay," Diane said, waving her hand, so as not to be confrontational. "When do I start?"

"Have that paperwork completed by tonight. The manila envelopes contain directives, plane tickets and a per diem. You will meet Bart, your crew and soundman tomorrow. Your first assignment will be in Madrid, Spain, and you'll leave the same day, tomorrow night."

"What? I'm going to Spain tomorrow?" Diane's eyebrows bounced on her forehead.

"Yes. Take the rest of the day to settle your affairs," Richard said.

"When will I return?" Diane said.

"Listen, I'm happy to have you onboard, but this isn't Professor Stanley's class. I'm not going to hold your hand any more than I have to. Do as you're told, and you'll be taken care of. Too many questions will indicate to me that you're not right for the job," Richard said gruffly.

"Okay. I understand."

"I told you once to observe, and now I want you to observe and report the truth and keep your nose clean." Richard pulled a red tie from his inside jacket pocket and began to put it on.

"Will do. What about the Middle East, the things we saw in Yemen?"

"I have spent a lot of time there. Our focus—*your* focus—will soon be there too," Richard said.

"But all those beheadings and bombings . . . is it safe?"

"I'm not here to sugarcoat things. You will face danger at some point, just as we all have," Richard said solemnly.

"Is it all right to be nervous?" Diane asked in a whisper.

"Nervous? Yes. Scared? No," Richard said plainly. "And as far as Jack Quaid goes, slowly break ties with him. You have no room for love in your life right now," Richard said, completing a perfect Windsor knot.

"Love?" Diane said weakly.

"Trust me, it's better to go it alone for a while." Richard looked at his watch again. "I must go. Take a few moments and gather yourself. When you're ready, Sam, who let you in, will let you out."

"I just want to thank you. I mean—" Diane began.

"The best thanks you can give me is a job well done. I expect nothing less," Richard said. He extended his right hand, and Diane shook it firmly before he turned and headed down the hall. The echoes of his footsteps were deep and far-reaching.

Diane looked at the papers in her hand, leaned against the wall and slid down. She exhaled and blew her bangs off her forehead.

"Ms. Babel, you have five minutes," Sam's voice was loud and direct.

Diane opened the manila envelope and took out a laminated press pass. There was also her graduation photo, a roundtrip plane ticket, $100 in cash and a pocket-sized Spanish dictionary, which she opened. She searched for the word that best described her feelings and quickly found it: *Asombroso!*

Richard was already blocks away, standing in a pay phone booth in a nearly empty playground. A few kids were playing basketball. He looked down at a piece of paper that read: "Zbigniew Kazimierz Brzezinski," followed by a phone number. Richard looked around a few times before dropping a dime, and the phone rang three times before it was answered.

"Brzezinski, it's Dick."

"I've been waiting for your call," a voice returned.

"Don't speak. Just listen. She is onboard. Babel is a go. I'm counting on you to keep your end of the deal. I'll make sure the Islamic Green Belt is kept in check and free of Russian influence. Let the Shah stay where he is, and let him try and mediate these oil contracts. Trust me, we are both looking for the same outcome, even if we're coming at this from different angles. Babel's reporting will distract both sides so we can meet our objectives. Don't screw with me on this, Brzezinski. Carter looks like a lock, and we have to put our differences behind us. When you are the United States National Security Advisor, remember this conversation."

Richard hung up the phone, lit a cigar and pulled out a picture from his inside jacket pocket. He was depicted smiling, standing in front of a Christmas tree with his wife, Molly, and daughter, Deborah. The bottom of the picture read: "1968." A tear ran down his cheek. He wiped it away and slowly walked away from the phone booth, watching the children play ball.

Chapter 8

Diane sat on her couch. The once bright yellow sunflowers from her graduation sat wilting in the vase, all but faded. She looked at her ITN press badge and smiled.

The phone began ringing. She thought it was Jack again; the phone had been ringing and ringing since she'd returned from the meeting with Richard. After the last ring reverberated through her otherwise still stuffy apartment, she took the phone off the receiver. She walked over to the kitchen table, grabbed her leather bag and fished out her notebook. She sat down and began writing:

Dear Jack,

I'm sorry to be distant. My dad pulled some strings and got me a job, and I will be working oversees a lot. You might not know the company, but it's ITN. I wanted to tell you in person. I really did, but I have to leave for Spain tomorrow.

You are one of the closest friends I have . . . well, more than just that. I know that probably sounds strange, but it's true. I think about us often, but I don't have room for a relationship. I'm not sure it's possible to only have a friendship with you. I ran into Clarissa from class at the market, and she told me you have an interview at the White House, to possibly work for the press secretary. I wish you all the best.

ITN is working with PBS on newscasts, special reports and breaking news. I guess you can find me there if you want. I hope to

*write to you again in the not-too-distant future, but for now, I just
need my space. Please understand.*

With love,
Diane

The following morning, Diane took one last look at her apartment
before going to meet her crew at the airport. She had a few bamboo plants
that she overwatered, but nothing else would live unattended in that space
until she returned. Before slipping the key in and locking the door, she
dropped her bags and headed back into the apartment. She walked over to
the wall and grabbed the picture of herself that she'd taken in Yemen. She
walked back to the door, opened one of her bags and slid the photo into
her copy of *Black Like Me.*

She dropped Jack's letter in the mailbox and followed the directions
provided in the manila envelope. Diane, hurried and visibly nervous,
hailed a cab to the airport, where she would meet Bart, her cameraman
and field producer. As she sat in traffic, she held her leather bag close to
her chest. At times she was prone to panic attacks.

She heard screams to her right and quickly looked to a rusted brown
Buick. With the morning heat on the rise, the windows were open. Inside,
a young couple was screaming at each other. The girl looked so helpless
to Diane, until she threw a Coke bottle across the front seat, just missing
the man's head.

"You fucking bitch!" he screamed. "That's it! It's over this time."

"Fine!" the girl yelled back. She opened the door as the light was
turning green and stomped away.

Diane's driver was an older man with a dark complexion and graying
hair. As he drove, he shook his head. "It is difficult for a man laden with
riches to climb the steep path that leads to bliss," his voice was foreign,
distant to her.

"Excuse me?" Diane said, leaning forward.

"These are words from the Quran," the man said softly.

"Where are you originally from?" Diane questioned; the coincidence
was not lost on her.

"Egypt, but I have been here driving since 1969," he said, stopping at
a red light. "Those two young people were fighting, and for what? Allah
says He does not love those who reject Him, does not love those who are

transgressors, does not love those who are evil-livers. He does not love evil talk."

"Maybe they do not believe as you do," Diane suggested.

"Maybe, but it is the only truth you see, Allah." He continued to drive, and Diane noticed his pleasant smile in the rearview mirror. "Okay, we are here. Pan Am is a very good airline. Eleven dollars please."

Diane opened her purse and handed him fifteen. "Keep it," she said with indifference.

"Bless you, bless you," the driver said. He turned to her and smiled. His eyeteeth were missing, and he had hair growing on the bridge of his nose.

"Right," Diane said and grabbed her two bags and shut the door. She banged twice on the roof, and the cab pulled away.

"So where is this Bart?" she murmured to herself.

She walked among countless travelers, some on business and others for leisure. One little girl was on a bench crying, while her father tried to console her. It reminded her of the first trip she'd taken with her parents, when she was only nine. They were going to London, but Diane had forgotten her favorite doll, a Raggedy Anne that she named Sue. She cried and cried in the airport. Her father took off his tie, wadded it into a ball and took out his yellow handkerchief and wrapped it around the balled tie. Then he reached into his briefcase and grabbed a rubber band, which he secured around the handkerchief to create a head. With a pen, he drew two eyes, a nose and a smiley face. Diane remembered her tears drying, and she named that makeshift doll Timmy.

"Diane Babel?"

She was snapped back to the moment and turned to see a fiery redhead approaching.

"Diane Babel? I'm Bart, your producer and cameraman. I know. Big budget, right?" he said, extending his hand with a smile. "Mike, the soundman, is already inside, and we have checked the equipment. Let's hope it gets there with us."

Diane nodded. "Yes, it's . . . well, nice. I mean, uh . . . hi." The words fell from her mouth. "Sorry. It's been a long day, and I didn't sleep much last night. Let me start over. I'm Diane, and I look forward to working together with you."

Bart's skin was pale and populated by more freckles than she had seen on any one person in a long time. He was short and rotund and a few years older. He had an angelic face, but he was wearing a devil's smirk. He pointed to the airport doors. "Spain awaits our arrival." He handed her a few Spanish newspapers. "How's your Spanish?" he asked with a smile.

"It's okay. I have a dictionary," Diane said pointing to her leather bag.

"Well, we have a translator, Sandra, meeting us on the other side, and also our driver. Hector's a good guy. I've used him before. Anyway, read up as much as you can, because tomorrow is supposed to be the big news day. Franco's death is finally taking hold."

"Yes, there was some information on this with my assignment, but it's good to have the newspapers. Thanks," Diane said.

Diane wasn't seated next to Bart or Mike; rather, she was in the back of the plane. By the time she passed their seats, Mike already had his sleeping mask on.

Bart just smiled and waved. "See you in Spain."

It had been almost a year since Francisco Franco, the Spanish dictator, military general and head of state of Spain died from complications of Parkinson's disease. He ruled from October 1936 until his death. He came to power as a prominent member of the far-right Falange movement. Falangism, likened to Italian fascism in certain respects, shared its contempt for Bolshevism and other forms of socialism and harbored a distaste for democracy, Diane learned. Not unlike the Italian Fascist Blackshirts, the Falange had its own party militia, the Blueshirts. Diane recalled that the Falange's National Syndicalism was a political theory different from the fascist idea of corporatism, instead inspired by Integralism.

In Franco's wake, a political uprising occurred throughout the country. While Spaniards were split on Franco's legacy, many recalled how he killed as many as 50,000 countrymen during the first Spanish Civil War dating back to the 1930s. There was a cry for democracy, but it wouldn't come easy. Unrest and protest filled the streets, and blood was shed daily.

Diane had picked up a copy of *The New York Times* to brush up on recent events, as she knew the Spanish newspaper would be a challenge. She was excited and inspired to learn that only months earlier, over 500,000 workers had protested in Vitoria, but police violence called for more bloodshed. In total, more than twenty-seven people had been killed in similar protests since Franco's death. Diane wondered if she might be number twenty-eight.

An older woman, roughly Diane's mother's age, sitting two seats away, pointed to the newspaper. "*La libertad tiene un precio*," she said.

Diane searched for her Spanish dictionary and hurriedly flipped through it.

The woman leaned closer and, in a thick Spanish accent, repeated, "Freedom has a price." The woman softly nodded her head and smiled at Diane and looked out the window into the black night. Diane continued reading the article.

In March, Spain celebrated its first International Women's Day. There were over 17,000 labor complaints, and thousands of workers went on strike, often going without pay for months at a time. As the people continued to rebel, King Juan Carlos the First of Spain and Queen Sophia, who had recently visited the Shah and Shahbanou of Iran at the Mehrabad Airport, said the government was "impotent in front of the labor offensive."

As a nod to the people, the king later dismissed Arias Navarro. After serving in various positions, including Mayor of Madrid from 1965 to June 1973, he was named Minister of Governance in June 1973. After the assassination of Prime Minister Luis Carrero Blanco, he was appointed to that office, a position he held after the death of Franco. But civil unrest continued with more deaths and assassinations. This was trial by fire for Diane, and she knew it.

Hours later the plane screeched its wheels, landing at Madrid Barajas International Airport. As Diane deplaned, she could see Bart's red head. The site was oddly comforting to her. When she entered the waiting area, she was approached by Mike. He was tall, with John Lennon-style glasses, bushy black hair and long sideburns like Neil Young's. His Rolling Stones lips-logo t-shirt was wrinkled and worn.

"Sorry I was so out of it on the plane. I didn't hear about this gig until yesterday morning, and I had a quite a night before that," Mike said with a smile. "Anyway, I'm Mike. Anything you need, just let me know."

Diane smirked, caught off guard by his affability and soothing voice. "I'm Diane. Thanks, Mike."

After forty minutes of waiting, they gathered their bags and equipment and headed to curbside pickup. Standing in front of a nondescript blue van was a short man with oily hair, dark sunglasses and a toothpick rolling back and forth across his mouth. He held a sign that read, "ITN."

"Hector," Bart bellowed, "it's good to see you."

"Yes, my friend. *Si*! Did you have a nice trip?"

"We did, *amigo*. We did."

"And who is this?" Hector said, pointing toward Diane, who was wearing sunglasses and was clutching her leather bag tightly.

"I'm Diane Babel," she said sternly.

Hector grabbed her hand and kissed it. "Let me be the first to welcome you to Madrid. The city is dangerous now, but do not worry. With me, you are in good hands." Hector motioned to grab her bag, but she leaned back.

"It's okay. I've got it. The other bags are on the cart," Diane said. The airport was busy and loud, distracting.

Hector spat out the toothpick and smiled. "Okay."

As they drove through Puerta del Sol en route to central Madrid, Diane watched as large areas of city squares were taken over. It reminded her of the sit-ins of the 1960s, though it felt more violent—something akin to the Kent State shootings. She watched as people of all ages marched through the streets carrying signs, many of which read "*Libertad!*" Others depicted Franco in effigy.

"So, Diane, how long have you been in the business? I got your résumé and watched a few clips, but to be honest, I'm sort of surprised they are throwing you into this lion's den," Bart said. He lit a cigarette and rolled down the window.

"I'm sort of surprised myself, to be honest, but I've been briefed, and I'm quick on my feet. I just need your help—both of you guys," Diane said, looking at Bart and Mike. "As far as I'm concerned, we are a team, and that is all that matters—that and getting the best news we can."

"I'm all for that," Mike said.

"Well, that's the attitude I like. I'll keep my eye on you but prefer you to act on instinct the best you can. That always gets the best results," Bart said, flicking his cigarette out the window.

Diane looked to Bart. "Okay, then let's forget the hotel and start working now. Can we? Are you guys set up?"

Bart looked to Mike, who shrugged. "We have a location to shoot in central Madrid. I'm sure the scene there is more intense. Stick to the scripted questions the best you can though—the ones they gave you. I have a copy of them. By the way, who is your contact ay ITN?"

"Um, I'm not at liberty to say," Diane quietly said.

"That was what my boss said you would say," Bart said with a grin.

Hector interjected, "Yes, for so many months now, it has been violent, but change is happening. My friend's sister lost her brother in the riots. He was beaten to death, then trampled."

Diane took out her notepad and began writing down everything she saw.

As the van slowly pulled through narrow streets, protesters slapped the windows and screamed.

"Is this what The Beatles felt like?" Mike wondered.

There was a silence in the van for nearly five minutes, until Bart spoke.

"When we arrive, keep your eyes on me and Hector. Diane, Sandra, our translator, will be on location for you. I want you to go into the crowd, get the vibe, the feeling and put together a three-minute piece. Mike, you secure sound, and I will shoot B roll until Diane's ready. Diane, dig deep as you can. We don't need a *Times* rerun," Bart said. His demeanor had morphed into a lieutenant.

"Got it," Mike said.

Diane looked up from her writing and nodded.

In the distance, they heard gunshots. Hector slammed the brakes, then brought the van to a crawl toward the location. More shots were fired.

"That's only a few blocks away," Bart said. "I did a camera gig in Saigon in '74."

"Is this safe?" Diane said. Her face had lost its color. She thought back to her meeting with Richard at the Washington Monument, and her heart sank.

"Hector, keep a slow pace. They won't be shooting forever. See? No more shots," Bart encouraged as a rush of people ran toward the van, away from the square to which they were headed. "We'll be fine."

Hector pulled the van across the street from a café. Bart and Mike began assembling their gear. A knock came at the van door. A young woman around eighteen, skinny, with long blonde, wavy hair smiled.

"That's our translator," Bart said.

Diane opened the door. "*Hola*! I'm Sandra."

"*Hola*!" Diane said softly.

People were running through the streets, and there were placards on the ground. Other people were leaning out of windows, screaming.

"Can we walk around so I can talk to some people?" Diane asked.

"Of course, but we must be careful," Sandra said, her voice melodic and warm.

They mingled in with a crowd that was going in many different directions, like bees fleeing an upset hive. Music streamed from nearby apartments, and student protestors stood back.

"They are saying people have been shot in the street by the police," Sandra said. "Five are down for sure—maybe more," she said.

"The police? Are you sure?" Diane questioned.

Sandra grabbed an older gentleman who was out of breath. She whispered loudly in his ear, and he whispered just as loudly in response. "He says it might be the fascists," Sandra said to Diane.

With Sandra's help Diane questioned many of those fleeing the scene, taking answers from anyone who would listen. She took notes as fast as she could as she pushed her way toward the center of the square, surrounded by sirens and police officers. Many officers were swinging their clubs, trying to hit something, someone, or anything they could.

Diane noticed Bart's camera trained on the varied action. She stood on her tiptoes and saw officers dragging bodies over cobblestone streets. Their legs were limp and lifeless, their heads bloody.

"We have seen enough, yes?" Sandra questioned. She looked nervous.

"Yes, we can go back now."

Diane returned to the van and shot Bart an exasperated look. "Give me fifteen minutes and then let's roll."

"You got it!" Bart yelled.

Diane feverishly wrote in her pad. She scratched out nearly every other word, then finally yelled, "Okay! I got it." She handed the copy to Bart for review. She pulled a small compact mirror from her purse and applied the only makeup she had accessible: red lipstick. She fixed her hair the best she could and made her way back into the streets.

Sandra looked on and smiled. Mike was in place, and Bart handed the copy back to her, with a few notes written in red ink. He steadied the camera. The microphone felt heavy in Diane's hands, which were clammy and sweaty. Bart raised his left hand and counted down from five to one, then pointed at her.

"Of the nine people shot, five were killed, and the others are left in critical condition. Those gathered are members of the workers' commission trade union and the clandestine, the communist party of Spain. The suspects are believed to be members of the Falange and the Franco Guard, both far right parties opposing the communist neo-fascist movement. We will report updates as they become available. This is Diane Babel, reporting for ITN. Back to the studio."

Bart held his hand up for a few seconds, then gave the thumbs-up. "Okay, that's a wrap. It's too dangerous here. Maybe we'll get more tomorrow. We have to see how this plays out," he said.

Hector walked over to Diane and again tried to help her with her bag. She tried to refuse again, pulling away from him, but this time he grabbed her hand. "I'm just trying to be polite," he said in a dry tone.

"I'm okay, thanks," Diane said. Her heart was beating fast. The noises in the street slowed slightly, and panic was no longer the prevailing feeling. She walked over to Sandra and said, "Thank you. You're a big help." Diane exhaled. "That was . . . a little crazy back there."

"*Si, si,*" Sandra said with a half-smile, then looked at Diane expectantly for a long time.

"Oh, right. Money. Let me ask Bart," Diane said.

As she turned, Bart was heading toward Sandra with a small white envelope. "Thank you. If we need you, the number I have is the one to call?"

"Yes, *si*. Thank you, Mr. Bart."

The four piled back into the van and headed to their hotel located a few miles back in Puerta del Sol.

Even inside the van, Diane was still sweating and out of breath. Her nerves were running high. She looked over at Mike, who seemed unaffected. "So, Bart, that was okay?" she questioned.

"You did good. That was a real man . . . er, woman-on-the-street piece. Sure, it was a little dangerous, but I love those, and we don't always have the chance to get them. We seemed to be at the right place at the right time."

"Do you need help editing?" Diane said.

"Nope, that's my deal. You just write and report. Great scoop though. I guess I shouldn't second-guess you again," Bart said.

Mike looked over at them both.

"I didn't know you second-guessed me a first time," Diane said.

Mike smiled.

"So, who are these sources of yours? We are hired as contractors, and they don't tell us shit. Just, 'Go here . . . go there.' Right, Mike?" Bart said.

"Yup," Mike said.

"Bart, if I told you, I'd have to kill you," Diane said with a slight smirk.

Bart laughed. "Heh. I think we're going to get along just fine. I have a good feeling about you, and I've seen a bunch of you greenhorns who might have shit themselves back there."

Hector looked into the rearview mirror at Diane. "I think she is just fine too."

"Okay, enough already, Hector. Zip it and drive," Bart directed, rolling his eyes.

When they arrived at the hotel, Diane saw a bar off the lobby. She did a double-take when she saw a man sitting at the bar—a man who looked exactly like Jack, at least from behind.

"Do you want to check in?" Bart said to Diane.

"I'm going to grab a drink first. You guys go ahead."

Bart looked at Mike and shrugged. "Okay. Let me know if you need anything. Otherwise, we'll be down later."

Diane made a beeline for the bar. There were only a handful of people drinking. Peter Frampton's "Do You Feel Like We Do?" was playing on the jukebox. Diane sat right next to the man, so close she could smell his cologne. "Merlot please," she said to the bartender.

The man turned to look at her. His eyes weren't as blue as Jack's, but he radiated welcoming warmth nonetheless. "There are many other great Spanish wines," he said with an endearing broken English inflection.

"Maybe you can show me on the next drink," Diane said. She blew her bangs from her eyes. They sparkled, but she was really just running on fumes and adrenaline.

"It would be my pleasure. I am Paul," he said, extending his hand.

"Diane Babel," she said, taking his strong hand in hers. She held it for a few extra seconds before letting go. "This is my first time in Madrid."

"The night is young then," Paul said, smiling.

"Yes, yes it is." Diane blushed slightly.

Diane noticed breaking news on the television behind the bar. The spot depicted the area they'd just left, then cut to the King of Spain, Don Juan Carlos I, speaking. She leaned close to Paul. "Can you tell me what the reporter is saying?"

Hector's voice came from behind and interjected. "As rebellions continued to populate the country, the king proclaims principle of popular sovereignty, promises a democratic system."

"And who is this man?" Paul questioned.

Diane rolled her eyes. "Hector, my . . . um, *our* driver." She then picked up the glass of wine and swallowed it down in one gulp, causing the two men to look at her with surprise. "Hector, you can get this glass of wine. Paul, it was a real pleasure." She grabbed her bag, headed to the front desk, checked in and took the elevator to her room.

The room had no frills—just two beds and a small balcony. On the dresser was a bottle of red wine with a card that read, "We're counting on you . . . Richard."

Diane opened the bottle and poured a glass. She walked over and looked over the city and smiled. "I did it," she murmured, looking at Richard's note. She opened her leather bag and *Black Like Me* fell to the floor. The picture from Yemen stayed safely tucked inside. She grabbed her small black book and found Jack's number. She walked over to the phone, picked it up, asked the operator for an outside, international line and provided the number, half-certain that the call would probably cost her a per diem. She let it ring and ring and ring.

"Hello," Jack finally said, his voice weak and hoarse, as if he'd been sleeping. "Hello? It's two in the morning. Who is this?"

Diane slowly hung up the phone, leaned back on the bed, looked at Richard's note and drank more wine.

SECTION TWO

"Conformity is the jailer of freedom
and the enemy of growth."

~ John F. Kennedy

Chapter 9

The presidential election season of 1976 was in full swing that September. The success of the Georgia peanut farmer was tantamount to a Cinderella story, especially his winning the Iowa caucuses and the New Hampshire primary. Governor Jimmy Carter had selected Walter Mondale as his running mate, and the pair was gaining traction; many pundits believed they could pull off what had seemed impossible only one year earlier.

It had been over one month since Jack had heard from Diane. He kept her letter in his nightstand and read it when he couldn't sleep, which was often. Jack wondered where she was and what she was doing and if she was *doing it* with someone else. He dated one girl, Veronica, who found the letter by his bedside one evening and questioned him about it. "This is . . . weird," Veronica said when she spotted it. Jack smoked, but Veronica went through twice as many cigarettes, and she sounded like a woman three times her age. "What? Do ya still have the hots for her or something?"

They'd been drinking, and her scratchy-throat speech was slurred, skewing her homegrown Bronx accent, making it all the worse. At twenty-eight, she was divorced and on her second city. Boston hadn't worked out, and Jack ran across her while she was bartending on K Street. Jack wasn't that attracted to her and knew it was simply a matter of convenience.

He raised his eyebrows, and she drifted off to sleep. Diane's letter fell to the ground. Jack picked it up and left Veronica in his bed alone. He awoke in the morning with cotton-mouth, fully clothed. The letter was on the coffee table, as was another from Veronica: "Don't bother calling me anymore, you slouch!"

Jack had just completed a one-month research contract for a Republican senator seeking reelection in Virginia. He had never met the three-term politician but was charged with the responsibility of digging up dirt on his Democratic opponent, who was gaining traction in the polls. Apparently, the former college football player-turned-politician liked to dress in women's clothes, Jack was told, though he was never able to substantiate it. Nevertheless, the rumors were enough to help Jack's interim boss. Jack was paid well and on time, but he wasn't fulfilled.

One night, while he was home alone, the phone rang. "Hello?"

"Jack Quaid?"

"Yes?"

"It's Professor Stanley." Jack recognized the voice immediately but was surprised to hear it.

"Yes, hello. How have you been?" He lit a cigarette and rubbed his chin.

"Oh just fine, Jack," he said. "Listen, how are you fixed for work these days?"

"Well, I actually just finished a research assignment for a senator seeking reelection, but it's over now."

"Well, if you're finished with that, I believe I might have an excellent opportunity for you. However, it may require you to switch teams, as it were," Professor Stanley said and coughed.

"Switch teams? I don't get it."

"I have an old, dear friend by the name of Jody Powell."

"Wait . . . Powell? You mean Jimmy Carter's guy?" Jack snubbed his cigarette and sat erect; the professor now had his full attention.

"Yes, the same. It's good that you know of him. He needs to fill a spot on the campaign and asked me for a recommendation of a recent graduate. You were the first one who came to mind."

"Really?" Jack asked, sounding somewhat flattered. "Well, I appreciate that, but can you give me any details?"

"Honestly, I don't know much, nor can I guarantee you the job, because he is meeting with other candidates. What I do know is that if you're interested, you will need to jump through some hoops and meet with some other people from the campaign first. If all goes well, Jody will meet with you, but with November right around the corner, we have to get the ball rolling on this right away—as in tomorrow."

"Of course! I'm so thankful, yes of course."

"Okay, Jack. I'm glad I caught you. They will expect you at ten a.m. at the Carter campaign headquarters; I think it is on K Street."

"I'll be there."

"Great. I have to run now, but good luck with this, Jack. Oh, and if you're not tuning in to the first presidential debate, you should. It's on now," Professor Stanley said and hung up the phone.

Jack walked around his apartment, completely dumfounded. He went to his bookcase and opened the diploma he'd received seven weeks earlier. He searched behind it again and checked every crease, hoping he'd somehow missed the hidden note. *Is this job lead my reward?* he wondered. He walked into the bedroom with this diploma, opened his nightstand drawer and pulled out Diane's letter. He carefully folded it, placed it inside the diploma, closed it and walked back to the bookcase in his living room, where he tucked it behind a stack of books.

He poured a glass of bourbon, lit a cigarette and turned the radio on. He moved the dial until he heard the closing remarks of the first presidential debate between President Gerald Ford and Governor Jimmy Carter.

"For a long time, our American citizens have been excluded, sometimes misled, sometimes lied to. This is not compatible with the purpose of our nation. I believe in our country. It needs to be competent. The government needs to be well managed, efficient and economical. We need to have a government that's sensitive to our people's needs, to those who are poor, who don't have adequate healthcare, who have been cheated too long by our tax programs, who've been out of jobs, whose families have been torn apart. We need to restore the faith and the trust of the American people in their own government," Carter continued. "I don't claim to know all the answers, but I've got confidence in my country. Our economic strength is still there. Our system of government, in spite of Vietnam, Cambodia, CIA and Watergate, is still the best system of government on Earth. And the greatest resource of all is the 215 million Americans who still have within us the strength, the character, the intelligence, the experience, the patriotism, the idealism, the compassion and the sense of brotherhood on which we can rely in the future to restore the greatness to our country."

Jack grabbed a yellow legal pad and began taking notes.

The commentator called on President Ford to offer his remarks, and Ford said, "On November 2, all of you will make a very, very important decision. One of the major issues in this campaign is trust. A President should never promise more than he can deliver, and a President should always deliver everything that he has promised. A President can't be all things to all people. A President should be the same thing to all people. On the Fourth of July, we had a wonderful 200th birthday for our great country. It was a superb occasion. It was a glorious day. In the first century of our nation's history, our forefathers gave us the finest form of government in the history of mankind. In the second century of our nation's history, our forefathers developed the most productive industrial nation in the history of the globe. Our third century should be the century of individual freedom for all our 215 million Americans today and all that join us," President Ford continued. "In the last few years, government has gotten bigger and bigger. Industry has gotten larger and larger. Labor unions have gotten bigger and bigger, and our children have been the victims of mass education. We must make this next century the century of the individual. We should never forget that a government big enough to give us everything we want is a government big enough to take from us everything we have."

Jack turned down the volume on the radio dial and tapped his pen on his forehead. He looked to his coffee table and picked up an issue of *Newsweek* that depicted the White House on its cover, with a headline reading, "The Race Is On." Pictured underneath were Ford and Carter. Jack began reading an article about security and terrorism. Soon after, he leaned back, closed his eyes and drifted off to sleep.

The next morning, Jack was anxious and nervous as he walked down Pennsylvania Avenue, one of his favorite things to do. He loved the White House and often thought about what George Washington had called the historic stretch, Grand Avenue. On that day, however, his destination was K Street.

Upon arriving at the Carter campaign headquarters, he was greeted by low-level staffers who took his résumé and letters of recommendation and asked him general questions about political affiliations and his understanding of the campaign.

"You're from Georgia," one interviewer said; he seemed younger than Jack. "That'll score points with Jody."

"Does that mean I will get an interview with Mr. Powell?" Jack asked hopefully.

Phones were ringing off the hook, and staffers and volunteers were weaving around the office, making Jack feel dizzy. The fluorescent lights cast dull warmth.

"Well, I can't lie. It's a tough job to get. I'm interviewing too, you know," the staffer said. He had thick glasses and dark, thin, receding hair. He wore a Carter button on his vest.

"You are? With all due respect, I just . . . well, I don't get it," Jack said.

"I'm not here to do this, you know, interviewing people. That's not why I got into politics. But it's all about upward mobility, or you're dead in the water. Anyway, we got a call about you, so you'll be back to meet with Jody. Your résumé looks good, but didn't I read that you worked for a *Republican* last month?"

"Know your enemy?" Jack said with smile.

"More likely that you needed the money," the staffer said dryly. "Anyway, come back on Thursday. If you wanna do yourself a favor, study up on Jody. He's no slouch."

"What?"

"I said he's no slouch."

"Yeah, okay. That's what I thought you said." Jack gathered his things and looked across the busy room. Through frosted glass, he saw Jody Powell's office, where a shadowy figure paced back and forth.

As Jack's meeting with Powell approached, he studied everything he could about his interviewer, leaving no stone unturned. Powell had been with Jimmy Carter as his press sectary since he'd been elected as Georgia governor in 1971. Jack came to admire Powell's tough approach to politics. A political opponent once called Carter a "gutless peanut brain," to which Powell immediately responded with a note that respectfully encouraged the man to "take a running jump and go straight to hell." Jack figured it came off a little sweeter with a Southern drawl; Powell, a Georgian, had that in spades.

Powell's moxie impressed Jack, and he was excited that he'd made it so far in the interview process. Jack owned one good suit, a Luke Soeron in gray bird's-eye. He accented it with a handful of different shirts and ties. His bought a blue tie and white shirt that almost screamed "*Democrat!*" As he walked into the campaign headquarters on the day he was to meet with Powell, he was struck by the energy that bounced around the room like a laser-light show. Phones were ringing, and staffers worked effortlessly, like trained dancers. Campaign signs and slogans covered walls and desks. One read, "Remember Your List of Enemies: Vote Carter/Mondale."

Jack looked around for the person who had interviewed him earlier in the week, but he didn't see the balding man anywhere. He stood adrift in a political stew, not yet cooked, until a young, dirty-blonde-haired girl with a bright smile and large glasses approached him.

"Jack Quaid?" she said sweetly but abruptly, pushing her glasses up on her nose.

"Yes." Jack stood erect.

"Follow me. Mr. Powell is on a call . . . well, calls. You might have to wait for a while. I hope you don't mind." She weaved in and out of desks and supporters, all of whom were working toward a common goal.

"Yeah, no problem," Jack said as he tried to keep up. He saw a woman from behind with a thick brown mane of hair; though he knew she wasn't Diane, he wished she was.

The young woman led him to a back room, encased and separated from the mayhem of the main office. He could see a figure, one he presumed to be Jody, behind the frosted glass wall.

"Okay, just sit here, and he'll be out shortly. There are some magazines there on the table if you'd like to do some reading, and the bathroom is down that hall. And don't worry. He is actually a nice guy." She smiled at Jack as if she had sat in the same seat once before.

Jack returned her smile. "Thanks."

As he sat there, he felt sweat dripping from his underarms and down his ribcage. Jack looked down at the same issue of *Newsweek* that he'd been reading at his place, the one with the White House on the cover. He had never finished the article on security threats and thought it was as good a time as any to finish it.

Things have changed quite a bit since President Thomas Jefferson held office, Jack thought as he read. On his second inaugural in 1805, Jefferson held an open house at the White House. Following the swearing-in ceremony at the Capitol, he was followed to the Blue Room for festivities by onlookers, citizens.

The article, however, depicted America as a different place, no thanks to a couple of strange birds who literally took to the sky, trying to hurt their own country. In 1974, Robert Preston, a U.S. Army private, stole a United States Army UH-1 Iroquois helicopter from Fort Meade, Maryland and flew it to Washington, DC, where he hovered for six minutes over the White House before descending on the south lawn, about 100 yards from the West Wing. He lifted the craft back into the air and was followed by two Maryland State Police helicopters. Minutes later, Preston returned to the White House, where he was fired upon and injured; he finally landed the aircraft without further issue.

Five days later, Samuel Joseph Byck, an unemployed tire salesman, attempted to hijack a plane flying out of Baltimore-Washington International Airport. He intended to crash into the White House in the hopes of killing President Richard Nixon, then waist deep in the Watergate scandal. Jack recalled studying that very case with Diane while they were both undergraduates. He also recalled being fascinated by the attempts and wondered what it meant for the future of the country.

He remembered with a smirk that Diane had quoted Plato in class during one of their related debates: "Laws are partly formed for the sake of good men, in order to instruct them how they may live on friendly terms with one another, and partly for the sake of those who refuse to be instructed, whose spirit cannot be subdued, or softened, or hindered from plunging into evil." As he sat waiting for Powell, he also remembered the snug red sweater Diane had been wearing that day.

Jack read that Byck had driven to the Baltimore-Washington International Airport, where he shot and killed Maryland Aviation Administration Police Officer George Neal Ramsburg before boarding a DC-9, Delta Airlines Flight 523 to Atlanta. When the pilots told him they couldn't take off until the wheels were unlocked, he shot them both, killing one. Byck had homemade explosive bombs in a briefcase, which he used to threaten passengers and crew. With the plane grounded, through a closed door, police officers fired at Byck, wounding him. Before the police made it onto the plane, Byck shot himself in the head. He didn't die immediately and was heard saying, "Help me," as he took his last breath.

More than thirty minutes had passed, and there was still no sign of Powell. Jack's foot nervously tapped the air. He thought back to all the research he'd done on the man. Carter had once said of Powell, "Jody probably knows me better than anyone except my wife." In the early years of campaigning, the two even bunked together while on the road.

After a few more minutes, Jack began to feel over-prepared, and that made him nervous. He looked at his watch, which had stopped ticking. *Perfect*, he thought. Finally, a door opened, and he heard a familiar *twang*, one he'd tried to get rid of over the years.

"Jack Quaid. C'mon on in now."

Jack couldn't see who was behind the door until he reached the archway. He slowly opened the door. A television was on in the corner, but the volume was turned all the way down. One of two windows were open, and the other's ledge was stacked with a haphazard, overflowing pile of papers. A news wire ticked by in the other corner. Pictures of Jimmy Carter and other dignitaries were strewn about, as were various diplomas, trophies and pictures of little kids playing baseball.

Jody Powell was on the phone. He smiled and motioned for Jack to take a seat. He turned his chair around so his back was to Jack. "It's out of context is my point. I'm not saying it's not what the governor said, because he did say that about the gas situation, but you are spinning this, and you know it. You can't run this quote as is. Get back to me please. I know you will do the right thing here, Sam." Finally, Jody turned his chair around and slammed the phone down with a smile. "Donaldson is a good guy. All in a day's work, right?" he asked in a distinct Dixie drawl.

"Sure," Jack said.

"So, Mr. Jack Quaid, I presume?" Jody said, looking down at a piece of paper. "Is all this the truth?" he said, pointing at Jack's résumé. "I do have a bullshit detector, as I'm sure you're aware."

"Yes, Mr. Powell."

"Jody."

"Excuse me?" Jack said.

"Call me Jody." His slightly shaggy brown hair was brushed over to the right, though a part was hard to find. He had a warm, disarming smile that gave a sparkle to his otherwise serious eyes. His white dress shirt was unbuttoned at the neckline, and his dark blue tie had vertical red pinstripes.

"You're a peach, if I'm not mistaken," Jody said with a smirk.

"Georgia, born and raised," Jack returned.

"Welcome to the mafia."

"The mafia?"

"The Georgia mafia," Jody said with a laugh. "We've got your back. I grew up outside Atlanta, and I think you know who my boss is and where he is from."

Jack forced a laugh.

"So, G.W. '76, huh? A young gun."

"Yes, sir . . . er, I mean Jody. But I . . . well, I do have experience." Jack's voice was shakier than he would have liked.

"Let's get serious here. You should thank Professor Stanley for helping you get your foot in the door. Stanly and I go back a bit. Now you've had what? Two interviews so far? You've made the cut till now, so it's my turn to have a little fun. I won't go into your Republican work background. We all get confused from time to time. Do you know what my job is?" Jody said. He took a sip from a can of Tab cola.

"The press secretary is primarily a spokesperson for the campaign, the administration."

"Hmm. That's a decent Webster's definition, but what do you think I *really* do?"

"You're a filter."

"Go on."

Jack loosened his tie slightly. "You decide what the American public needs to know and what they don't need to know."

"Do you believe in that philosophy?" Jody questioned.

"I believe Americans have the right to know exactly what is happening in the world and how it affects them. However, just because they have the right to know doesn't mean they should. Sometimes protecting citizens means protecting them from the truth."

"What do you know about the truth?" Jody said, lighting a cigarette. He offered Jack one, and Jack obliged, leaned over Jody's desk, and took a light from him.

"Well, I used to like Nixon and supported him when he ran for President. I have a kid brother, and we grew up watching all those old World War II movies—you know, the real heroes. Anyway, my brother graduates college, Northeastern, and comes back home and decides to enlist for Vietnam. I mean, by then, I didn't believe the truth coming out of Washington, but he still did. We argued about it quite a bit. Now, he has a metal plate in his head and walks around Walter Reed like a zombie. I know all about perceived truths."

"Sorry to hear that. Sometimes something has to hit close to home before we really understand it," Jody said. "My job is to control the message. If hired, your job will be to do the same—what I say and what Jimmy says."

"Jimmy?" Jack questioned.

"Yes, Mr. Carter. He is the boss," Jody continued. "Listen, the tough work has been done on this campaign, but someone important to me just dropped out. We need to make the final push to November 2, though, and I need a twenty-four/seven commitment. We win, and you have a job in the White House."

"So are you offering me the job?" Jack said, sitting up straight in his chair.

"You have great credentials, and you're young. We can work you like a mule, and you have Professor Stanley's vote. That's a ringing endorsement in my book." Jody smiled and extended his hand. "Welcome aboard . . . and don't disappoint me."

Chapter 10

With the presidential election only days away, Jack was working around the clock. It wasn't uncommon for Jody to call him at four a.m. and rouse him out of bed. And while he worked hard, long hours, Jack hadn't personally met Jimmy Carter. Carter had addressed the room to "bolster the troops," as Jody would say, but Jack was seen as Jody's shadow, his right-hand man. Jack's life was a series of trains, plains, automobiles, speeches, banners, handshakes and coffee—lots and lots of coffee.

"What we have going in our favor is that Ford has no charisma. Also, he wasn't *elected*," Jody said to Jack as they sat in his office, looking over the latest poll numbers.

"You know I want him to win. We all do, but don't worry about his limited experience as one-term governor or—of all things—the press's belittlement of him as a former peanut farmer," Jack said.

Jody interjected, "We had the same issues in Georgia, and we won there. Is it an uphill battle? Yes, but the American people want something new, something different, and that is Carter. Some might ask if it's for the better or worse, but I say it's for the better. And don't forget, he served as the chairman of the Democratic National Committee."

"We all want him to win, of course, and I never thought I would say that, even if you had asked me that this time last year," Jack said.

Jody stopped Jack and pointed to the television in the corner of the room. "Turn that up, will you?"

As Jack walked toward the television, he almost tripped; there was Diane, on the screen right in front of him, reporting the news. He turned up the volume and caught her last few words: "This is Diane Babel, reporting for ITN." His cheeks warmed at the sight of her. She looks so . . . worldly, Jack thought.

"I've been hearing things about this reporter, Babel. Every time I try and catch her, I miss it—like now. She's making waves for sure, though I don't know much about this ITN she works for," Jody said.

"You haven't heard about her from Professor Stanley," Jack said.

"Huh? Was she in class with you?"

"Sure was," Jack said and smirked.

"No shit, Jack! Did you go out with her?"

"Well, we're just . . . I don't know. I guess you could say we're only friends now. It's best to leave it at that, if you don't mind, Jody."

"Stanley did mention something to me about ITN a few months back, a new partnership with PBS or something. I didn't give it much thought, as there are too many things to think about—mainly getting Jimmy elected. But this Babel seems to be getting some good scoops, giving Donaldson and his cronies a run for their money, which is always good. And she's young like you—hungry."

*   *   *

Two days later, Jack woke up to the phone ringing again. He looked at the clock. It was five thirty a.m., Election Day, November 2.

"Hello, Jody?" Jack said, half-asleep.

"No. Jeez, I'm sorry. I didn't realize the time difference."

"Who is this?" Jack said, rubbing his left eye and holding the receiver with his other hand.

"It's Diane, Jack. I'm overseas. I just . . . well, I know the election is today and just wanted to wish you, well—you know, good luck and all."

Jack rubbed his eyes and lit a cigarette. "Thanks. I mean, I'm just surprised you're calling. Do you know what time it is?"

"Sorry. I'm in London on a layover. I was able to mail in my vote, but I wish I were there to actually vote and put a final nail in the Nixon coffin. It's time to get rid of Ford."

"It's just so weird to hear from you. I'll tell you, a national campaign is nuts. I must have been in thirty cities over the last four weeks. I think we have this though. It'll be close, but I think we have this wrapped up."

"Oh shit! I'm running late here. I have to go," Diane said in a hurried voice.

"I saw you on television," Jack muttered before he heard the line go dead.

*   *   *

Jack walked to the street and grabbed a copy of *The Washington Post* and read an article entitled, "The Presidential Roundup." Whereas Carter had a double-digit lead, he'd made a major misstep that put Ford back in the game; Carter's interview in *Playboy* magazine crippled his polling numbers. The gaff was that he discussed a number of personal issues and admitted to having lusted "in his heart." Ford had a gaff of his own, claiming, "There is no Soviet domination of eastern Europe." And while the press hounded Ford for a retraction or an explanation, Ford stood by his statement, further weakening his chances. Between the two gaffs, Jack thought, Carter still had a slight edge.

It was well after midnight, November 3, 1976, and supporters were cheering and clapping in the Carter campaign headquarters. Red, white and blue balloons filled the room; a few were in the shape of peanuts, decorated with Jimmy Carter's smiling face. As Jack and Jody manned the phones and watched the polling returns on the news, Jack looked down at a button on his shirt: "Jimmy Carter for Bicentennial President." The poll numbers were close, and it was definitely a nail-biter.

Jody's special phone, the one Jack referred to as the "Bat" phone, rang. It wasn't red, but when it rang, important news was always on the other end. Carter and only a few others had the number, and Jack was not on that list. When that phone rang, everyone paid close attention, and the room fell to whispers. Jody picked up the phone and turned his back to the room. He slowly turned around with a widening smile.

"What?" Jack exclaimed.

"It's official!" Jody bellowed.

"C'mon, Jody! Tell us. What!"

"We carried Mississippi. NBC will announce it shortly! We won, folks!"

The room erupted in applause. Hugs and kisses floated heavily across the room like an early morning fog over San Francisco.

Jody signaled Jack into his office. He picked up the Bat phone and dialed quickly. "Did you hear the news, Mr. President-elect? Congratulations! We did it!" Then Jody hung up the phone and hugged Jack. "Next stop, 1600 Pennsylvania Avenue!"

*   *   *

President Jimmy Carter was inaugurated on January 20, 1977, and Jack looked on with pride. He listened closely as Carter repeated the oath: "I do solemnly swear that I will faithfully execute the office of President of the United States and will, to the best of my ability, preserve, protect and defend the Constitution of the United States."

As the crowd erupted in applause, Carter kissed his wife and quickly shook outgoing President Ford's hand; he looked like a prisoner pardoned from death row. Carter next turned to Walter Mondale, shared a bewildering smile and feverishly shook his hand.

Chief Justice Warren Burger leaned in to the microphone as a marching band played "Hail to the Chief." In a deep baritone, Burger bellowed, "Ladies and gentlemen, the President of the United States."

Perhaps no other words could fall harder on a man's shoulders, Jack thought.

Carter looked around as people clapped and cheered. His trademark smile, the same one that had graced his face during a tough campaign, was not as wide, but his face took on stoic quality. Jack looked at Jody, who looked like a proud younger brother.

Nearly thirty seconds passed before Carter waved his hands in a calming fashion and addressed the nation for the first time as its President. "For myself and for our nation, I want to thank my predecessor for all he has done to heal our land." Carter again motioned to Ford who shook his hand, this time longer. "In this outward and physical ceremony, we attest once again to the inner and spiritual strength of our nation. As my high school teacher, Miss Julia Coleman, used to say, 'We must adjust to changing times and still hold to unchanging principles.'"

Jack held a quiet confidence; he'd had a small hand in the speech-writing process. It was Jack who had suggested to Jody that Carter read a passage from the same Bible on which Carter was sworn in, and he did just that.

Carter continued, "He hath showed thee, O man, what is good; and what doth the Lord require of thee, but to do justly, and to love mercy, and to walk humbly with thy God (Micah 6:8)." The words echoed as if they bounced off the walls of history.

As Jack looked out over the Washington Mall, he began to believe again in his country. He looked at Carter and thought, *Anything is possible now.*

Jack was appointed assistant press secretary, to report directly to Jody Powell; that sent shockwaves throughout the staff, since he leapfrogged many others who wanted the same position and had been there longer. He was promptly assigned his own office and secretary.

As directed, he kept a close watch on Diane, though he hadn't heard from her personally since Election Day morning. She had been in Egypt, Morocco, London and Geneva, among other places, reporting. He thought about her from time to time, but he almost always missed her PBS broadcasts, which aired on Sunday evenings at eight p.m. He had to order transcripts. When he read them, he could almost hear her voice and inflections.

Before the inauguration, however, Jack did watch one broadcast with interest. Diane was covering the Egyptian Bread Riots, January 18-19, 1977. A spontaneous uprising protesting the World Bank and the International Monetary Fund-mandated termination of state subsidies on basic foodstuffs gripped the country, and thousands took to the streets. Jack watched as Diane reported, "As many as 79 people were killed and 800 wounded in the protests, which ended with the deployment of the army and the reinstitution of the subsidies."

Little did Jack know, but Diane was now in Washington DC often. She kept a low profile and met with Richard sometimes, just blocks away from the White House. On a nippy March morning, she stood in front of the Lincoln Memorial, waiting. Tourists surrounded her, snapping pictures. She wore a green down coat and blue wool scarf. On occasion, she was recognized by strangers, and that made her feel important.

"Best President ever," Richard whispered in her ear after he stealthily sneaked up behind her.

Diane didn't turn away from the statue but was soothed by his voice. "I was too young to remember him in office," she quipped.

Richard smirked slightly. "Your work has been good. We're meeting our objectives with every report, and people are tuning in more and more. It's working. PBS executives are happy too."

"That's great to hear, because Bart and I joke that we're always playing to an empty room." Diane said, looking directly into Richard's eyes. She noticed that his graying temples had begun to spread to his bushy eyebrows.

"Listen, that's enough back-patting for now. In about four hours, a group of Iranian students, along with a few armed black gunmen, are going to attempt to seize and take hostages in the Islamic center."

Diane looked around and leaned closer to him and whispered, "What? It hasn't happened yet?"

Richard took her off to the side and shook his head. "No."

"Shouldn't we warn them? Someone? The police?"

"You're a reporter. You're job is to *report* the news, not stop it from happening."

"But if we can prevent this from happening—"

"There is no if. We just . . . can't. The best we can do is inform the people of why it is happening. Bart has been apprised of the situation and is standing by. Off you go. Be careful."

A few hours later, Diane and Bart and the rest of the crew arrived at the Islamic Center. The impressive structure was built in 1957 and was the first mosque in the capital, as well as the largest in the Western Hemisphere. Hundreds of thousands of Muslims visited over the years. The architecture was imposing, with an inspiring 160-foot minaret. But on this day, it was under siege, teeming with chaos. Police and Special Forces surrounded the buildings behind and around the mosque, and curious onlookers lined the perimeter.

As Diane approached the scene, she made eye contact with Bart. Moments later, she was handed research files.

"We just need to tell the story, get some B roll and get out here," Bart said to Diane. "I want to shoot you in front of the gates, as close as possible. PBS is going to run this as a live feed, a special broadcast. It'll be the first time for us, so get it right. We are without a net here."

Diane looked at the news truck and noticed it had more bells and whistles, including a satellite. She read over her notes, spoke to a few officials and started writing her script. Ten minutes later, she gave the signal to Bart. He read over her script, nodded and ordered the crew to roll film and sound.

Across town, Jack was seated in Jody's office. "Turn on PBS, will you? I just got word that a live report is coming in from this issue at the Islamic Center. Shit! This all we need," Jody said. "The Hanafi Siege is what they're calling it."

"What?" Jack walked over and turned on the tube. Diane was dressed in a plaid, tan, one-piece suit with a purple ascot tied tightly around her neck. She looked nervous and tired.

"A group of students/militants along with a few black Muslim men, have seized three buildings in downtown DC, including the district building, where the mayor's office is located. Apparently the men have demands that include the release of several convicted killers responsible for the deaths of the children of group leader Hamaas Abdul Khaalis, presumably by execution."

"She is out ahead on this story," Jody said. "Didn't I tell you to watch her?"

"I have been, but I-I knew nothing of this," Jack stammered.

"Well, then maybe you should be doing your job better," Jody snapped.

"Yeah. The press corps will be waiting for you," Jack said, motioning to the door.

The White House halls were buzzing. Jody stood up from his desk, stopped writing notes and watched Diane's report with more attention.

"Other demands include a visit by Muhammad Ali and Nation of Islam founder Luis Farrakhan. Their final request is for the destruction of *Mohammed, Messenger of God*, a film that . . ."

Jody walked across the room and shut off the TV, and Jack stood aside, watching.

"Ali? Farrakhan? How does she have better intelligence than us?" Jody scoffed.

Jack simply shrugged.

"So how well do you know this Babel gal?"

"Like I said, we went to GW together."

"Listen, I don't have time for this now, but you have to find out where she's getting her information. There's no way the news feed is faster than us. And that is not my order. It's Jimmy's."

"Okay, got it, but we haven't spoken—"

"No excuses, Quaid—not now," Jody snapped.

"I'll do my best, but what do we do about this hostage situation?"

"The only thing we can do is hope for the best."

Jody grabbed his notes and headed out of the room, and Jack followed behind. Moments later, Jody was standing in front of countless reporters. In an array of flashing lights, he fielded bullet-like questions coming from all directions. Jack looked on from the wings, taking mental notes.

"Steve, your question," Jody said.

A reporter in his mid forties and paunchy read from the notebook he was holding. "Is the administration going to meet their demands?"

"It is not in the Carter administration's policy to negotiate with terrorists," Jody said plainly, his twang softened.

"How many are held captive?" Steve returned.

"About 130, I believe, though there are reports that three of them are in critical condition from gunshot wounds. Next . . . Barbara."

A blonde reporter with piercing green eyes and a blue blouse stood up. "Can you release the names of the injured?"

"We cannot. We are still receiving details that are considered confidential. The best thing you all can do is pray for the hostages' safety. That is all for now."

As Jody left the podium, reporters called out with more questions. Cameras clicked like rifle fire. When Jody was free of the public eye, he chugged a glass of water and leaned against a wall, where a picture of President Jimmy Carter hung.

"They don't let up, do they?" Jack said.

"It's all part of the job."

"Who are the injured hostages? Can I know?"

Jody paused as a staffer handed him papers. He studied them quickly. "Dead."

"What?" Jack questioned. "Who?"

"Two of them are confirmed dead."

Jack stepped back, shocked. "But you didn't—"

Jody leaned close to Jack. "They don't need to know yet. For now, they just need hope."

*   *   *

The occupation and hostage takeover lasted more than thirty hours, while Diane and Bart left for downtime and rest. They returned as the thirty-ninth hour commenced, and they heard loud screams and cries—and even some cheers.

"We're rolling!" Bart yelled.

They watched as the Muslim militants were taken into custody by police. The hostages were dazed as they left the building, and some received immediate medical attention.

Diane ran around, speaking to anyone she could who could provide details on the release. She wrote quickly in her notebook, then ran back toward Bart. "Let's roll this so you can get the action—them leaving, being arrested in the background," Diane blurted.

"You have your script ready to go?" Bart questioned.

"Close enough."

Diane held the microphone tight in her hands, and after Bart counted down from five and pointed at her, she said, "The police commander, trusted by Khaalis, was able to convince the Hanafis to turn themselves in. They were revealed to be a group of Iranian Islamic students trying to gain recognition for the injustices in their country. The thirty-nine-hour standoff claimed two victims. Our thoughts and prayers are with their families. I'm Diane Babel, reporting live from downtown Washington DC."

Bart pulled the camera away and gave Diane a thumbs-up. As he did, he saw something approaching quickly from behind her. "Who's that? Hey! Diane, be careful! Someone's coming."

Diane turned to find Jack. He stopped ten yards away and motioned for her to come over. "It's all right, Bart. He's an old friend, now with the Carter Administration." Diane then walked toward Jack. "Jack? It's great to see you! Really!"

"Thanks, Diane. You too. Can we grab a coffee? We need to talk." Jack pointed across the street to a small café.

In the cozy eatery, Jack sat across from Diane at a booth.

A waitress with an orange and white uniform and thick blue eye shadow approached with a smile. She snapped her gum often. "Hey! I've seen you on the tube," the waitress said. "You're the news girl, right?"

Diane looked slightly embarrassed and nodded. "Yes, you're right. Thanks. We're just going to need a couple cups of coffee please."

"Sure thing, honey."

The waitress filled their cups as the jukebox played Johnny Cash's "Ring of Fire." The lyrics stood between them in the awkward silence:

Love is a burning thing,
and it makes a fiery ring,
bound by wild desire.
I fell into a ring of fire.

Diane took a deep breath and then exhaled slowly. "So . . . it's been a while. The White House? Really? Congratulations! Sounds like a great gig," she said.

"I'll admit it's quite inspiring. I feel like I've found my place," Jack said, having trouble looking directly into her eyes.

"Me too. I feel the same," Diane said with a stronger air of confidence.

"I see you're doing very well for yourself. You look good on TV," Jack said.

"Well, thanks. Yeah, it's been a crazy few months."

"Okay. All right, enough of this bullshit. Is Professor Stanley behind this?" Jack whispered strongly.

"Huh? Behind what? What's with your attitude?" Diane leaned back.

"You report on things that even the White House doesn't know about yet. How is that possible? Is Stanley involved somehow?"

"What does *he* have to do with any of this?"

"That job he promised. He's helping you, isn't he? Does he have ties to ITN?"

"I hate to disappoint you, but—"

"I don't buy it," Jack said sternly.

The waitress approached with the coffee and a dish. "Here you go. Have a few donuts on the house. It's a special day for us, with a famous reporter in the restaurant and all."

Diane smiled. "Thanks, but that wasn't necessary."

The waitress smiled and walked off, still snapping her gum.

Diane pushed the donuts aside and whispered. "Did Powell send you to see me? Is he getting nervous?"

"What do you think?"

"That you're jealous."

"Jealous? You just want to be a star."

"That's crazy." Diane crinkled her nose.

"I'm sure you know about the two victims from the takeover."

"Of course."

"You know, one of those killed at the Islamic Center was a journalist."

"Yeah, Maurice Williams, a radio reporter for WHUR. I met him once," Diane said softly.

"You could have saved him."

"That's not my job, Jack. I'm a reporter, not a hero."

"Well, this time the reporter was a victim. How long before you get too close to these breaking stories and become a part of them?"

Diane paused for a moment and looked out the window. She watched Bart standing next to the news van, waiting. "I'm just doing my job."

"And I'm just doing mine," Jack said and slammed his fist on the table hard enough that a few customers took notice.

"Jesus, Jack! Lower your voice."

They looked away from each other for a moment.

Diane fished around her pockets but could produce only foreign currency. "Um . . . can you get this?" Diane said.

Jack scoffed at her and slammed five dollars on the table. "And what about us?" he asked in a huff.

"What do want me to say? We talked about this already, Jack."

"Talked? Wrong, Diane. You only left me a note. I just want the truth. Are you really telling me you don't think about us?"

"You know I care. It's just that . . . well, how can we . . . ? Things have changed," Diane said. She looked concerned, stood up and walked over to Jack's side of the table. She leaned in, as if to kiss his cheek, but instead she whispered in his ear, "I don't want to be a star. Take care of yourself." When she reached the door, she looked back at Jack with a slight gleam in her eyes before leaving.

The bells on the door jingled, and Jack watched as Diane crossed the street, walking toward Bart and the ITN news van.

Chapter 11

Washington DC has a distinct way of enveloping and eclipsing one's personal life. Time had passed since Jack and Diane's encounter, and as Diane prepared for her next assignment in Turkey, she sifted through old mail, a process she did only a few times a month. A letter from her parents had arrived a week earlier. She opened it:

> *Diane,*
>
> *I trust this letter finds you well and busy with exciting pursuits. My friends ask if I still have a daughter. I smile and nod. All the other girls your age are having babies and starting families of their own. "Not my Diane," I tell them. We watch you on PBS. You're quite "the wonder," the ladies say.*
>
> *You are like your father, a traveler. He, too, has been gone more than he is here. He sends his love, as do I. My teaching is going well, but I continue to threaten myself with taking a sabbatical. For now, I will continue. It is my hope to see you soon.*
>
> *Mom*

Diane walked over to a pile of books that sat idle in the corner of the room. Halfway down the stack was a photo album, barely filled. She flipped through until she saw a picture of her and her parents, taken at Christmas when she was in high school. Though her mom was Jewish, they had a Christmas tree, mistletoe and all the traditional fixings. A warm feeling came over her as she looked at the picture. In her parents she saw elements of herself: her mom's eyes and her dad's chin. They possessed a quiet confidence that was not lost in the camera's translation. It spoke to Diane in the same way Richard spoke to her: succinctly.

*   *   *

Days later, Diane landed in Istanbul, Turkey, early on May 1, 1977. She was there to cover the nation's Labor Day celebrations. Richard had briefed her, and she had done her due diligence, reading newspapers and reports, even though, as usual, she'd been notified of the assignment only days earlier.

"When we arrive at Taksim Square, we may encounter some violence," Bart said to Diane as they were driven in a rented van through the busy streets. The weather was hot, and the street smells of spice and smoke were almost tangible. "We have been down similar roads before, so let's get in there, get our story and get out."

"They went from 1928 to 1975 without a celebration," Diane said, looking up from her notes. She was holding a cup of coffee that dripped and spilled as the van careened. "The Confederation of Revolutionary Trade Unions of Turkey, DISK, organized the first rally on Taksim Square last year. *The Times* says there could be as many as 500,000 people there today," Diane said.

Bart shook his head. "Bigger than Woodstock." He had put on a few pounds over the last year. "Too many beers and not enough sex," he often joked, slapping his belly.

"The leadership of DISK support Workers Party of Turkey, you know—the Socialist Workers Party of Turkey. The Communist Party of Turkey banned the participation of the so-called Maoist block. They are also known as the Liberation of the People, the Path of the People and Union of the People. It's expected that these groups will clash with each other. This is the story, Bart."

A translator, whom Bart hired at the airport, chimed in, "Yes, there will be violence. People have waited a long time for this celebration." The man smiled and said his name was Joe, though he was clearly of native descent. He chain-smoked cigarettes and scratched his thick, black beard often, and he spent too much time looking in the rearview mirror.

The van screeched to a halt a block from the square. People filled the streets, chanting and holding signs, although some ran in the opposite direction. There was a military presence, and it was chaotic. Bart and the crew embarked on the scene, grabbing as much B roll and sound bites as possible.

Diane grabbed Joe, the translator, by the arm. "You're with me."

They spoke with shop owners and young protestors, and Diane noticed that they didn't smile. Their faces were illustrated by fear and hope.

"They are saying shots have been fired and people are dead in the streets," Joe said.

"When was the last shot fired?" Diane said, ducking into an archway.

"They say maybe a half-hour ago," Joe said.

"Let's go then," Diane said. She walked toward the square that was littered with papers, protest signs and—to her amazement—countless injured people, some crying for help. She looked across the square and saw Bart, being harassed by what appeared to be police. She watched as a mother and father, both bruised and bloodied, tried to shield their young child. Diane signaled to Joe, and they headed toward the van, with Bart following closely behind. "I'll be ready to tape in five minutes and then we need to get out of here," Diane said as Bart rushed back to the van.

"You got it. We can edit in the studio," he decided, slightly out of breath.

*   *   *

A day later, across the world in the White House, Jack sat in Jody's office, watching Diane's report. He took diligent notes and checked her information with the wire service report. Jody was on the phone.

"Reportedly only four people were actually shot and killed. The other thirty were trampled by the pandemonium created by law enforcement," Diane said.

She looks so tired, Jack thought.

"Is she getting this right, Jack?" Jody asked, cupping the receiver of the red Bat phone.

"Yeah, all seems to check out. We're just not sure about the number of dead. Some say twenty-four, some say thirty-six, and some put it near a hundred. In any case, it looks bad over there," Jack said.

"That whole region is ripe for more upheaval," Jody said, hanging up the phone. "Have you had any further contact with Babel?"

"Not since that day in the coffee shop. It's been a while. I try to call every now and then, but she never picks up," Jack said, looking down.

"Well, Jimmy is putting the pressure on about this. Any other classmates you can call on to help out?" Jody asked, taking a chug of Tab.

"She was a loner. She's an only child, keeps to herself."

"Well, in that case, it seems like you're the man for the job. Keep working on her, and consider it an executive order. Now, off you go. I have a few things to do," Jody said with a half-smile.

Jack stood up to leave. He nodded at Jody, grabbed his papers and left the room. When he reached his office, he sat at his desk and bit his lip. He picked up the phone and dialed Diane's number, already knowing she wasn't home. As the phone rang and rang, Jack thought back to the Fourth of July. His mind wandered to the way Diane had smelled and her understated beauty. That night, she'd been full of promise and hope.

*   *   *

The following day, Diane was back in Washington. Jetlagged, her sleep schedule was off. She went to the corner and picked up a copy of *The Washington Post* before heading back home to enjoy the rare treat of sleeping in her own bed. The headlines were of the events that occurred in Istanbul. It already seemed to Diane that so much time had passed. Not yet 28, hours began feeling like days to her.

As her eyes grew more tired, Diane read with interest a story at the bottom of the fold of the paper about the Shah of Iran and the oil crisis. The article explained that according to U.S. government documents, during the summer and fall of 1976, in the midst of the Ford-Carter presidential campaign, President Gerald Ford's "economic advisors" worried that another big surge in fuel costs might trigger a global financial collapse. The Shah enforced his 1973 declaration to end existing oil contracts and called for all contracts to cease between 1977 and 1979.

Diane recalled that three years earlier, the Shah had engineered the "oil shock" that made oil prices skyrocket, shaking the foundation of Western prosperity. She continued to read the article: "To pay their exorbitant oil bills, countries in southern Europe took out huge loans from private lenders and banks on Wall Street, including Bank of America, Citibank, Chase Manhattan and Morgan. The banks lent so much money so quickly that by late 1976, they were dangerously overextended, even as European governments were pushed closer to insolvency," the article noted. "The fear of Alan Greenspan and others in the administration was that Portugal, Italy and Spain might default on their debt repayments and unleash a devastating financial contagion."

Since her time in Yemen, Diane had remained curious about the Shah and his motivations. When asked if he would not ask for an oil price increase at an upcoming meeting of OPEC leaders in Venezuela, the Shah responded, "I am ready, as far as my country is concerned, to take that chance and responsibility, to go along with you and give you a spell, a break, provided you also take the necessary measures and steps for conservation and finding new sources of energy." It was curious to Diane that the issue of the oil contracts didn't make bigger headlines.

Nearly asleep, Diane heard the phone ring. "Hello? Hello? Who is this?" Her voice sounded sleepy.

Jack didn't say a word and hung up.

She shook her head, hung up the phone, laid the paper down and fell asleep.

The next day, after a long, deep slumber, Diane was back at the Washington Mall to meet Richard. Spring had sprung, with an air of new possibility. Diane found herself walking with a bit more confidence. She saw a cloud of smoke in front of a pond and approached. "You are always alone. I often wonder if you are ever with people, with family and friends," Diane said. "By the way, did you call me yesterday? Someone did, and it was weird. I could hear something, but whoever it was just hung up."

"My personal life is none of your concern," Richard said sternly. "I didn't call you. Was it just once?"

Hordes of tourists milled about.

"Yes, once . . . and I was half-asleep. I thought maybe I dreamt it."

"Tired or not, always be on guard. We are playing high stakes here."

"I'm just reporting, doing my job and trying to mind my business otherwise."

"You are doing more than that, young lady, and my contacts are very satisfied with your work so far, Diane."

"When do I meet them?" Diane asked as she pulled her thick hair into a ponytail. Her skin glowed slightly darker from the strong spring sun.

"I'm afraid that's not possible. It's best to keep the information and informant separate. Legally, we'd like to keep things clean."

"Legally? Are we breaking laws here?" Jack's face flashed in her head. She lifted her sunglasses and rubbed her eyes.

"Anytime you cut through bureaucracy, the higher-ups will be sure to find a law that you're supposedly breaking," Richard said. "Trust me, you'll be safe though. You're a public figure now. My contacts and I, on the other hand, are not. We could disappear easily."

"Safe? I thought I was in danger in Turkey and other areas not back home in Washington DC. I take it your neck hurts from always looking behind you."

"Our main threat is Zbigniew Brzezinski," Richard said and looked around.

"National Security Advisor Brzezinski?" Diane said, also looking around suspiciously.

"We were colleagues once—or more like rivals actually. He's been suspicious ever since I went rogue. Brzezinski is topnotch. He received his B.A. and M.A. from McGill University and his PhD from Harvard. He is on the faculty of Columbia and Harvard University. He holds honorary degrees from Georgetown University, Williams College, Fordham University, the College of the Holy Cross, Alliance College, the Catholic University of Dublin, Warsaw University and Vilnius University," Richard said and slid his aviator sunglasses on.

"Wow. That is impressive. I mean, *he* is impressive. I've seen pictures of him before. Seems like a tough guy," Diane said. "So why the fallout? Do you ever speak?"

"What do you mean by *speak*?" Richard asked gruffly.

"Just that Washington is small, especially in the circles you run in," Diane said. Her voice was shaky. "I just thought—"

Richard cut her off again, just like he had in the desert of Yemen. He looked around again and whispered. "No, we don't speak, and even if we did, it would be none of your concern, Ms. Babel."

"I apologize," Diane said, startled; it was the first time since Yemen he had referred to her in that way, and it made her feel like an intern again. "But why do you keep looking around so much?"

"You can't trust anyone," Richard said.

"Do you trust me?" Diane asked sheepishly.

"I want to. In my position and experience, you see many things. Friends are hard to come by, and trust is always elusive. Let every eye negotiate for itself and trust no agent, which is what Shakespeare said and I agree."

"Fair enough, but what about you? Do *you* trust *me*?" Diane asked, leaning closer.

"Time tells all. For now, I have no reason to doubt you. Listen, speaking of which, we are short on time. The Shah of Iran has requested a personal one-on-one interview."

"I was just reading about the OPEC oil conference and his siding with the U.S. Is that the angle? He knows who I am?"

"Yes, he knows of you, at least a little, and no, the oil issue is secondary. He's currently under a significant amount of pressure from the Carter administration and feels like he needs to tell the American people his side of the story. He's also trying to clean up his image."

"Okay. I'm just surprised he knows me—I mean, the Shah of Iran."

"I haven't gotten much into my past with you, but I have connections with his family. I was a part of Operation AJAX in 1953. Do you remember what I told you years ago?"

"Sure. The U.S. and Britain sponsored a coup that ousted Mohammed Mosaddeq and put the Shah back in power," Diane said.

"Good, and right you are. I can't be specific, but I was in charge, along with Kermit Roosevelt."

"The grandson of President Roosevelt? That's pretty big."

"It was and still is. We put the Shah in power for a reason, and we want to make sure he stays in power. It came at a great loss," Richard said and stared as a young couple with a baby stroller passed by.

"What loss? Did you lose something in all of this, Richard?"

"Never you mind about the loss. That is not your job, nor is it a story for you to investigate. Just do as you're told, and all will work out."

"Is he in trouble? The Shah I mean," Diane said and watched as two squirrels fought over a piece of stale bread. "Why aren't we or anyone else reporting on the oil contracts—that he is going to pull them soon?"

Richard straightened his tie and squared his sports jacket. "It is a fair question, but I have my orders, and we are not to report on that—at least not yet." Richard leaned closer. "Are you familiar with the Green Belt project?"

"I remember reading about it in the Old Testament, but not as a project as much as a way of protecting trees and land from destruction," Diane said quizzically.

"Well, this is a CIA project, and the green here denotes Islam. The concept here is to surround the Soviet Union with Islamic religious regimes because the CIA believed Islamists would be easier to control," Richard said. "This is the Carter administration's stance too, and it includes the overthrow of the Shah and the support of Afghan guerillas, the Mojahedin, against the Soviets."

Diane looked around. "So Brzezinski wants the Shah out? Is that what you're saying? And if so, why aren't I reporting on this?"

"I'm simply educating you on the region you'll be traveling to. I want you to have all the facts," Richard said.

"I see," Diane returned.

Richard leaned closer to Diane's ear before walking away. "When you meet with the Shah, you will follow a list of questions." Richard looked around again, as if to make sure no one was listening in. "If you go off topic—and that includes any talk of the oil contracts—you can consider yourself fired."

*   *   *

In mid-June, Jack was buried in paperwork. As he did every day, he poured over reports, articles and declassified intelligence. Jody had been on a press tour the previous week with the President, which left Jack in charge of the press corps for the first time since accepting the position.

Jack was re-reading the President's commencement speech, which he had given the previous weekend at Notre Dame University. Jody had recently fired a speechwriter and asked Jack to edit and tweak the speech for him. While Jack had limited experience in writing speeches, he was well versed in Carter's message; he read over the transcript with pleasure: "Democracy's great recent successes—in India, Portugal, Spain and Greece—show that our confidence in this system is not misplaced. Being confident of our own future, we are now free of that inordinate fear of communism, which once led us to embrace any dictator who joined us in that fear. I'm glad that that's being changed.

"For too many years, we've been willing to adopt the flawed and erroneous principles and tactics of our adversaries, sometimes abandoning our own values for theirs. We've fought fire with fire, never thinking that fire is better quenched with water. This approach failed, with Vietnam the best example of its intellectual and moral poverty. But through failure we have now found our way back to our own principles and values, and we have regained our lost confidence. By the measure of history, our nation's 200 years are very brief, and our rise to world eminence is briefer still. It dates from 1945, when Europe and the old international order lay in ruins. Before then, America was largely on the periphery of world affairs. But since then, we have inescapably been at the center of world affairs.

"Our policy during this period was guided by two principles: a belief that Soviet expansion was almost inevitable but that it must be contained and the corresponding belief in the importance of an almost exclusive alliance among non-communist nations on both sides of the Atlantic. That system could not last forever, unchanged. Historical trends have weakened its foundation. The unifying threat of conflict with the Soviet Union has become less intensive, even though the competition has become more extensive."

It was nearly noon when Jack's assistant, a young brunette with a Harvard pedigree and sharp smile, entered the room. She cleared her throat but couldn't get his attention. "Mr. Quaid? Mr. Quaid?"

Jack didn't look up.

"Jack!" She raised her voice and cleared her throat again, as if she was readying herself for song.

"I'm busy here, Kara. Can it wait? And why didn't you call first?" Jack said without looking up at her.

"Jack, there's someone here to see you."

"One moment. I'm mid-sentence here."

"This is important," Kara said directly.

"Right. So who is it?" Jack said.

"It's, uh . . . well, it's President Carter."

Jack looked up slowly and found himself staring right at Jimmy Carter, who was standing there next to Kara, wearing his typical wide, bright, toothy smile. He stood five-ten and was otherwise unassuming, considering he was the leader of the free world.

"Mr. Quaid, do you have a moment?" Jimmy said warmly. His Southern drawl was comforting to Jack, and it reminded him of home.

A rush of blood hit Jack's face, as if he'd been hanging upside down. He looked down at the speech, then back to the President. "Yes, of course, Mr. President." Jack stood up and walked over with his hand extended. "It's a pleasure, *my* pleasure," Jack said. He had met the President before, but always with Jody. "This is Kara, my—"

"You're a true Southern gentlemen, Jack. Kara and I had the pleasure of meeting only minutes earlier."

Jimmy nodded at Kara to dismiss her, and Jack quickly shot a look at her. Her eyebrows raised inquisitively.

"It's a beautiful afternoon, and the sun is generous to us today. Will you take a walk with me, Jack?"

"Of course, Mr. President."

"After that speech you wrote and all the fine work you've been doing, please call me Jimmy. Pretense has its place, but there's no need for it here."

They proceeded down the hall, heading toward the South Lawn. Secret Service followed like shadows, and colleagues looked on with curiosity. When they entered the lawn, Jack could see Secret Service men around the perimeter. The sun was hot, and the grass was an Irish green.

"I miss walking alone," Jimmy said.

Jack noticed his gray sideburns, thick hair parted to the side and the fact that he wore a blue shirt, plaid tie, and gray pants but no suit jacket. Almost every word was followed by his signature wide, toothy smile.

"Should I leave or . . . ?" Jack stammered.

"No, Jack," Jimmy said with a laugh. "I appreciate company, but it's just that I'm never alone anymore," the President explained, thumbing back to the black suits following them.

"Oh right. I guess privacy goes out the window in exchange for protection."

"I knew sacrifices would have to be made, but sometimes I just want to jump the fence and run freely around town." Jimmy looked around. "I hope you don't mind being taken away from your work. I like to get to know everyone who works for me, personally if I can."

"I appreciate this time with you," Jack said, turning to Jimmy as they slowly walked across the lawn. Jack clasped his hands behind his back and squeezed his left wrist tightly with his right hand to release tension.

"How's Jody holding up?" Jimmy said. He stopped, took a white handkerchief from his back pocket and wiped sweat from his forehead.

"He's doing a great job," Jack said and quietly questioned why he didn't carry a handkerchief too. Sweat beaded around his eyebrows and dripped down the bridge of his nose.

"I knew he would," Jimmy said. "He's the best."

They walked silently for a few more steps. Jacked looked up and could see a passenger jet high in the sky. Beyond the black wrought-iron gates of the White House lay a world Jack felt disconnected from. He marveled at the fact that the South Lawn had been open to the public until World War II. Now, only select few could visit during the annual Easter egg rolling contest.

"He tells me you are friends with that reporter, Diane Babel," Jimmy said, snapping Jack back to the moment.

Jack, surprised his attention had drifted, bit his lip as Jimmy slid on a pair of sunglasses. "Yes, we were, uh . . . classmates," Jack said.

"Right. Just classmates . . . at G.W., a fine school," Jimmy said. "We need you to keep an eye on her, Jack."

"Jody has had this talk with me about her. Diane is just a reporter, as far as I know. Is there something more I should know about her?"

"Yes, she may be *just* a reporter, but I hope the request holds more significance coming from me. I can tell by your change in demeanor that you two have a bit of a history."

"Well, Mr. President, to be perfectly candid, I'm not sure I'm comfortable speaking about this," Jack said, breaking eye contact.

Jimmy stopped walking and put his arm around Jack. "I understand. I was young once too, and you know what I told *Playboy* about having lust in my heart. There is a lot at stake here, Jack. We are a team. She's been raising a lot of red flags as of late. She knows too much and reports the same—too much. We just want to make sure she's on our side, on the side of America. Keep her close if you can."

"Is that what you're supposed to do with friends? I mean, I don't even know if *friend* is the right word anymore."

"Well, then in your case, keep her closer," Jimmy said, lightly patting his back.

"Yes, Mr. President . . . er, I mean Jimmy. I will try. We haven't spoken much. She is a bit of a loner. I suppose that's good for her profession."

"She has a big interview with the Shah of Iran coming up. We need to know everything she finds out—not merely what she reports about."

"The Shah? Really? Wow. I'll try my best."

"That's all we ask, Jack. The more information you can give us, the more we can give you, if you catch my meaning."

"More access, more responsibility," Jack said softly.

"Whatever a fellow Georgian needs, he gets. That's my point. We have an opportunity, and we have the ability to make some real changes in this country."

"Look there," Jimmy said with a proud smile. "The future."

"What are they doing? Is that the new energy initiative I heard about, all that banging the last few days?"

"Yes, we're installing solar panels. We're going to show the world that America can be energy independent. The oil prices are killing us. In a few years, the panels could be installed on all houses. Can you think of a better place to start?"

"You think it will work?"

"With enough hindsight, you can get anything to work."

Jimmy motioned to the Secret Service agents. "Okay, Jack. It seems duty calls again. I have meetings to attend. I trust I made myself clear with regard to Diane Babel and what I will expect of you?"

"Yes you did—perfectly clear, Jimmy. I just hope I can deliver," Jack said.

"I'll leave you with the words of William Faulkner. 'Everything goes by the board: honor, pride, decency to get the book written.'"

* * *

Later that night, Jack sat at home drinking bourbon, smoking cigarettes and thinking about what Jimmy had told him. He was unsure of what "book" was being written and whether or not he was a willing contributor like Jody.

He took a deep gulp of his Maker's Mark and picked up the phone. He dialed Diane's number. As the phone rang, his heart began beating faster.

"Hello?" Diane said. "Hello? Who is this?"

"Hey," Jack said softly.

"Who is this?"

"It's Jack, Diane," he said, exhaling a large cloud of smoke.

"Jack? Hey." Diane's voice was lightly strained.

There was a brief silence, and they both sat still.

"So . . . you called me," Diane finally said.

"I know."

"Well, why?"

"I was just thinking of you, wondering how you are. So how have you been?"

"Busy," Diane said sharply.

"That's it?" Jack returned quickly.

"Jack, you're lucky you caught me. I'm hardly home, and when I am, I'm usually sleeping, which I should be doing now since I have an overseas flight in the morning."

"Where are you headed?"

"You don't know?"

"Why would I?" Jack scoffed, his words slightly slurred.

Diane stood up and walked toward the window. She pushed the curtain aside and looked up and down the street. "Seems to me you White House guys know everything."

"I can say the same for you. So where you headed?"

"Watch the news. You'll find out soon enough."

"Diane, what is with your attitude? Can you just talk to me?" Jack's voice was tense.

"Me? What about you? Can't you have conversation with me without fishing for information?"

"The Shah. That's where you're headed."

"Well, the news wire announced the interview already, so it's public information," Diane said.

"Are you prepared for that?" Jack asked.

"Rather condescending, don't you think, Jack?" Diane snapped.

"Well, what are you planning to cover?"

"Are you kidding me, Jack!? Who do you think you're talking to? This isn't Professor Stanley's class. This is the real world, and the stakes are high."

"I know that, Diane. We're supposed to be friends. Can't we just take off our respective hats and be there for each other?" Jack said.

"Jack, are you saying you're in over your head?"

"Why?"

"Because you are smarter than this transparent approach, unless this is part of some larger plan. You are confusing me, and I really don't have time for all this. I mean, I guess it was nice to hear from you, but I really have to go now."

"Diane—" Jack began, but then he heard the line go dead. He quickly redialed, only to get a busy signal. He tried for the next fifteen minutes, but the line remained busy. *Must be off the hook,* he assumed. The busy signal pounded against his head like a jackhammer.

*   *   *

The following morning, Jack found himself back at George Washington University, waiting for Professor Stanley to finish his phone call. Jack was dressed in his best suit. He now owned three, and they could be mixed and matched with various colors of ties. On this day, he went with red over a dark blue suit.

With a smile, Professor Stanley gestured to Jack that he would be a minute. Soon, his chair turned around away from Jack. Behind him, on his wall, Jack noticed numerous pictures and diplomas. Jack focused on one picture that depicted a much younger professor with another man Jack didn't recognize, both dressed in fatigues. He stood up and walked closer, studying the picture. Next to it was a more recent picture of the professor and Jody Powell.

Professor Stanley slammed down the phone. "Jack, it's always good to see students," he said, extending his hand. He walked with a greater limp without his cane. "Do you like those pictures? That's me with my old buddy General George Grady, although I just call him Richard. He went on to fight wars and then on to the CIA; and of course, you know Jody."

"Should I recognize him, this Richard guy?" Jack questioned.

He smiled. "Perhaps you should. In any case, what brings you here?"

"Diane Babel."

"Ah, another promising student reaching great heights. Everything okay?" He busied himself with his briefcase.

"Did she win? You know, at graduation," Jack asked as he walked back toward his chair.

"Oh, Jack, I pulled some strings to get you that interview with Jody Powell's people, and now look at you! You got the job, and as far as I can tell by that suit, you're doing well. I would say *you* are a winner if there ever was one. Now I have a class to get to—"

"Professor, I'm worried about her."

"Jack, don't worry about who won. Worry about yourself. I'm sure Diane will be just fine, as will you."

Chapter 12

"I can't believe the network can afford this flight," Mike, Diane and Bart's soundman, said as he duck-walked around the cabin on the small private jet flying somewhere over the Atlantic Ocean. Mike was in his early thirties, tall and skinny and usually not talkative, which Diane found odd, given his profession.

"Yeah right, like the network is paying for this," Bart said. He was on his second scotch and water. He had grown a bushy beard, which had turned an auburn color.

"Who is paying then?" Mike said. He popped open a bottle of Heineken.

"Mohammed Reza Pahlavi," Diane said, looking up from her notes. She was dressed down in jeans and a t-shirt. Her hair was in a bun, and she was sucking on the stem of her glasses as if she was preparing for a final exam.

"Who?" Mike said.

"The Shah of Iran," Diane said sharply. "Bart, didn't you tell him?"

Bart showed little interest and didn't bother answering with anything other than a shrug.

"Oh, I thought his name was Shah," Mike said.

"For someone I've brought around the world, could you be any less cultured?" Diane said, shaking her head and wearing a half-smile.

"Give him a break," Bart said.

"So we're clear, Mike, *shah* is an Iranian term for monarch or leader," Diane said.

"So he's like the king of Iran?" Mike said.

"Well, if it helps you to think of it that way, I guess so," Diane offered.

"Why does he want to talk to you? What's the angle this time around?" Mike said.

"That's what we're here to find out," Diane said. "Jeez, Mike. This is as much as you have spoken since I've known you."

"I guess I'm just taking more of an interest," Mike said and sat down a few seats from Diane.

The cabin fell silent, and Diane looked out the window. The night was dark, and she couldn't tell whether they were flying over water or land. Wisps of clouds obscured her view.

"I was given orders, Diane. You have to keep to the scripted questions," Bart said.

Diane broke her gaze. "I know, but there is so much to study. He's quite a man," Diane said.

Hours later, the jet came to a bumpy, screechy stop at Mehrabad International Airport. Diane, Bart and Mike had all fallen asleep, and the reporter was surrounded by papers. As she looked out the window, she was reminded of one of her father's favorite movies *A Poppy Is also a Flower*, starring Omar Sharif. The movie, she recalled, centered on an attempt by narcotic agents working for the United Nations to stem the heroin trade from Iran. Diane liked the part of the film when a mysterious woman, played by Angie Dickinson, was introduced, doing her own investigation. Diane thought that woman was cool.

Diane, Bart and Mike were met at the airport by members of the Shah's Immortal Royal Guard.

"The Shah wishes to welcome you to Iran, to Tehran," the lead guard said. His voice had a velvet quality to it, and Diane thought it seemed as if he'd learned his English from the British. He was highly decorated. He stood nearly six feet tall and wore an impressive rounded imperial black hat with gold bands that culminated into a silver medallion above his forehead, topped by a small golden crown. His uniform was pressed perfectly with more gold, looped tassels and medals signifying experience and success—an impressive uniform Diane had first seen in the mountains of Yemen years earlier.

"Thank you," Diane said, looking around and smiling politely.

Three underling guards with less decoration also smiled politely and picked up bags and equipment; all the while, Bart looked over the equipment with watchful, bloodshot eyes.

"Let's be careful," he said, walking beside them through the airport, modern and full of travelers.

"Please, we'll take the best of care of your belongings," the lead guard said, adding that his name was Abida.

"My name is Diane Babel, and this is Bart, my producer, and Mike, our soundman," Diane said as Abida opened the car door and gestured for them to enter.

"My pleasure to meet you all," Abida said.

As Diane sat down, she leaned her head out the door and asked, "That's a nice name. What does it mean?"

"Thank you. It means 'one who worships,'" he said and slowly closed the door.

Much like the private jet, the limousine was ornately decorated with gold and jewels. A phone was positioned on one wall, and a full bar, complete with finger sandwiches was made available.

"According to the itinerary, we are to be dropped at the hotel for a few hours, and then the interview is scheduled. They have given us ninety minutes for the interview but prefer less time," Bart said. He opened a bottle of Coke. "Are you set with the questions?"

Diane nodded. "We're in good shape. Do you guys feel good and ready?"

"Just fine," Mike said.

Bart nodded.

"They are providing production support as well," Bart said. "Along with my camera, I will be directing two others. I don't want to miss anything, our jobs depend on it."

"Our jobs?" Diane questioned.

Mike sat straighter in his seat. His hair was still unkempt from sleeping on the plane.

"I've never asked too many questions, Diane," Bart said. "I've worked at a few networks, but ITN is different. I mean, think about it . . . we never meet at a studio. We are all given our assignments by phone or in writing. There are no production meetings where we sit together. I'm supposed to know more than you, the reporter, but that isn't the case, so I just go with it. And the person I report to—"

Diane interrupted, "And who is that?"

"John Phillips," Bart said. He cocked his head. "Whom do you hear from?"

"Yeah sure. John Phillips too," Diane said quickly.

"Right. Well, he said ratings are suffering, and if we don't get a better angle than Barbra Walters or Mike Douglas, we're dead in the water."

"We will be fine—even better than fine." Diane looked out the window. She was pleasantly surprised by what Iran offered. It didn't look all that different than the U.S., she thought, with its highways and byways, traffic and architecture. While people dressed differently, especially the women, they lived their lives one step at a time.

Diane had read about the once lush gardens of Tehran, plentiful with plane and pomegranate trees; however, they were now few and far between as the once quaint village had grown into a metropolis, an environmental sacrifice suffered by every great city.

As the car weaved through traffic, Diane looked out the window to the north, where the southern slopes of the Alborz mountain range stood, defiant and beautiful. Snow was visible at its peak, nearly 19,000 feet, as the driver pointed out. She learned the Caspian Sea was only fifty miles on the other side of the mountain range, home to a dormant volcano. She wondered what secrets those mountains might hide.

Hours later, Diane stared at her notes and questions. She was picked up from the hotel by the same guards and limousine. Bart and Mike had left ahead of her for pre-production. As she sat in the back of the car, she felt her palms begin to sweat. She wished Richard was there with her, and she wondered what Jack was doing. Aside from her father, those were the men in her life.

The limousine pulled up to an old palace that was home to one of the Shah's many offices. Standing outside was Bart, and he looked different. He had shaved his beard down to a mustache and pork chop sideburns and wore a brown sport coat over a blue button-down t-shirt.

The door was opened for Diane; she stood up with an armful of notes and papers. She stared in amazement at the impressive, ornate building. The palace was a huge, castle-like structure.

"Just a little nicer than my studio. Jeez," Bart said. "You should see inside."

Diane looked at Bart and smirked.

Bart leaned closer to her. "Stay cool. This will be great."

Mike came down the walkway. "Bart, we need two microphones, and I think some of the cables are questionable." Bart pointed to another vehicle where equipment was stored. Mike ran over and grabbed two cases, handing one to Bart.

Diane, Mike and Bart headed toward the entrance, where two imposing guards stood. They stopped them and inspected the equipment boxes and looked through Diane's notes and pocketbook.

"Boys, boys, c'mon! Easy with my gear," Bart said.

They didn't listen.

"Hey, what is this? Russia?"

There was no response.

Shortly later, they entered a room that seemed as wide as a football field but a quarter as long. Beautiful Persian rugs with colors of red, black and gold covered the floor. An etched glass and wood conference table that seated twenty anchored one side of the office. Floor-to-ceiling windows were covered in golden drapes and curtains. Mirrors lined the walls, and Diane couldn't count how many crystal chandlers hung, illuminating the room.

Bart and his crew were set up on the other side of the room, where a long couch faced an empty chair. A coffee table was directly in front of a large seat. Bart brought over a hand mirror. Diane took a long look at herself. Her hair was down, falling past her shoulders. She wore an olive-toned lipstick that highlighted the hue of her cheekbones. Her hazel eyes were bright and brilliant. She showed her teeth and rubbed them with her pointer finger to make sure they appeared clean.

She smoothed out her eyebrows, sat up straight and signaled for Bart to retrieve the mirror. She placed her notes outside the scope of the camera view. She sat patiently and looked to the same door she'd entered. Two guards stood there, stone-faced. Moments later, they parted, and the Shah entered the room. As he approached, Diane recalled that he was a secular Muslim and wondered if he knew she was part Jewish.

Diane stood up to formally greet the Shah. He was in his late fifties, and though small in stature, his presence was large and commanding. Diane reached out her hand respectfully. Bart signaled Mike and the other cameramen to start recording.

"It's an honor to meet you, Your Majesty," Diane said. Her voice was strong and measured.

"My pleasure. Please sit down," the Shah said, waiting until she was seated before he sat.

Diane sat on the lavish couch adjacent to him, and their arms were only a foot apart.

"How was your flight?" the Shah said.

"Quite nice, thank you."

"And your accommodations?"

"More than enough. We really appreciate your hospitality." Diane motioned to Bart and Mike, who both nodded at the Shah.

"It's not how you pictured it, is it?"

"Excuse me?" Diane said. She quickly studied his tailored gray suit and purple tie. His temples were gray.

"Iran."

"It's a beautiful country."

"Did you expect that?"

"I wasn't sure what to expect."

"And what did you expect?" the Shah said.

"To be honest?

"Of course."

"I expected a third-world nation."

"You are not alone in your assumptions of my country. I recently met with Mike Wallace and David Frost, and they concur that Americans and the British have no idea what it is like here. There is poverty, yes, but there is poverty in all countries. We are a prosperous nation on a very successful technological, social and educational path."

"I see that."

"Of course surface beauty is important, but it's all for show. I'm saying Iran is prosperous because of what you *can't* see."

"And what is it, Your Majesty that we Americans can't see?"

"A nation determined to create peace." His eyes were direct, with a softness that made Diane feel at ease.

"Your Majesty, how will you create this peace?" Diane said.

"It all comes down to creating strong allies. That's how it begins. I have seen too many people die in my lifetime. If I do not concentrate on what my neighbors are doing, what they have, we can see more death."

"You've also been supplying military resources to Saudi Arabia and your other Persian Gulf neighbors. For what purpose?" As Diane asked the question, Bart double-checked his notes to make sure she was on script.

"Yes, as well as Lebanon. My Royal Guard, along with American operatives, are fighting Islamic Extremists in Oman as we speak. My other friends, Egypt's President Sadat and Israel's Prime Minister Begin, are also trying to fight these Islamic fundamentalists to protect U.S. and Israeli interests and preserve peace in the Middle East."

"And why all the outreach? Why now?" Diane asked, leaning slightly closer.

"We must stop the Islamic radicals. They will be the downfall of society and provide a long-term instability for the region. Right here in my own country, there are radical groups looking to overtake me. You know of Ayatollah Khomeini?"

"As I understand it, he was once a political and religious leader, now exiled in Iraq under the care of Saddam Hussein," Diane said.

"Yes. Khomeini is supposedly organizing a revolution. He wants to overthrow me with his fundamentalist ideas, and it seems as if certain Western leaders are planning a plot against me under some human rights initiative. All my allies and I have done to create peace will be destroyed when the radicals come into power. Does this make sense?"

"I see. If it comes down to another overthrow plot, would you kill your own people to save your empire?"

The Shah paused and looked deeply at Diane. Bart focused the camera squarely on the Shah's face. His eyes grew dark and cold, more resolute.

"I love my people and the people who support Iran. I would never want to see a drop of their blood in my streets. Just as in 1953, when I came back, I specifically asked that not a single soul be killed. My people should have the right to come to me directly and address their issues with my government. I'm establishing a twentieth-century society, built upon the first kingdom of Cyrus, 3,000 years ago. Do you keep up with your history book, Ms. Babel?"

"I know about King Cyrus, your civilization, history and how this nation of yours was once led by a great leader who was a visionary and, even back then, provided his people with freedom of speech, religion, liberty and justice for all races through the Persian Kingdom. Of course I know, Your Majesty, but are you suggesting that you're trying to duplicate what Cyrus did 3,000 years ago?"

The Shah shifted in his seat slightly and leaned closer to Diane. "Allow me to be very candid with you. It's been my plan all along to build new pathways toward a greater civilization for Persian people and my country. I'm sure you saw a sample of our modern society in the last few days. That's my only intention. If you're asking me if I would kill my own people, absolutely not! Under no circumstances."

"Your Majesty, with all due respect, I was being hypothetical. America will not let there be another coup," Diane politely countered.

Bart looked to Mike, raised his eyebrows then focused on the camera.

"If things continue on their present track, the disintegration of Western societies will occur much sooner than you think under the umbrella of fascism and communism. Freedom has a breaking point, and our enemies would like to bring us to that point," the Shah said.

"Our leaders will say America is stronger than that," Diane said.

"I appreciate your esteem for your nation. You think very much like me in that regard. I think the most difficult thing for me to accept is that when the time comes, it will be my Iranians who overthrow this government. I can forgive those who try and kill me and try to abduct my wife and my child, but I cannot forgive those who betray Iran. If I execute twelve who betray, I will also execute the next twelve who betray. This is my policy. These men are Marxists."

Diane nodded solemnly.

"I studied your last name, Babel," Shah said, rubbing his eye with his finger.

A noticeable flush came over Diane's face.

"The city and its tower, so it says in Genesis, is the tower we know as Babel in the Shinar plain. The whole Earth was of one language and of one speech. Do you know this, Ms. Babel? This passage? God felt by building a tower to the heavens, the people were competing with him," the Shah said earnestly.

"It was an act of hubris in God's eyes, I believe," Diane said. She knew they were far off script, so she didn't dare look to Bart.

"Yes, Ms. Babel, hubris indeed," the Shah said. Then he sighed and sat back in his chair, pleasantly waving his arm to stop the interview.

Chapter 13

As Jack often did, he sat in his office reading, with music lightly playing on the radio. Jody always scoffed at that, so he kept it under his desk. He was tapping his feet and singing along to Elvis Presley's rendition of "My Way."

> *I've lived a life that's full.*
> *I've traveled each and every highway . . .*

Jack was busy with a side project that had been handed to him by Jody: figuring out the latest computer released from a small San Francisco company, Apple. He looked at the Apple II, which included a case, keyboard, power supply and screen; the whole thing was a foreign concept. While he set up the system on a side desk, he looked at his electric typewriter as superior.

The music played on:

> *Regrets? I've had a few,*
> *but then again, too few to mention.*

While Jack's door was ajar, he didn't hear the knocking until it got louder.

"Mr. Quaid. Mr. Quaid!" a stern voice bellowed.

Jack looked up to see Zbigniew Brzezinski, National Security Advisor. He was in his mid-fifties, dressed in a dark, vested suit with a pin-striped blue and white collared shirt and matching tie. His face was rugged and rife with wrinkles. He seemed to carry on his back the weight of every struggle, trial and tribulation of his Polish ancestors.

120

"Oh, hello. Sorry," Jack said, startled. He leaned down and turned down the music, then tossed the Apple manual on his desk.

"The President tells me you're someone we can trust," he said.

Jack knew Brzezinski was the strong hand in the otherwise typical left-wing administration. "I am," he answered.

"We will be intercepting the footage Diane Babel has recorded in Iran with the Shah. I need you to review it and write me a report, especially on any item that might not make it to air. We know you have had personal relations with the journalist. Will this compromise your ability to do your job?"

"Not at all."

"I believe Iran could be a large threat to us and the world, especially with the Shah in power."

"I see."

"Jody will give you the details, but I expect a thorough report, Mr. Quaid."

"Yes," Jack said, "and please call me Jack."

Zbigniew nodded and walked out of the room. He was there less than three minutes, but Jack felt like he'd been run over by a bus. Jack leaned down and turned the music back on. He walked over and closed his office door. He slid down the door until he was seated on the ground. He thought about Diane. "The Shah of Iran," he said and smiled.

Jack played coy; he had studied Zbigniew as a student and remained in quiet awe of the man. Like his first meeting with Carter, Jack looked forward to his first interaction with him and was embarrassed that Elvis's croning was party to the experience.

He knew Zbigniew was a Harvard professor who often argued against the policies of then President Eisenhower, believing that antagonism would push Eastern Europe further toward the Soviet Union. A later strike in Poland, coupled with the Hungarian Revolution in 1956, supported his stance that the eastern Europeans could gradually counter Soviet domination. Jack learned about him in greater detail when he was teaching at Columbia University and wrote, *Soviet Bloc: Unity and Conflict*.

*　　*　　*

Later that evening, Zbigniew was riding in the back of a black town car. "Pull over there, on the side of those trees," he told the driver. It was pitch black. He lit a cigarette, pushed the door open and slid to the right across the back bench seat.

"I prefer the phone," Richard Harden said, sitting down. He was dressed in dark clothes and spoke in a hushed tone.

"Nixon taught us all a lesson. You're aware that Jack Quaid is working for the administration, are you not?" Zbigniew said plainly.

Richard didn't speak and motioned toward the driver.

"Hey, Bill, go grab a smoke, will you?" Zbigniew said.

The driver did as he was told.

When the driver's side door closed, Richard returned his focus. "Babel told me, yes. This shouldn't change anything."

"They were lovers."

"And we were once friends. What's your point?"

"I know Babel is en route home. We have to review these Shah tapes. There is no room for movement here."

Richard raised his hand and started shaking it in defiance. "That wasn't our deal. If you compromise the Shah, our deal is off."

"We continue to fear the Afghanistan and Russian alliance. Keeping Russia in check is our main goal, the Carter administration's goal. If that is compromised, *we* are compromised. That is the deal—America's deal."

Richard lit a cigar.

"This one time, take the damn tapes. I'll cover the overseas interests, but make this a habit, and we're gonna have trouble. That interview has to air soon."

"You handle your sources and keep Babel in check. I'm putting Quaid in charge of reviewing the tapes. It'll give us a chance to see what he's really made of," Zbigniew said coldly.

Richard snubbed his cigar in the ashtray. He opened the car door and stuck his head back into the smoked-filled cabin. "No bullshit here, Zbigniew," Richard said and slammed the door.

*   *   *

The following day, Diane, Mike and Bart were waiting for their luggage to arrive at the Washington National Airport. They were the last ones left, and only one bag went around and around on the conveyor belt.

"I don't think our luggage is coming. It's been more than an hour," Diane said. She was visibly tired and frustrated. Her hair was askew, and bags were forming under her eyes.

"What if we lost all our footage?" Bart said and threw up his arms.

"Does this mean we could lose our jobs?" Mike said.

"Everything," Bart snapped.

An hour later, the three were standing in a security office that smelled of burnt coffee and stale smoke.

"I've just been informed that your baggage has been flagged and confiscated," a black woman in her late forties said. She was slightly overweight, and her uniform was creased. Her white shirt wasn't fully tucked into her belt.

"Confiscated?" Diane said, her voice shrill.

"Yes, a national security matter. You shouldn't have anything to worry about, unless you're carrying a bomb," she joked.

"No bomb, just video. We have a story to air!" Diane said.

"Oh yes, I thought you looked familiar. Babis something, right? Well, we'll call you once everything is sorted out. This happens all the time with people traveling in and out of that area. Should only be a few days."

"A few days? What area?"

She looked at her clipboard. "The Middle East—a real dangerous place."

"This is bullshit."

"C'mon," Bart said, grabbing Diane's arm. "They've got us by the short hairs."

*　　*　　*

That night, Diane returned to her apartment. It seemed as if months had passed since she'd been home. Her plants drooped, and all that remained in her refrigerator was butter, grape jam and soy sauce. She dropped to the couch and picked up the phone. Her eyes were half-open as she dialed.

"Hey, Dad," she said. She listened for a few minutes. He spoke rhythmically but in sentences that never seemed to end; but when they did, they were always in the form of a question. His voice always soothed her. "Yes, it went well—very well, I think. The Shah, the palace was just amazing. I thought about you when we landed in Tehran, that movie you love with Omar Sharif . . .''

The following afternoon, Jack was attending a press conference with Jody. President Carter was fielding questions in preparation for a visit from Israeli Prime Minister Yitzhak Rabin. Jack grew to admirer Carter's charm and his uncanny ability to mediate while staying on message. He called on a reporter from *ABC News* for the first question.

"Mr. President, there has been a lot of talk about defensible borders lately and what that means in regard to the Middle East. Could I ask you, sir, do you feel it would be appropriate in a Middle East peace settlement for the Israelis to keep some of the occupied land they took during the 1967 war in order to have secured borders?"

To Jack's amazement, Jimmy didn't break eye contact with the reporter. He smoothly answered in a measured, hospitable tone, "The defensible border phrase, the secure borders phrase, obviously are just semantics. I think it's a relatively significant development in the description of possible settlement in the Middle East to talk about these things as a distinction. The recognized borders have to be mutual. The Arab nations and the Israeli nation, have to agree on permanent and recognized borders, where sovereignty is legal as mutually agreed upon. Defense lines may or may not conform in the foreseeable future to those legal borders. There may be extensions of Israeli defense capability beyond the permanent and recognized borders.

"I think this distinction is one that is now recognized by Israeli leaders. The definition of borders on a geographical basis is one that remains to be determined, but I think it's important for the world to begin to see, and for the interested parties to begin to see, that there can be a distinction between the two; the ability of Israel to defend herself by international agreement or by the sometime placement of Israeli forces themselves or by monitoring stations, as has been the case in the Sinai, beyond the actual sovereignty borders as mutually agreed by Israel and her neighbors."

The earnest reporter continued his line of questioning. "Well, does that mean international zones between the countries?"

Jimmy paused and gathered his thoughts. He looked to Jody and also caught Jack's eye. "International zones could very well be part of an agreement, and I think I can see in a growing way, a step-by-step process where there might be a mutual agreement that the ultimate settlement, even including the border delineations, would be at a certain described point. In an interim state, maybe two years, four years, eight years, or more, there would be a mutual demonstration of friendship and an end to the declaration or state of war.

"I think what Israel would like to have is what we would like to have: a termination of belligerence toward Israel by her neighbors, a recognition of Israel's right to exist, the right to exist in peace, the opening up of borders with free trade, tourist travel, cultural exchange between Israel and her neighbors; in other words, a stabilization of the situation in the Middle East without a constant threat to Israel's existence by her neighbors. This would involve substantial withdrawal of Israel's present control over territories. Now, where that withdrawal might end, I don't know. I would guess it would mean some minor adjustments in the 1967 borders, but that still remains to be negotiated.

"But I think this is going to be a long, tedious process. We're going to mount a major effort in our own government in 1977 to bring the parties to Geneva. Obviously, any agreement has to be between the parties concerned. We will act as an intermediary when our good offices will serve well. But I'm not trying to predispose our own nation's attitudes toward what might be the ultimate details of the agreement that can mean so much to world peace."

Jody, smiling confidently, leaned over to Jack as Jimmy fielded more questions. He whispered, "Are you finished reviewing the Shah tapes?"

Jack nodded. "Just about. The report will be ready soon."

"Get back to it now. I'm fine here, and Zbigniew is breathing down my neck on this. We have to get those tapes back to ITN."

"Got it," Jack said and slipped away from the press conference.

Hours later, he sat sequestered in his office, listening to tapes, watching footage and reviewing his report. The phone was ringing, but he didn't answer.

Finally, a knock came at his door. It grew louder and louder until Kara opened the door. She was dressed in a brown pantsuit and a yellow turtleneck. "Jack!"

"What?" he said, looking up.

"Diane Babel, that reporter, is at security demanding to see you."

"She's here? Now?" He picked up a brown box and began placing tapes and evidence in it. "Okay. Wait five minutes and send her up."

"Really? She seems mad and more than a little impatient."

"Just do it."

Jack removed his radio from under the desk and put the box of tapes in its place. He quickly checked his breath, fixed his hair and straightened his tie. Moments later, Diane burst into his office authoritatively. Kara couldn't stop her.

"Where are my fucking tapes?"

"Keep your voice down." Jack walked over to his door and looked up and down the hallway. He waved off a Secret Service agent and closed the door.

"Where are my tapes?"

"Jesus, Diane. I haven't seen or heard from you in months, and this is a how you approach me? Your tapes are under review."

"What does that mean? You're enjoying this, aren't you? You love this power you have over me."

"This is my job," Jack said. He couldn't help noticing how tired and distraught Diane looked.

"We aren't in grad school anymore. This is real, Jack."

"We're standing in the White House. You are in *my* office. I know what is real."

"Where are my tapes?"

"This is just protocol. We need to review everything."

"Brzezinski is behind this, isn't he?" Diane scowled.

"He's my superior, so to a certain extent, yes."

"He is to review everything the Shah says because he doesn't trust him?" Diane blurted.

"We did the same thing with Mike Wallace, so relax. The Shah is our ally. Why would he not trust him?"

"Because he's becoming too powerful, Jack."

"That's ridiculous."

"What's ridiculous is how blindly you follow other people," Diane scolded.

"Other people? I follow our President. There's nothing blind about that."

"Will I ever get the tapes back?"

"Right now, that remains confidential. I'm sorry, Diane, but ITN will be informed as soon as we are done."

"It depends how much is revealed, doesn't it?"

Jack stood in silence, wondering if she cared more about the tapes or him.

"Do me a favor and watch the interview. You might learn a thing or two," Diane said before she turned toward the door.

"Where are you going?"

Without turning back, Diane answered, "Back to work."

"Diane, wait," he said.

"For what, Jack? For what?" He looked at her and tried to break through the veneer that had become their professional lives. Her demeanor hadn't changed.

"I need to call security to have you escorted back out," he said, shaking his head.

"Kara!" Jack yelled down the hall.

Kara came running.

"Please kindly escort Ms. Babel out," Jack said. He mouthed the words, "I'm sorry," to Diane, but her face was as impervious as the Wailing Wall.

"Sure, Mr. Quaid," Kara said.

Jack closed the door and sat back at his desk. He turned on the radio to hear Stevie Wonder's "Sir Duke" in mid-song:

> *Music knows it is and always will*
> *be one of the things that life just won't quit . . .*

Jack pulled the box labeled "ITN, Babel, Diane—The Shah Tapes" from under his desk. He then pulled out his report and read it over. After a few minutes, he turned down the music and picked up the phone. "Hi, Jenny. It's Jack. When Jody gets back from the press conference, tell him he can pick up the report. He'll know what I mean. Thanks."

Chapter 14

Two days later, after returning from a trip to New York, Diane was worn out from yet *another* flight. She shivered from the cold November DC winds. Christmas decorations were being strung about by airport personnel, but holiday cheer had yet to envelop the city. A feeling of time slipping away toward a new unknown was tangible.

The chilled, unforgiving, whipping winds snapped her cheeks and crusted her runny nose. With luggage in hand, she waited outside for a cab. Bart had traveled with her to New York, despite her insistence that he stay behind. They had developed a brother/sister relationship that always seemed to turn incestuous after Bart's third bourbon. He was still in the airport, opting to capitalize on their downtime and grabbed a connecting flight to Tampa to visit with friends. She was alone.

"Excuse me, but might you have light?" a man asked. He was tall, dressed in a tan trench coat and a fedora.

"Sorry, but I don't smoke," Diane returned.

"Having a tough time finding a ride, are you?" the man offered.

Diane noticed he was wearing black leather gloves, and she wondered if he smoked at all. "I'll be fine," Diane said as passersby waved and smiled, embracing loved ones, while other people looked panicked and out of breath as they headed toward the entrance for a future undetermined and out of their control.

"You're that, uh, that reporter, right?" the man said, stepping closer. "I know your face."

"Yes. I report for ITN," Diane said.

"Aren't you ever scared?" the man asked. He tipped the brim of his hat, revealing bluish-green eyes.

"Of what? Traveling in foreign lands that are considered dangerous?" she offered.

"No," the man said and stiffened. "That your reporting will put this great country in harm's way. I didn't fight in Vietnam for the freedom of the likes of you."

"Excuse me?" Diane said.

Before the last word left her mouth, the man walked away into the late November afternoon. Shorter days were realized, and the sky was fading to a creamed orange blue.

Diane shook her head and looked toward the curb and smiled. "I didn't expect curbside pickup," she said, looking puzzled at the black town car.

The window was half-down, exposing Richard's face. He looked worn and troubled. "It's not like that exactly, I'm afraid," he said, opening the door. "Come sit down. Just don't get that comfortable."

Diane forced her bags toward the door.

Richard grabbed them and placed them to his left. "Now close the door. It's freezing out there," he said.

Diane sat down. The car smelled of stale smoke and forced hot air that did little to warm her cheeks. "So what's up?"

Richard handed Diane an airplane ticket, and she promptly inspected it. "Israel?"

"Anwar Sadat, the president of Egypt, is going to be making a visit there. We need you there," Richard said, relighting his cigar.

"The leader of an Arab country is going to Israel?"

"Exactly."

"Well in that case, you're right. I do need to be there."

"Your flight is leaving soon. You better get going." Richard handed her a bag and an envelope. "Some background information, questions to be asked and a stipend," he explained.

Diane hurried toward the gate and made it through security quickly. She was now a frequent flyer and had begun to recognize the faces of the airport employees. One guard, a black man around twenty with a domed afro always said, "There she is" each time he saw her. Diane didn't mind his attention. He was from Trinidad, didn't own a television and only cared about playing soccer; he mentioned these facts nearly every time he saw her. He had no idea that she was on the news and often said, "Punch my calf. It's like a rock. I'm the next Pelé. I can do flips and all."

On this day, she didn't see Pelé, but she heard another familiar voice.

"Do you know how close I was to getting on the plane to Tampa?" Bart said with a grin. "Those bastards had me paged. I guess they got you too."

"Oh, but this will be so much better than Florida, Bart," Diane said with encouragement. "Plus, you don't seem bikini-beach ready," she whispered, tapping his stomach with her hand. "Let's go!"

Hours into the flight, Diane opened the envelope Richard had given her. She placed the $200 in cash in her purse and began reading about Menachem Begin, the prime minister of Israel. She knew of him and had studied his impressive career before, but with so many interviews, stories and research swirling in her brain, she always enjoyed Richard's profile updates.

Begin was the sixth prime minister, but his political lineage was long and varied. He founded Likud in 1973, an alliance with several right-wing and liberal parties. Richard had underlined the following: "Likud's victory in the 1977 elections was a major turning point in the country's political history, marking the first time the left had lost power."

Before this achievement, Diane read with interest that Begin was the leader of the Zionist militant group Irgun, the revisionist breakaway from the larger Jewish paramilitary organization, Haganah. What Begin hated most was the British. In February of 1944, he proclaimed a revolt against the British mandatory government, opposed by the Jewish Agency. Begin targeted the British in Palestine.

As the plane cruised through the air, Diane watched a stewardess flirt with a man rows ahead in first class. The leggy blonde giggled and, in a curtsy-like dip, lit his cigarette while taking away his glass. She couldn't see the man: only his pressed slacks, dark socks and well-shined, wing-tipped shoes. It could have been any man, she thought. He could have been her father.

She continued reading, next about the Sadat. She recalled more about him. In school, Jack had been fond of him for his participation in the clandestine revolutionary Free Officers Movement, which overthrew the Muhammad Ali Dynasty in the Egyptian Revolution of 1952. In 1970, Sadat became the third president of Egypt. In the previous eight years, he became a trusted ally among many world leaders, but the road was not without barriers.

What surprised Diane most about this historic meeting she would soon cover was the Yom Kippur War, or, as Professor Stanley referred to it, the 1973 Arab-Israeli War, which was fresh in the minds of many. It was fought from October 6-25, 1973, between Israel and a coalition of Arab states led by Egypt and Syria.

It was a joint surprise attack on Yom Kippur, the holiest day in Judaism, which coincided with the Muslim holy month of Ramadan. Egyptian and Syrian forces crossed ceasefire lines to enter the Israeli-held Sinai Peninsula and Golan Heights respectively, which had been captured and occupied since the 1967 Six-Day War.

What Diane remembered most and recalled fearing was that both the United States and the Soviet Union supported their respective allies during the short-lived war that almost led to a nuclear showdown between the two superpowers: World War III.

As Bart slept, the stewardess batted her eyes, and the seatbelt light flickered. Time had marched on and would continue to do so. She wondered why she didn't feel a connection to Yom Kippur or care that much about that aspect of her own lineage. Equally, Ramadan meant nothing to her. She thought about a quote that had long troubled her, one by Henry Ward Beecher: "I never knew how to worship until I knew how to love."

Diane knew she loved her parents, perhaps a few friends, and maybe even Jack, but not in a way that equaled the ability to worship peacefully or to bask in a light that would make her feel so confident and resolute in her feelings. She was jealous of this in others, even those who could simply fall in love.

She looked at the black-and-white head shots on Begin and Sadat, those Richard had provided. The men were, in many ways, the same. They were of similar age and balding, and both possessed strength of character in their eyes that only served to highlight their respective strong, defined nose and sculpted face. They stood at nearly the same height, and one was slightly darker than the other, including in hair. Their faces were worn and beaten but worthy of adoration not unlike the small, waved pounded rocks that survive the cold winters on Maine's coastline.

Diane reached into her bag and pulled out a letter she had received from a Texas Iranian-born student who only identified himself as Arman. It was written on yellow legal pad paper in crude cursive. He explained that Iranian students from all over the country were organizing into groups to protest or support the Shah's next visit to the White House, and he wrote, "November 15, 1977 will be a day Americans see the Shah for who he is. For the most part, you will hopefully witness pro-Shah supporters. These are considered the left-minded Iranians, but the Shah will also see the hatred coming from the Islamic extremists. These people are tied to the Ayatollah Khomeini and receive support from his advisors, including Dr. Ebrahim Yazdi and Mr. Sadegh Ghotbzadeh. I know people receiving air fare and bus tickets to attend the event with hotels and meals being paid for—all in the name of propaganda. They intend to insult the Shah on a world stage. Ms. Babel, you must cover this story and make sure the Shah is protected, or extremist Iranian interests will continue to seek his ousting. He is good man who kept our country together after World War II, built a power stance against Iraq and Russia and forwarded women's right, something for which I think you could be thankful as a woman. I am just a university student, but you are a person with a platform. Please help our cause."

Diane placed the letter back in her bag, making a mental note to discuss the issue with Richard upon her return. She remembered that Arman meant "hope" and wondered if Jack knew the Shah would be welcomed by a protest.

She returned her focus to the cabin of the aircraft as it prepared for landing. Mike, the soundman, wasn't on that trip, and Bart made arrangements for a stringer to fill in. They had but a few hours after landing to make it to a hangar at Ben Gurion Airport, where Sadat would be welcomed in grand fashion on a whirlwind thirty-six-hour visit. Throngs of dignitaries, reporters and select onlookers filled the space. Night had fallen. Moments later, an Egyptian 737 jet slowly taxied down the runway.

Diane watched as Bart took B roll of the expecting faces. In the distance, Begin was reading papers and notes. As the plane drew closer, he handed the papers to an assistant, straightened his tie and placed a half-smile on his stern face. His suit was navy blue, and he wore a black tie. To his left stood Israeli President Ephraim Katzir, a rotund man with a shock of gray hair. His smile was less welcoming. To their right, past the red carpet that led to the stairs that would soon meet the plane, were soldiers prepared to fire an honorary twenty-one-gun salute.

As the plane met the ascending steps, the crowd began to cheer. Diane looked around the perimeter, fearing an assassin might be in their midst. The crowds cheered more. Eventually, the plane doors opened. Moments later, Anwar Sadat appeared, waving his arm and offering a big smile. Diane was reminded of when The Beatles had first landed in New York. He slowly made his way down the stairs. The assembled crowd tightly surrounded the staircase. As the two leaders drew closer, it was like watching a solar eclipse. Onlookers with square Kodak cameras snapped pictures, and the lightning-like illuminations of flash bulbs filled the air. Diane tried to get close to hear the exchange and only hoped any words between the two men would be translated.

When Sadat placed his feet on Israeli ground, the crowd cheered louder. Amidst the noise, and with deliberate motion, Begin walked closer to Sadat, who was dressed in a beige suit and blue-and-white polka-dotted tie. Diane found him oddly handsome. His confidence was equaled by that of Begin. The two men shook hands for what seemed like three minutes. Their up and down motion and solid grip signified years of turmoil and bloodshed. It was as if they could rid the worst of the past away by pressing their foreign flesh together. There was a unity of spirit reflected in their still skeptical eyes.

Diane stepped away from the crowd and prepared to tape her segment. Bart steadied the camera and instructed Nagib, the fill-in soundman, to get as close to her mouth as possible without being in the frame. He smiled and nodded.

"This is Diane Babel for ITN News, reporting from Ben Gurion Airport on what is certainly a historic day." Diane postured to her left to allow a better shot for Bart.

In the distance, his camera caught Begin and Sadat walking together as the twenty-one-gun salute rang out.

"Egyptian President Anwar Sadat is the first Muslim leader to visit Israel. This is a giant leap forward in Arab Israeli relations. It is reported that the two are possibly considering a peace treaty between their nations . . ."

Diane and Bart were given an agenda but not press credentials to attend any other event. Bart tried to fight it, but it was of no use. The Israeli government wanted the greeting captured for the American media, but it seemed clear that they were just as unsure of how the rest of the visit might turn out.

From the airport, Sadat was to be driven to Jerusalem for an hour-long meeting with Begin. The following day, Sadat would address the Israeli Parliament, the Knesset. His speech would be broadcast live to hundreds of millions of people all over the world.

"I wish we could have gotten more," Diane said to Bart while they sat at the hotel bar, waiting to make their return flight the following morning.

"We will have spent more time in the air than on the ground this trip," he said. He motioned to the bartender for bourbon, then leaned closer to Diane. "You looked good out there today."

"*Bart*," Diane said.

"What? I can't compliment you or your work without it being something more?" He lit a cigarette.

"I suppose you're right. Thanks. You know, we'll be in the air when he gives his speech tomorrow."

"Yeah, I know. We will have copies of it when we land in DC, though, and we can edit it into our footage."

"Yeah, but we have to cover the Shah's visit to the White House first."

"Shit. Is he back again? At least he's on our turf," Bart said.

*   *   *

When Diane returned to her apartment, she nearly slid on a telegram that was pushed under the door. It read: "Get some sleep and get the crew to Lafayette Park to cover the Iranian protest by ten thirty. There are already people there. This could be interesting. Richard."

Without much rest, Diane, Bart and Mike arrived at Lafayette Park the following morning and were stunned at the commotion. Hundreds of student protestors were arguing and battling. They wore hooded black garments or covered their faces with paper bags and carried signs, some in support of the Shah, but most in opposition. Diane noticed more than twenty police officers, some on horses, trying to control the crowd.

A young man, nearly twenty, approached Diane. He carried a sign that read, "Welcome to Washington." A picture of the Shah and his wife, Farah, were underneath. He had dark, disparate light scruff on his smooth, tan face, that appeared to Diane as yet-to-be-shaven, coarse hair.

"It is my great honor to meet you, Ms. Babel. I am Arman," he said, extending his hand. "I thought my letter would be dismissed."

Diane looked at his face, full of idealism and vigor, and realized she was older, in a new age subset only gleaned through such experiences. "Of course, Arman. I appreciate you writing to me and educating me on this situation. It is my pleasure to meet you. Now, please tell me what is happening. What have you seen?"

"These are the anti-Shah demonstrators," he said, pointing to Layette Park. "*We* are across the street."

Diane looked over to the crowd that grew in numbers and chants as the minutes elapsed. Some men and women had covered their faces in makeshift cardboard masks and held signs that read: "Down with the Shah!"

"Stand back!" police yelled. "Stand back!"

Bart was rolling film, and Mike operated a boom microphone. With each passing moment, the tension increased between the factions.

"There have been some injuries," Arman said loudly over the chants. "The police have been . . . combative."

The crowd of anti-Shah demonstrators began shouting, "*Marg bar Shah!*"

"What are they saying?" Diane questioned as she watched many young children stand for the Shah with their parents and grandparents.

"Like the signs, it means, 'Down with Shah.'" Arman said sternly. Arman pulled out an Iranian flag from his vest and waved it toward Bart. "We, too, were asked to come here to support the Shah. My trip was paid for, and the same goes for those people," Arman said, pointing to the anti-Shah protesters some of whom carried sticks, waving them in anger.

"You see only a few hundred people here, and you can see the majority are against the Shah. They are being paid for that opinion. Can you imagine what it is like in Iran? They want the Shah ousted . . . or worse," Arman said coldly to Diane as she watched a policeman club a protestor who swung a stick at an opposing protestor.

"I have been to your country and interviewed the Shah, and I believe he is a good man," Diane whispered in Arman's ear, "but I am here to cover this story and must move on for now."

Arman quietly nodded, held up his pro-Shah sign high, and crossed the street, where his supporters stood. He turned around and mouthed, "Thank you."

Across the street, in the White House, Jack and Jody watched as the Shah, his wife Farah, and Jimmy Carter looked out the window at the unfolding events.

"I'm not sure our scheduled public greeting is wise, given this unfortunate display," Carter said peacefully to the Shah. His smile seemed hollow to Jack.

Jack watched as Shah looked out on the growing crowds, some of whom were beaten down by police as they attempted to climb the gates. "I will not be seen as cowering to these demonstrators, Mr. President. With all due respect, I wish for the ceremony to continue as planned."

Carter called Jody over and whispered in his ear, "Get this under control by any and all means . . . NOW!"

Jack watched as Jody quickly exited the room. Aside from Secret Service, Jack was left with Carter, the Shah, his wife and the Shah's press secretary, who urged the Shah to stay inside. The Shah brushed off this request as if it was a waiter, asking him if he wanted more water. Jack looked outside as the planners set the stage for the official welcoming ceremony. The pageantry was in direct opposition to the violent, teeming protest occurring less than a football field away.

Thirty minutes later, the protestors were contained, and Carter opened the doors, inviting the Shah and his wife to the garden. Proudly smiling for the approved media, which didn't include Diane, the Shah waved to the small invited crowd, all of whom looked nervous. He embraced in a long handshake with Carter, as if time was slipping away.

As their extended handshake hung in the air, protestors began rushing the White House gates. Jack watched as protestors were beaten with nightsticks. Yells, screams and anti-Shah chants invaded the otherwise pristine White House garden. Tear gas was thrown, filling the air with a stinging sensation that brought tears to the Shah's eyes. Jack watched as Carter wiped the tears from the Shah's cheeks with a brilliant white handkerchief. He also noticed the countless cameras documenting the historic and telling moment. The Shah, lost in forced tears and smoke, held his head low before being escorted back into the White House.

*   *   *

The following week, November 21, 1977, Jack burst into Jody's office.

"Have we passed a knocking-before-entering-my-office relationship?" Jody said sternly.

Jack was startled to see he wasn't alone.

"This is General Robert Huyser, Jack."

"Of course. My apologies," Jack said, extending his hand. "It is an honor, sir."

"Mr. Quaid," General Huyser said plainly. His face was worn, tough like a baseball glove. His eyes were deep and dark. "Well then, we will continue this conversation on my return. Good day, gentlemen."

With that, the general left the room. Jody closed the door behind him.

"You are aware he is NATO's deputy commander-in-chief, aren't you?" Jody said to Jack.

"I am. Where is he going?"

"To Iran."

"Iran? Why?"

"Jimmy trusts him to deal with the Shah, especially in light of what happened last week. That Shah is a stubborn man. He should have just stayed inside. And this is not Huyser's first trip. This is all to do with that OPEC speech the Shah gave years ago—oil stuff. This is not just public policy. Do I make myself clear."

"Yes, of course."

"So is it true?" Jack said.

"Is what true?"

"The peace treaty. Is it really going to happen? I mean, with all due respect, the Shah crying on international TV was hard to watch, and I imagine it weakens him, even if it was just from tear gas."

Jody lit a cigarette. "Oh, that's why you burst in? The Shah's tears? Time moves on. Sadat was not happy with the Geneva Convention. He wants more to be done."

"Could Israel and Egypt ever really have peace after all they've been through? Not to mention how much Egypt's reputation would suffer in the Arab world," Jack reasoned. His time in the White House hadn't yet overshadowed his student tendencies.

"It sounds pretty daunting, doesn't it? Our boss thinks it's possible."

"But is it real?"

"Not just real, but guess who's going to mediate it?"

"They're replaying Sadat's speech now, you know," Jack said, pointing to the radio.

"I already have the transcripts," Jody said, pointing to his desk.

"Let's just listen. Hear his voice," Jack said.

"Okay, but I have a briefing to get to. A few minutes only," Jody said as he buttoned his shirt closer to his neck and picked up his tie that was draped over his chair.

Jack flipped the radio on and caught the speech in motion. A translator conveyed Sadat's words: "I come to you today on solid ground to shape a new life and to establish peace. We all love this land, the land of God, we all, Moslems, Christians and Jews, all worship God . . . I do not blame all those who received my decision when I announced it to the entire world before the Egyptian People's Assembly. I do not blame all those who received my decision with surprise and even with amazement, some gripped even by violent surprise. Still others interpreted it as political, to camouflage my intentions of launching a new war.

"I would go so far as to tell you that one of my aides at the presidential office contacted me at a late hour, following my return home from the People's Assembly and sounded worried as he asked me, 'Mr. President, what would be our reaction if Israel actually extended an invitation to you?'

"I replied calmly, 'I would accept it immediately. I have declared that I would go to the end of the Earth. I would go to Israel, for I want to put before the people of Israel all the facts . . .' No one could have ever conceived that the president of the biggest Arab state, which bears the heaviest burden and the main responsibility pertaining to the cause of war and peace in the Middle East, should declare his readiness to go to the land of the adversary while we were still in a state of war.

"We all still bear the consequences of four fierce wars waged within thirty years. All this at the time when the families of the 1973 October war are still mourning under the cruel pain of bereavement of father, son, husband and brother. As I have already declared, I have not consulted as far as this decision is concerned with any of my colleagues or brothers, the Arab heads of state or the confrontation states.

"Most of those who contacted me following the declaration of this decision expressed their objection because of the feeling of utter suspicion and absolute lack of confidence between the Arab states and the Palestinian people on the one hand and Israel on the other that still surges in us all.

"Many months in which peace could have been brought about have been wasted over differences and fruitless discussions on the procedure of convening the Geneva conference. All have shared suspicion and absolute lack of confidence . . ."

Chapter 15

"Can you believe we have this much downtime?" Bart said to Diane. They were seated in a recently rented no-frills editing room off of K Street that had a smell of mold and/or rotten food. "ITN are slave drivers with shit pay for sure, but time off? Not bad," Bart said. He looked at Diane with a mix of admiration and attraction, which he masked in humor. "You know, you aren't half-bad, kid. I've been impressed by your work."

"You're not so bad yourself," Diane said and winked. "So, no word on the Shah tapes yet, huh?"

"Nope. Just a few more days I think."

"I paid a visit to my old fried Jack Quaid," Diane said.

"At the White House?" Bart questioned.

"Yes."

"And?"

"And still we wait."

Bart walked over to a college-sized refrigerator, opened two beers and slid one across the desk. "So they're asking for a reel, a sort of highlight of international events, and I thought the Israeli airport trip a few weeks back with Menachem Begin would be a good addition. Let's check it out," Bart said.

"Okay. I just hate watching myself," Diane said and sipped her beer, wincing at the taste.

"If you did like watching yourself, that would be worse," Bart said with a smile. He rolled the tape on the monitor.

Diane reported from the tarmac, "A large jetliner carrying Egyptian President Anwar Sadat arrived only moments earlier. A band played celebratory music. Awaiting Sadat on a red carpet was Israel's Prime Minister Menachem Begin and a host of other dignitaries," Diane said. Her voice was over B roll that Bart shot.

Sadat waved widely and smiled broadly as he walked off the plane.

"Sadat was greeted like a rock star, with cheers from the hundreds of onlookers who had gathered. In what might be the most important meeting of Middle Eastern leaders in recent history, Sadat embraced Begin and kissed each side of his face, as per custom. This is a giant leap forward in Arab-Israeli relations. It is purported that the two leaders are possibly considering a peace treaty between their nations. For now, the people, the world, patiently wait. This is Diane Babel, reporting for ITN."

"See? That's good stuff, and the camera work isn't half-bad," Bart said.

"Well, thanks . . . and I mean thanks for everything, Bart. You've been really great, all around, just great," Diane said and tipped her beer toward him.

"Aw, stop. Just doing my job," Bart said. His cheeks flushed, adding new dimensions to the red hue of his hair. They sat in an awkward silence before the phone rang, and Bart left the table to answer it.

*　　*　　*

A few weeks had passed. It was an early winter evening. The sidewalks were covered in thin ice, and mounds of crystallized slush were in random piles. Diane approached the entrance to the Glenwood Cemetery.

Gravesites gave her the chills but also piqued her curiosity. She knew George Atzerodt, co-conspirator of John Wilkes Booth and assassin of Abraham Lincoln, was believed to be secretly buried in an unmarked grave. Diane recalled a late summer afternoon when the sun was as hot as Haiti. She and Jack carelessly frolicked between stones, monuments and statues, looking for the unmarked grave with no success. They did find Emmanual Leutze's grave, and he painted "Washington Crossing the Delaware." Diane recalled Jack saying, "Could you have imagined what it must have felt like to be on that boat?"

As instructed, Diane entered on the west side of the cemetery. She pushed a heavy iron gate ajar and followed the path to the left for fifty yards. In the distance she saw a figure in black. Smoke swirled around the man like a thick cloud.

"This is different. Sort of morbid, no?" Diane said.

Richard didn't turn around. His tone was terse. "Don't worry. You'll get the tapes back eventually. We are postponing the airdate of the interview by one week. We've reached out to the Shah's people as well. This protest and crying spectacle didn't help matters."

"It doesn't seem legal to keep the tapes from us and from the public, especially when the people need to hear from the Shah," Diane said, flustered. She had a red scarf wrapped around her neck. A matching knitted wool hat was pulled down to her ears, a gift from her mother, who always tried to protect her only daughter, even as an adult, against weather.

"Anything's legal when you make the laws," Richard said and turned around. His eyes were bloodshot, and it appeared he had aged. One hand held a cigar; the other he grasped the collar of his jacket tight against his throat. He bent his head slightly downward, trying to escape the chilly winds that swept by with an agenda.

"Is the Shah going to be okay? Are we really not going to help him?" Diane said.

"What do you think?" Richard said and exhaled a large nebulous cloud of smoke and chilled air.

"I need to see the other side. I need to know more," Diane countered.

"Well, you've got your chance. You need to go back to the Middle East and expose the roots of the Islamic uprising that's taking place there. They were right back in Yemen. They were right," Richard said and moved away from the gravesite he was obscuring.

Diane looked at the grave. The stone was etched with an Irish blessing: "May the wind be always at your back. May the sun shine warm upon your face. The rains fall soft upon your fields. And until we meet again, May God hold you in the palm of his hand." Underneath that were two names: Molly Harden (1936-72); Deborah Harden (1956-72).

"My God, Richard. I'm so sorry. I didn't know," Diane said. She covered her mouth and gasped.

"Yeah, well Deb would be about your age now. And Molly . . . well, both of them, they were just so . . . they were it for me, you know," Richard said. He seemed to have more of a sparkle in his eye when he reflected. A half-moon helped to illuminate his face. "That damn Operation AJAX. Yeah, we ruffled many feathers, but so many years had passed. I was stationed in London. It was Christmas Eve. I drank too much the night before, and the girls wanted to go to an early Mass. Ever since we were married, Molly had always hated driving over there—you know, the opposite side of the road. I was just too tired that morning, so off they went. I thought it was an earthquake. The ground shook. The explosion was so loud it blew out the windows in the cottage. I didn't have to look. I just knew. Thank God I didn't hear any screams."

Diane's hand was still over her mouth. Her gloves muffled her response. "My God."

"You figure over there you got to watch the Irish bombing the English, but it wasn't them. It was traced back to an extremist group, Islamic fuckers who hate the Shah and what he represents. They hated me too. Still do," Richard said. He turned and looked at the grave.

"How do you move on from something like that? I mean, when we were in Yemen only a few years later, and you were acting so . . . aloof," Diane said.

Richard pulled out the Christmas picture of his family, struck his Zippo lighter, and showed it to Diane. "Sometimes in order to get complex answers, you have to ask simple questions. You sort of remind me of Deb. That's one of the reasons I think Professor Stanley thought I would like you. This is not about your career or us being perceived right or wrong. This about the truth, Diane."

"It's always been about the truth," Diane said.

"Has it?' Richard countered.

"What is that supposed to mean?" Diane snapped.

"Just remember that I am responsible for you being here, over there, anywhere and everywhere," Richard said.

"I haven't forgotten that," Diane said softly.

"In the cloud of travel and glory the best of us can lose our way, trust me on that," Richard said.

"I'm on your side, Richard," Diane assured him. She felt like hugging him, if only to console his loss, but he was a rock, like a cemetery stone, and it seemed at no point would moss ever have a chance to grow.

Before she could say goodbye, Richard turned around and in a strong but hushed tone began praying: "Hail Mary, full of grace, the Lord is with thee . . ."

Later that evening, Diane sat next to the warm radiator, sipping tea and looking out the window. She thought about Richard and his loss, and she cried softly. Her bell rang, and she walked over to the door and opened it to find a yellow envelope on her welcome mat. She barely saw the courier as he quickly turned the corner down the hall. Diane opened the package, skimmed the details and learned she was heading to Tehran, following Carter's New Year's visit to Iran. She would leave on December 30.

She dropped the papers on her kitchen table and walked over to her records. She sifted through until she came across one of her favorite albums, *The Concert for Bangladesh*. It was named for two benefit concerts organized by former Beatle George Harrison and famed satirist Ravi Shankar. Diane attended the concert, which took place in 1971, at Madison Square Garden. Harrison conceived the idea to raise funds for relief efforts for refugees from East Pakistan following the 1970 Bhola cyclone and atrocities during the Bangladesh Liberation War. Bob Dylan, Eric Clapton and Ringo Starr were among the performers.

She recalled listening to that album with Jack. She dropped the needle on his favorite track, "Something." The music filled the room, and for a moment, Diane wasn't a reporter or a seeker of truth, but a lonely girl who knew the power of lost love and connection. She closed her eyes and sang softly with George Harrison:

> Something in the way she moves
> attracts me like no other lover.
> Something in the way she woos me . . .

Almost in a trance, Diane fished out her address book from her bag. She flipped to the letter Q and found Jack's number. As the music slowly faded, she dialed his number. The rotary phone dial clicked and retracted with each spin. The phone rang for several minutes without an answer; she finally hung up.

She then walked over to her desk and picked up a telegram sent by her parents, which she had received the previous day. "Continue to take the world by storm—stop—We are off to Anchorage for two weeks—stop—We figured you would have plans for the holidays—stop—We hope to see you in New York in January—stop—Love you always, Mom and Dad—stop."

For years Diane had received these telegrams, and until recently, she collected them. Her parents never seemed content in one place for too long, and her father's job afforded them world travel. Her mom's teaching career suffered, but she didn't complain all that much. They weren't a family that celebrated holidays. "We celebrate whenever we are together as a family," her father would often say.

The following morning, Diane walked down to the street dressed in her robe to fetch the paper. It was two days before Christmas, and it was the first time in months she'd had a few free days. She watched as kids ran in the streets playing, throwing snowballs and laughing. Christmas decorations were strung about. There was a fleeting feeling of peace.

She was snapped back to her reality when a black town car quickly approached and pulled toward her. The door opened, and Richard stepped out.

"Richard?" Diane said, confused. He never came to her apartment or her neighborhood.

He looked around and whispered. "I have some news, I'm afraid."

"What is it? What? Is Bart okay? The Shah?" Diane said. She dropped the paper and rubbed her arms for warmth.

Richard motioned to the car.

"Would you rather come in?" Diane said, pointing to her apartment.

"Please, in the car," Richard said solemnly.

Richard closed the door, and the warmth of the car instantly made Diane feel better.

"A private plane your parents chartered to Anchorage has not been heard from. It's been three days. I have made calls on your behalf, looking for answers. There was a mayday from the pilot, but the plane has all but vanished. I'm so sorry, Diane." Richard leaned over and put his hand on her shoulder.

"What? I just got a telegram from them. How does a plane disappear? What do you mean lost?" Diane looked around like a child lost in a supermarket.

"Take time off and do what you need to do. We'll find someone else to cover for you," Richard said. His bedside manner was clearly lacking. "They are considered lost right now. I have many calls out, including the National Guard and local police. Your father is an important man, and that is another reason we want to keep this quiet until we have the facts and to make sure there isn't foul play at hand."

Diane buried her face in her hands and began crying. Richard slid across the seat awkwardly and did his best to console her in a fatherly manner.

"Three days, Richard? Alaska? We both know they're dead," Diane said. Her eyes were red, her cheeks wet from tears.

"Well, you never know."

Diane took a deep breath, turned her head toward the window, wiped tears from her face and turned back to Richard. "I'm still going to Tehran."

"Diane, I said time off."

"Richard," Diane said. Her sobbing was light and rhythmic. "This is all I have, my work. Just promise me you will keep looking and keep me posted. Find them, Richard. Just find them." Diane reached for the door but was stopped by Richard's hand.

"You have my word, Diane."

Chapter 16

After stops at several different Middle East countries, Diane, Bart and crew landed in Tehran, Iran as the last stop of Jimmy Carter's Middle East trip. In the early morning hours of December 31, 1977, Diane was sullen as no news came about her parents. She was finding it harder and harder to concentrate on work but she, along with countless other press, were following President Carter as he disembarked from *Air Force One* and was greeted with a pomp ceremony by the Shah of Iran.

Jimmy and Rosalyn Carter were embraced by the Shah of Iran and his wife, Queen Farah. The Shah wore a white military uniform adorned with countless medals, golden tassels, epaulets and blue pressed pants with gold stripes on the outer seam. Standing slightly taller, Farah wore a pinkish red gown with a silver sash. Her dark hair was off her face and adorned with a diamond-laced tiara. Their smiles and pleasantries appeared faked to Diane. The live music, the instruments, the smiling and clapping dignitaries all seemed contrived as if scripted for stage, and she was a paid-off theater reviewer.

She couldn't help but think about President Kennedy as the convertible Cadillac motorcade procession took Carter and clan past the Shayad Monument. The impressive structure, which reached toward the sky, was a portal into both the past and the future, Diane thought.

Bart filmed as the motorcade slowly passed through the Eisenhower Boulevard. Diane took notes and paid attention to a crowd of young and old men and women on each side of the boulevard happily chanting, "Long live Shah! Long Live America!" A fourteen-year-old Iranian boy, wearing an Evel Knievil t-shirt that had the number one wrapped with red, white and blue stars and stripes, waved an American flag and ran after the motorcade.

Diane's attention was averted when she locked eyes with a young girl. She had sun-baked skin, shoulder-length black hair and deep brown eyes. Her clothes were tattered and her hands were dirty. She was selling pieces of gum for pennies, seemingly to survive. Diane walked over and extended a dollar to the bubblegum girl. She passed Diane a stick of gum and smiled.

"Diane!" Bart yelled. She could barely hear as hundreds of people milled in and around the motorcade. She didn't turn around. She was transfixed by the bubblegum girl, who was on the outskirts of the parade and seemingly not impressed. Diane followed her.

"Hello," Diane said, bending down.

A boy only a few years older took the girl's hand and rushed away from the parade heading to the back streets of Tehran. Diane looked but could no longer see Bart. The motorcade had passed, and the tail end of the parade was trying to catch up.

"Where are we going?" Diane said to the boy and bubblegum girl.

"Come now and see the real Iran," the boy said. His hands were also dirty. He had hazel eyes like Diane. He was missing a front tooth but didn't smile.

"Is this is your sister? She is so young to be on the streets," Diane said.

"We have no father or mother. I am the man now. She has to work. This is life," he said.

Diane knelt down. The air was dry, but a tear came to her eyes. As they walked farther, Diane looked around at the slums. Windows were broken and doors ajar, and dogs roamed freely. There were also countless children in the streets, hungry and trying to survive.

"How do you live?" Diane said. A crowd of kids was curious and approached.

"Each day, we live. That is all we can do—try to live," the boy said. He seemed like a Bill Sikes prodigy. "Give us some money," the boy said gruffly.

Diane reached into her pocket and handed him a few bills. She looked at the little girl and knelt down. She hugged the girl, who showed little emotion but smiled. Diane stood up and walked in the opposite direction, leaving the children behind. She fought back tears and snapped pictures with a small camera she had in her bag. She looked for a taxi, eventually flagged one down, and in moments was whisked away. The taxi kicked up dust, obscuring Diane's view of the bubblegum girl.

"What the hell happened to you?" Bart snapped as Diane walked through the busy hotel lobby. She was dusty, dirty and preoccupied. His concern was palpable. She seemed adrift amidst the throngs of journalists and media also in Tehran covering the event. The hotel, unlike the slums she just walked with the bubblegum girl, was lavish with plush couches, oil paintings, brilliant, shining chandeliers and attentive staff.

Diane looked at Bart and shrugged. "The story took me somewhere else."

"We have an assignment, Carter and the Shah. You could have been kidnapped or worse, going off on your own," Bart said. He walked closer and put his arm around her. "We have been through a lot, and I need you to be safe. We got some good B roll, but tonight, just do your job, which is to observe."

"I was safe. There is more of a story going on here. We should at least look at these poor kids in these slums," Diane said to Bart. Her eyes were intent and now focused. "We can juxtapose the pageantry of this visit, the celebration tonight."

Across the room, Diane noticed Mike Wallace speaking with David Frost. They smiled and joked and looked at each other with mild contempt. They both wore dark suits. Wallace wore a blue, button-down shirt with no tie. While his eyes were piercing, his smile was tight, as if someone pulled his ears taught. Frost wore a white shirt and striped blue and white tie. Even from a distance, he seemed affable. Diane could barely make out the dryness of his English accent.

"Frost asked about you," Bart whispered in Diane's ear.

"What did he say?"

"Thought your interview with the Shah was impressive and wondered if you had another scheduled," Bart said with a sense of pride. "At least that interview finally aired."

"I wish I did have another, especially after what I saw today. Those poor kids," Diane said. She tried to fix her hair and sheepishly waved across the room. Frost tipped his drink and smiled. Wallace looked over without expression and lit a cigarette.

"I checked you in, and your bags should be up in your room now. Remember, tonight is social—no business. No cameras, just schmooze. Talk to people," Bart said.

"I know. I get it," Diane said.

"I'll ring you when we are to leave," Bart said. He leaned close to her ear. "Tonight's important, so please—"

"I'm onboard," Diane said.

"Here is your key. See you soon," Bart said.

Diane weaved her way through the lobby. As she approached the elevator, she heard notes ring from a grand piano. The pianist played "So What" from the Miles Davis album, *Kind of Blue*. She thought about the frigid backcountry of Alaska and felt tears percolate from within.

Upon entering her room, she found her bags neatly stacked in front of the king-sized bed that had too many pillows and a gold, satin comforter. The windows looked north to the Alborz Mountains. In the great expanse between, lights began to twinkle across the city as the night fell. The year was coming to an end.

Diane walked over to the bed. She unbuttoned her gray blouse, removed her ascot, kicked off her shoes and slipped off her skirt. Standing in her underwear, she caught a glimpse of herself in the mirror. Her face was dirty, but her body was still tight. She thought about the bubblegum girl and patted her tummy. She wondered about the miracle of birth and wondered if she could ever posses such power and strength to give life to another, and if she did, she didn't know if she could provide the right kind of care.

The phone rang, which startled Diane. She walked over to the nightstand and noticed a vase of red roses.

Diane picked up the phone. "Yes?"

"Diane Babel?" the operator questioned, her English troubled but passable.

"Yes."

"A telegram—for you."

"Please send it up."

Diane hung up the phone and walked to the bathroom. She washed her face, scrubbing away the day's memories. She found a white robe and slippers and felt enveloped by the soft cotton. The knock on the door came quicker than expected.

She opened the door to find a young porter, nearly twenty years old. He wore a red jacket with black buttons that ran down to his navel. His mustache was thick and dark for a young man. He offered the telegram with a smile. Diane feigned to look for money in her robe, but the young man waved his hand and quickly walked away.

Diane closed the door and read the message as she crossed the room. "No news yet—stop—So sorry—stop—Stay strong—stop—Call if you need anything—stop—Richard—stop."

Diane thought about her parents. Her eyes were wet and bloodshot but not yet had the dam broken. She knew what reality held in store but felt compelled to think they were simply traveling and out of contact. Holding the telegram, she sank into the bed and picked up the phone again.

"An outside line please. An international call," Diane said. She reached for her handbag and retrieved her address book. She flipped until she reached Jack's number. Diane read and reread the number to the operator several times before she heard the phone ring. Diane counted sixteen rings before hanging up. She balled herself into a fetal position and started to cry; within minutes she had to flip the pillow because it was wet.

An hour later, Diane and Bart entered the Shah's Niavaran Palace. The atmosphere was decadent and delightful. It was a black-tie affair; even Bart was dressed appropriately with a wide black bowtie that offset his newly grown beard. Diane wore high heels and a sleek black dress that hugged her body, an uncharacteristic look. The celebration attracted dignitaries, media and royalty. The room shimmered with light. Crystals hung from massive chandeliers. The walls were adorned with embedded crystals. Flashbulbs twinkled, and smiles were abundant. A huge banner in blue and gold read: "Happy New Year!"

"Remember, observe and mingle. Try and find out something new," Bart said handing Diane a glass of champagne.

She drank it in one gulp.

"Here's to a wonderful year working together," Bart added, clinking her glass. "And slow down, champ."

Diane smiled. "Yes, here is to 1978." In the distance, she could see President Carter and the Shah standing next to each other. They wore nearly identical tuxedos and bowties. Their height was also nearly the same. They shook hands with people who passed by as if they were a couple recently married, thanking those who attended the nuptials. But from Diane's vantage point, this wasn't a happy union, rather an arranged marriage.

"You're a little far from home."

Diane turned to see Jack's piercing blue eyes trained on her. He wore a smirk and was dressed in a tuxedo. He looked like a stunt double for Sean Connery. While half as handsome, he appeared more rugged and seasoned to Diane.

"Jack? You know, it's sort of weird but I tried to call. How are you?"

"A call? Diane, what?" He pulled the collar of his shirt out from his neck with his finger.

Jack studied her face and then looked her up and down from head to toe. "High heels on Diane Babel?"

Diane noticed Jody Powell a few people away speaking with Zbigniew Kazimierz Brzezinski, whose eyes scanned and pierced the room.

"I didn't have a choice, though it's nice to get dressed up once in a while," Diane said. She stopped a waiter who passed with a tray full of drinks. She grabbed two glasses of champagne.

"It's been a long time since the Fourth of July, back in '76," Diane said, handing him a glass. She let her fingers rest on his hand for an extra moment. She missed the touch of his skin.

"Last time we spoke, you were berating me and now you're offering me champagne?" Jack looked at her hand, and she slowly pulled it away. "How did you get to come to this party anyway?" Jack asked as he lit a cigarette.

Diane shrugged. "I'm friends with the guy who lives here. You might have seen the interview. It *finally* aired."

Jack didn't have time to respond before Brzezinski walked over and interjected, "Ms. Babel, it is my pleasure to meet you." He also lit a cigarette, but he wasn't drinking. "You know, we all do have something in common."

"Nice to meet you as well, Mr. Brzezinski," Diane said. "And what might that be?"

"Professor Stanley, of course," Brzezinski said.

"And how exactly do you know him?" Diane said. "Do we know anyone else in common?"

Jack looked uncomfortable.

"Oh, that's a story and a question for another time. This is a celebration. We are headed toward a new future. Now I must make more rounds," Brzezinski said and walked off into the crowd.

The room swirled with sounds, languages and dialects that reminded Diane of taking the New York subway in high school—so many differences but a common purpose. A twelve-piece band played an instrumental mixture of what seemed to Diane as disco and traditional Arabic standards. Across the room, she saw Bart speaking with David Frost.

Jack leaned closer. "Listen, here's the deal. We need to know what you know. It's a matter of security."

"You'll know if you keep watching the news, or maybe you learned by watching my tapes?"

Diane said and tipped her champagne glass back. "You could have protected the Shah from that tearful embarrassment, and there seems to be a reason why he wasn't protected and was rather humiliated."

Jack looked around and pulled her away from the crowd. Across the room he watched Jody and President Carter speaking. Jody signaled to Jack to pay attention. President Carter approached a podium. Jack nudged Diane to look on as the room slowly fell silent.

Carter smiled widely and politely signaled the crowd to be quiet. The Shah and his wife looked on. They were seated, regal and poised.

"Iran, under the great leadership of the Shah, is an island of stability in one of the most troubled areas of the world. This is a great tribute to you, your Majesty, to your leadership and to the respect, admiration and love your people give to you," Carter said, his delivery warm and measured.

The room erupted in applause. Jack put his drink down and clapped enthusiastically. He smiled across the room to Jody, who nodded his head. Diane showed no emotion but seemed loose on her feet as the party resumed.

"Not sure your boss has it right," Diane said. Her glass was empty.

"He's the President, not just my boss, but yours too. Listen, we need your information, Diane. Whatever doesn't make it on the air, we could use it for the greater good."

"So you can steal it? Your administration doesn't know what they're getting themselves into."

"*My* administration? You're still American remember?"

"Is that General Huyser? What is he doing here?" Diane questioned, pointing across the room.

"That's none of your concern," Jack said.

"Exactly." Diane turned to leave, but Jack grabbed her arm, and a few attendees took notice.

Jack whispered in her ear, "You need to let me in, Diane. You're losing yourself in all of this. Remember, your parents, a 'hard rain's going to fall'? The stories you told me."

"Don't you dare talk about my parents," Diane snapped, then brushed Jack off and walked away.

Jack threw up his hands and looked across the room at Jody. Jack watched as Carter and the Shah as well as Brzezinski, General Huyser and Iranian dignitaries were escorted into a private room. As the door to the private room closed, Jack wondered what was to be discussed. Jack looked to the other side of the room. Diane shouldered up to Bart, who was talking to David Frost. He then looked back to the closed door.

"Employment has risen 50 percent, and almost 90 percent of children are receiving free education. We have quality healthcare and trade, and above all, my people are happy. Women have more rights than ever before and have high positions in my administration," the Shah said from his place at a chair around a big wooden conference table.

A guard with a rifle and hip sword was positioned at each corner of the room. Champagne, water, fruits, cheeses and crackers were displayed on platters.

"It sounds impressive," Brzezinski said in a slightly sarcastic tone.

General Huyser remained silent.

Carter was intent but also silent.

"It is. Iran is a popular nation now, and I serve as the area police force. If I can continue to receive your support, I can keep peace in the Middle East," the Shah said.

Carter looked on without saying a word, and his body language was stiff. "Excuse me, gentlemen, but—and with all due respect to those present—I would like a word alone with the Shah."

Brzezinski and Huyser nodded and stood up; they were followed by three other Iranian men.

Carter motioned to the guards. "Everyone please. Actually, General Huyser, a moment."

The Shah nodded and signaled for the room to be cleared. General Huyser stood his ground at attention, and Brzezinski shot Carter a puzzled look.

When the room was cleared, Carter offered with a smile, "This is the first time we've all been in the same room together."

"You have a persuasive man in the general," the Shah said.

"General, where do we stand in regard to oil contracts? Are the British talking?" Carter questioned.

"Well, sir, Mr. President, I'm afraid we are running into trouble on that front. With all due respect, our position as negotiators is in a questionable state," General Huyser said, not making eye contact with the Shah.

"I understand you are allies, but why you continue to barter for the British concerns me," the Shah said. "Our talks should focus on our relationship. The British have a different approach and certainly a different history with this great nation."

"I trust you will consider our petition to your . . . well, your otherwise troubling request in regard to these contracts," Carter said to the Shah. He stood shoulder to shoulder with General Huyser.

"Yes, I will continue these talks, but we have matters to discuss privately, Mr. President," the Shah said, extending his hand to General Huyser. "I will look forward to future discussions."

As General Huyser walked toward the doors, the two leaders walked to the far end of the room. The party noise and music were barely audible.

Once the door was closed, the Shah said softly to Carter, "I want to thank you for your kind words earlier."

"It was my honor," Carter said. He tapped his pointer finger on his lip and looked down. "Let me first apologize again for what occurred during your last visit. I am familiar with the great improvements that has been made in your country, but I also know about some of the problems. You have heard my statements about human rights. A growing number of your citizens are claiming that these rights are not being honored in Iran."

"Mr. President, thank you again for your sympathy to what was a hardship for me, my family and my country. You must understand that the division you saw in front of your White House is a mirror of the trouble I face here in Iran. In regard to human rights, the only ones with that impression are those who do not support Iran or tried to assassinate me and my family. I will execute any person who betrays Iran. I'm trying to support and protect the rights of 90 percent of the people who get up every morning, go to work and try to support their families. You have the same situation in your country," the Shah said pensively.

"You mean the 10 percent who don't support you must be imprisoned?" Jimmy said sternly, with his hands clasped behind his back.

"You must trust that I am a just man. I'm a just leader and will forever be an ally of America. And whatever I do, I try to keep in mind your interests, as well as your allies in this region. In every society and country, there are those who are always unhappy with leaders," he said and walked closer to Carter, looking him straight in the eyes. "You should learn from your experiences in Vietnam and not repeat the mistakes in Iran when dealing with me, Mr. Sadat and Mr. Begin. We are confronting the roots of Islamic extremism in Yemen. The United States and other Western powers need to provide long-term economic development to reduce poverty and raise educational standards. This will help combat terrorism in the region in a more effective fashion than simply using military force. We are a nation in peace and would like to spread this peace through the Persian Gulf region. We feel there is a need for the United States to better understand the interactions of Persian society, from a sociological, religious, tribal and political standpoint," the Shah said.

Carter walked over to the table and poured a glass of water, then took a sip. "I'm afraid you're going to have to worry about this problem, Your Majesty."

The Shah was shaken by the direct comment and nervously replied, "I know my deal was with Nixon and Kissinger, but it was also with America. We paid for the A-WACS and F-14s. We had a deal! And since then, I have offered a bilateral deal for oil price-fixing because the cost for these spare parts, to keep this military equipment operational, has increased by 400 to 500 percent in the last few years. I will bring down oil costs for America if you can bring down these costs. This is only fair. Oil is all we have, yet I still separate it from politics. I consider the West our friend. All I ask is that you honor our deal."

"You understand you are placing me in a tough position. Nixon disgraced our country, and I haven't forgotten that you poured so much money into the Republican Party or about the oil embargo of '73. Yes, President Ford pardoned Nixon, but the country is still hurting in many ways. Any deal in regard to price-fixing has never crossed my desk. I see you using oil as a political tool now," Carter said. He placed the water on the table and pushed back his hair.

"The wounds from which you are healing are small compared to the problems America faces from the Middle East. You are forgetting that a business deal between friends, between America and Iran, does not have to be political," the Shah said.

"And you think having these planes, these weapons, will make the difference?"

"If I may speak bluntly, you are the man your people call a peanut farmer, right? My farm is the Middle East. This land I know, and you must trust in this." The Shah extended his hand for Carter to shake, and the President paused for a moment before shaking it.

"The experience of democracy is like the experience of life itself—always changing, infinite in its variety, sometimes turbulent, and all the more valuable for having been tested by adversity," Carter said. "Happy New Year, your Majesty."

SECTION THREE

"I am a firm believer in the people. If given the truth, they can be depended upon to meet any national crisis. The great point is to bring them the real facts."

~ Abraham Lincoln

Chapter 17

The new year brought no good news for Diane, at least not personally. The search for her parents was officially called off days after her return from Iran. Richard deployed some ex-military special operations officers to investigate, but it was as if the plane had just vanished. Diane was left with no family. She was adrift.

Weeks later, she knew her reporting had become erratic and even unprofessional at times; she'd flubbed a couple of on-air segments.

On one occasion, Diane and Bart were sent on a fluff piece to interview a representative from Volkswagen, when the company announced it would stop producing the famed Bug. Diane hated doing those kinds of pieces, but ITN's partnership with public television created certain politics and resulted in such marching orders. The Volkswagen story was broadcast live, and technology at ITN was still in the process of mastering. Bart, Mike and Diane were on location in Puebla, Mexico, where the plant was located.

After the interview, when Diane thought the camera was dead, she told the Volkswagen representative, a pencil-thin man with wire-rimmed glasses and a face pocked from acne, "You know, I lost my virginity in one of these in '69. That was some night!"

Before Bart could kill the broadcast, the sound bite went live to what *ABC News* would call a "horrified audience." Her on-air rivals capitalized on her gaff. Barbara Walters called her "unhinged"; Pat Robertson, of Regent University, identified her as "the problem with modern media"; while David Frost called her "spirited," adding that reporting comes with its own pressures and saying, "Ms. Babel could benefit from a rest or from a bit of on-air refinement."

Volkswagen demanded a public apology from ITN, which it received quickly thereafter. The incident sullied the young, upstart news station.

Overseas investors worried that the gaff could prove problematic to its integrity and overall mission. Internally, questions were raised as to whether Diane Babel was their girl after all.

With her parents gone and her friends few and far between, Richard was her only personal touchstone, almost like a long-lost uncle, but the lines were blurred. For the first time, on a cold February morning, she initiated a meeting with Richard at a little café near George Washington University. She had received a terse message from him after the Mexico incident and hadn't received an assignment since. The word "sabbatical" was offered by Bart as an explanation.

Diane sat nervously in the booth. Condensation outlined the café window that looked out onto a sleepy winter street. When Richard joined, the day grew colder. Diane found it hard to make eye contact with him. Seconds passed like minutes before Diane cleared her throat.

"I really do appreciate all you did in regard to my parents, Richard. Maybe it's best that their bodies were never found. I don't know. Sometimes I think they survived, you know—that they're somehow still out there," Diane said and signaled for the waitress to come over.

"Of course," Richard said. He wore a white turtleneck and had let his salt-and-pepper beard grow in. He clasped his hands together, and Diane noticed his college ring. The blue stone was nearly as big as one of her knuckles and reminded her of Jack's eyes.

"You know, my parents were my only family. We all had one thing in common. We were all only children, and my grandparents are all dead now. The United Nations had a ceremony, and Brooklyn College did something nice. It was well attended by colleagues, but like me, my parents never had too many friends. I was in New York for the ceremony. I flew up, as you know. To be honest, I haven't processed it. Their apartment is how they left it, as if they're just away on another one of their trips. That's how I'm thinking of it, I suppose. I need to put the apartment on the market soon though."

The waitress came over with menus. When she reached the table, she gasped and smiled. "Oh, you're Diane Babel, the reporter. Wow! I'm studying journalism and . . ." She pointed across the street to the university.

"We're in the middle of something. Just leave the menus," Diane said smugly.

Richard shot Diane a look and smiled at the waitress. "Thanks so much," he said.

The waitress slowly backpedaled. "I'll be back in a few minutes to take your order."

Diane looked over to the young waitress, who was behind the counter, speaking with another waitress. They busied themselves when Diane looked over. She turned her attention back to Richard. The Mexico incident was the elephant in the room.

"Talking about work makes me feel normal. I haven't had an assignment in weeks. I haven't really heard from you either, aside from that last letter. I'm just sort of feeling like everything is stalled."

"After Mexico, Diane, we seriously thought you might need a break," Richard said. His eyes were squarely fixed on Diane. "You have had a lot of pressure, a lot to deal with."

"A break?" Diane said. Not yet thirty, her eyes were awash with all the petulance of a thwarted teenager. "I apologized. ITN apologized. Yes, it was a major mistake, but c'mon, Richard. A fluff piece isn't—"

"This isn't up for discussion. You need to take a few months off to clear your head," Richard said, breaking a small but uncharacteristically warm smile.

The waitress came over with two glasses of water. Her hands shook, breaking the meniscus of the cold fluid that ran down the side of the glasses and onto the table. She shook her head, and her face turned red. "I'm sorry about that." She pulled a dirty rag from her waist and wiped the table.

"We need a few more minutes," Richard said.

After the waitress walked away, Diane leaned across the table. "What am I to do? I need my work," Diane said in a whisper.

"You need to find yourself," Richard said. "Process all of this. Talk to someone—a priest, a rabbi, a therapist or someone."

Jack was the first person to pop into Diane's mind. She recalled how they used to talk. He was the only one she would actually let in, albeit slowly. His warm, welcoming blue eyes caught her feelings—and sometimes her demons—in such a way that they were translated and redirected back to her in a manner she could better understand.

"Richard?" Diane said. "Not this, not now."

"Diane, it's just not me saying this, but everyone at ITN. Even Bart has come to us," Richard said.

"You met Bart?"

"No, but he was worried about you and thought you could use a break. That is why we've kept you regional. Plus, there has been some funding trouble, and honestly, we are also having a hard time securing interviews like before. I think the Carter administration is behind it. Something is off, and now you are off. We all need to regroup," Richard said, his tone hushed.

"I just think you're wrong. I can still do this job," Diane said.

"Diane, with hindsight, many things are gleaned. You might thank me one day for this, and your break won't be long. It's just . . . necessary. We will be in touch soon, as we're working on something exciting for you. If there is anything you need, just let me know. I'm on your side." Richard moved his hand across the table and gently tapped Diane's hand a few times.

"Actually, can you just leave me alone? I'm sorry you had to come all this way, but I just wanted to thank you in person for what you did and apologize for what I did." Diane said. "I know there is work to be done. Sadat, Begin—I know. I have been reading the papers."

Richard nodded. He opened his wallet and left ten dollars on the table. As he walked toward the door, he passed the waitress. "Thanks for your service," Richard said.

Diane circled her straw in the water. A few more tables had been occupied since she had first sat down. The clatter of forks, knives and conversation was drowned out by The Band's "The Night they Drove Old Dixie Down." The notes oozed out of speakers in the far corners of the café:

The night they drove Old Dixie down,
and all the people were singin'
They went, "Laaaaaa, la-la-la-laaaaaa
La-la, la-la
La-la-la-laaaaaa . . ."

Later that night, Diane sat in her living room. She was dressed in a t-shirt and shorts. Past a half-empty bottle of Merlot, the nightly news came on. Barbara Walters was reporting. Diane had once revered her, but after her latest comments, she found her to be crass. Secretly she was jealous that Walters's interviews with the Shah received more attention. She could tell the Shah liked Walters better and often opined as to why. Additionally,

Walters had conducted numerous one-on-one interviews with Carter, and even moderated the Presidential debates in 1976. Despite Diane's experience and connection to Jack, she had yet to even shake Carter's hand.

On this night, Walters was reporting on President Carter's announcement that a multimillion-dollar sale of state-of-the-art computer technology systems to the TASS News Agency would not be allowed to proceed. Additionally, she said, in her characteristically tightlipped tone, "New export restrictions are also in place for other technology that might be used to gain knowledge of the latest computer systems, including U.S. oil-producing technology. This shows a continuing depreciation in East/West relations."

The news broadcast had clips of Carter giving the speech earlier in the day. Almost off screen, Diane made out half of Jack's body. He had grown in thicker sideburns and was dressed in a gray suit and wore a blue tie. His hair was mop-like and longer than she recalled. If she didn't know him, he would have melted into the presidential administration backdrop, which, despite party affiliation, was always comprised of bright interchangeable players.

An almost weekly occurrence, Diane, emboldened by a few glasses of wine, picked up the phone. She would dial half of Jack's number, stopping at the fourth number, which was a nine. She let the rotary dial recoil. The counterclockwise slow draw-back always gave her enough time to second-guess the idea. As she had done countless times before, she hung up the phone.

Diane turned the volume off the television and flipped through stacks of records. She thought about what Richard said. His truths were clear to her, but she could only admit that when she was alone. With a wine glass in hand, she put on Gerry Rafferty's *Baker Street* album and played the title track. She swayed to the music. When the saxophone kicked in, she twirled. Soon, Rafferty's smooth voice entered her apartment:

This city desert makes you feel so cold.
It's got so many people, but it's got no soul.

Diane wiped a tear from her face, placed the wine glass down, picked up the phone again and dialed. As the music blared, the phone rang and rang. Finally, she heard a voice.

"Hello? Who is this? Turn down the music. Hello?"

Diane sauntered over to the record player and turned the music lower. She spoke softly into the receiver. "It's Diane. How are you?"

"Diane? Why are you calling?" Bart said.

"Oh, stop with the questions, Mr. Producer. Grab a bottle of bourbon and come on over."

"What? Are you serious?"

Diane turned up the music and hung up the phone. Surrounded by shadows and a muted television set, she slow-danced like a little girl following in the footsteps of her father.

Chapter 18

Spring had come and gone. Diane was given a small stipend from ITN but was listed as "on probation." She had gained nearly fifteen pounds by keeping too many late nights with Bart, who as a hired contractor, was also out of work. Their friendship had suffered as a result of their frequent dalliances. Diane only slept with Bart when she was drinking, and he made sure there was always plenty of alcohol to go around.

A pregnancy scare in mid-March woke Diane up, when her period was three weeks late. She visited with her doctor for a blood test. Since it would be hours before she'd hear the results, she walked around Washington DC. It was her favorite time of year, when the cherry blossoms were still in bloom. That springtime celebration always warmed her soul. It wasn't so much the beauty of the trees as the way they came to be there. In 1912, Mayor Yukio Ozaki of Tokyo, gifted Japanese cherry trees to the city as a sign of friendship.

As she walked under the majestic, flowering trees, panicked about the possibility of being pregnant, she wondered if the trees had knowledge of the deadly, world-altering decisions that had been made years earlier and only blocks away by President Truman, who ended World War II with the atomic bombing of Hiroshima and Nagasaki. She took the long way home, lost in thought.

When she returned to her apartment, she grimaced when she saw Bart sitting on the couch reading the paper. She had given him a key one drunken night and had a hard time getting it back. He knew the pregnancy test had been taken, but he had different hopes for the results. "Hey," he said. "Any news?"

"Not yet," Diane said, her voice monotone. "Listen, I have been doing some thinking today."

"I have too," Bart countered. "If you are . . . you know, let's make a go of it."

"I'm afraid I'm thinking quite the opposite," Diane said and dropped her keys on the kitchen table.

"You're not saying . . ." Bart stood up with a concerned look on his face.

"It's not as if there aren't choices, Bart," Diane said.

"Yes, but are you seriously considering options?"

"The couple we have been is a couple of drunks. I care for you, I do, of course, but this has all been wrong. You know it, too. Something is not right here, and I don't want to have a child from this. I want you to be my producer, not my boyfriend." Diane walked closer to him. The apartment shades were drawn. Spring, and all the life it represented, was trapped outside.

"I don't know if I can be only your producer, if we ever get called again for work," Bart said. He tried to embrace Diane, but she pulled away.

"We will get called again. I'm sure of it. I also know we can get past this. We make a good team, Bart, but we are not a couple," Diane said.

The phone rang. Bart looked at Diane like a boy seeking approval from his mother. Each ring echoed in the otherwise silent apartment.

"Aren't you going to answer that?" Bart said.

Diane walked over to the phone, took a deep breath and picked it up. "Hello? Yes, this is she."

Bart watched, but there was no expression on her face.

"Yes, I see. I understand, Doctor. I will. I promise." Diane hung up the phone and tightly closed her eyes. Moments passed, and the rattle of the refrigerator motor filled the air.

"Well?" Bart said. "Diane!"

"I'm not pregnant! He said stress and a poor diet and too much drinking might have thrown off my cycle, but I should be fine as long as I straighten up," Diane said. She grabbed a bruised apple from the table, found a sweet spot and took a bite.

"I-I don't know what to say. I know I shouldn't congratulate you," Bart said, "or maybe I should . . ."

Diane walked over to Bart and half-hugged him. "Listen, why don't you go? Let's just take some space, reset the clock and get back to what it is we do best. Bart, I do love you, but this has taught me that it's not the way you need me to love you."

"I sort of knew this wouldn't last. You've never even kissed me in daylight. I guess I'm a hard pill to swallow sober," Bart said. He grabbed his jacket, pulled the key out of his pocket and placed it on the kitchen table next to hers. He looked back at Diane with a slight smile. "You know this means I'm going to be a real cocksucker producer to you now."

"Yes, I know," Diane said, laughing slightly. It was the first time they'd shared a sober laugh in months. Bart slowly closed the door, and Diane walked over and quietly locked it. As she heard his footsteps grow distant, she slid down the door and began to cry. She wept not for the pregnancy scare or that she had hurt Bart's feeling, but because she finally accepted that her parents were gone.

Days passed and turned into weeks of confusion as to what the future would hold. Money was becoming tight. As she waited for the phone to ring with news from Richard, and on the urging of a few colleagues, including David Frost, Diane began compiling thoughts for a memoir. While she thought it was premature, Frost wrote, "Remember, dear girl, the power is not in the pen. It's how you observe and truthfully interpret experience."

After Frost's interviews with Nixon the previous year, his star was on the rise. Diane found him unquestionably charming and brighter than most assumed, Nixon included. It was with that sentiment she wrote to him, "I find you unquestionably charming and brighter than most assume." Every now and then, she received an encouraging note from him, almost a mild flirtation.

More than two months had passed. Diane had written nearly sixty pages of the memoir with no working title and had picked up a few freelance writing assignments from *The Washington Post* and *Time* magazine. She wrote on topics she knew, particularly the Middle East. She wrote commentary on the purported news that there was going to be a peace summit hosted by President Carter between Egypt's Sadat and Israel's Begin.

What was supposed to be a few months off began to turn into a much longer hiatus. ITN had used Diane Sawyer for a couple of oversees stories, which boiled Diane's blood. Much like her inclination to call Jack, she wanted to call Richard, but pride stood in her way. She also knew he was a man of his word. *He'll call,* she thought.

On a mid-June early morning, the phone rang. It was Bart. "Did you get a call today from ITN?" he asked.

"No!" Diane said.

"Well, sorry. I just thought. They are bringing me back, and I just figured—"

"Let me call you back," Diane said and hung up the phone.

She paced around her apartment. She picked up the phone to make sure it was working. Thirty minutes passed. When she could take the suspense no longer, she rushed to the phone and picked it up and dialed. "Richard?"

"Diane! I was about to call you. Can you meet me at the Tidal Basin in one hour?"

"Yes," Diane returned without hesitating at all.

"Good," Richard said and hung up.

Diane, back to her normal weight, jumped in the air and screamed, "YES!" She assumed and hoped she was right about what the assignment would be.

While Richard didn't specify where to meet, Diane knew as she walked the stone retaining walls that circled the massive body of water. She reached the Jefferson Memorial steps fifteen minutes early and waited, smiling.

"Do you have any favorite quotes of his?" Richard had appeared from around the opposite corner and was pointing to the domed building.

"None committed to memory," Diane said. She wanted to hug him but refrained. He looked absolutely no different.

"Bodily decay is gloomy in prospect, but of all human contemplations, the most abhorrent is body without mind," Richard said. "That was always my favorite of his."

"Is this to say you believe Carter is both body and mind equal to this historic task of mediation?" Diane said. She stood and walked closer to Richard.

It was just past noon when a mother and father with two small toddlers approached the monument. Richard waved them off. The father paused for a second but thought better of it and moved on.

"No way can Carter pull this off," Diane said in a hushed tone, feeling like she was back. Their rhythm hadn't faltered these many months apart.

"Don't be so pessimistic. Carter is a great ambassador. He's met with all the Middle Eastern leaders and has developed a good rapport. I read your *Washington Post* piece on this—not bad, albeit a bit dour. Believe me; this could work despite the pessimistic tone of the article."

"What would this mean? A peace treaty between Israel and an Arab nation?"

"If it succeeds, it's a light at the end of the tunnel. If it fails, the tunnel will collapse, quite possibly forever."

"High stakes, huh?"

"The highest."

*   *   *

Across town, Jody and Jack were arguing as they weaved their way through the White House maze of halls, en route to the press conference room.

"There's no way you can have Diane Babel there, at Camp David. There was that Mexico mistake, and now she's writing those Carter slam pieces for the paper. C'mon," Jack said. He was dressed in office casual attire, a short-sleeved white button-down shirt and gray slacks. For the first time in years, he was clean shaven.

"Oh, Jack. She'll find a way in anyway. Word has it that ITN is reinstating her. She's gained the trust of her subjects, as well as a growing number of viewers, according to a recent ratings report. Jimmy says he likes her moxy."

"Moxy? Listen to me. I know her, and I'm not sure I trust her motives."

Jody stopped and pulled Jack into an empty side room. "Jack, let's be frank. You *knew* her. Maybe you found some truth between the sheets, but that was long ago. She's good. Maybe she's not always on our side, but she *is* good, and I can't have this bullshit from you anymore. Focus on the big picture—the helicopter view."

Jack shook his head and stepped back, putting his hands up, as if to surrender unwillingly.

"Jack, listen, we need to get the world on our side for this one. America's trust is one of the biggest elements at play, but so are foreign audiences. She has a foot in both camps. Think big picture here, son."

"Yes, but I thought we were trying to *hide* information from her, not spoon-feed it to her."

"Consider this our way of controlling her, of controlling the message. Does that help?" Jody said. His tone was condescending like a calculus professor teaching geometry.

As they headed back toward the hallway, Jack whispered into Jody's ear, "I hope you know who you're dealing with."

Jody didn't respond and kept walking. Mid-conversation, they entered the press room, which was already teeming with reporters. As usual, as soon as Jody entered the room, cameras flashed and hands were raised. He reached the podium and lifted his hands in a calming gesture. He cleared his throat and took a sip of water.

The room fell silent.

"Thank you all for coming. I'm here to formally announce that beginning September 5 at Camp David, President Carter will be mediating a proposed peace treaty between the Arab nation of Egypt and the Jewish nation of Israel. Egyptian President Anwar El Sadat and Israeli Prime Minister Menachem Begin will represent their countries and try to make a huge step forward at a possible peace treaty in the Middle East."

The silence was broken as hordes of questions were shouted at the secretary.

*   *   *

Later that evening, Diane was seated at her couch, surrounded by papers and books, researching the two leaders. In the two months leading up to the treaty, ITN ordered two in-depth exposés on Sadat and Begin to better inform the audience."

Soon after Begin won power in Israel in 1977, he said, "The Jewish people have unchallengeable, eternal, historic right to the land of Israel, including the West Bank and Gaza Strip, the inheritance of their forefathers, and pledge to build rural and urban exclusive Jewish colonies in the West Bank and Gaza Strip." Diane next read a quote Sadat offered to a newspaper reporter, "Most people seek after what they do not possess and are enslaved by the very things they want to acquire."

Diane sat back with a pen in her mouth. Her hair was pulled back, and her eyes were red and growing tired. She wondered how such men could possibly find common ground.

When the phone rang, she half-expected it to be Bart. To her surprise, he was dating someone new and never mentioned what had transpired between them, though they had yet to share a drink together.

"Hello?" Diane said.

"Diane, it's Jack." His voice was shaky, and Diane thought she heard office background noises.

"Jack! Jack Quaid? Wow, it's been . . . a while."

"Yes, well they do keep me busy. I was sorry to hear you were suspended. Really, I am sorry." His voice was smoother and sincere.

"Did you see the Volkswagen story?" Diane asked sheepishly.

"Yes I did. Listen, you know how many mistakes I've made or things I shouldn't have said? If you've only screwed up once, you're ahead of the game."

"Well, thanks . . . but ahead of the game? I've been on the bench."

"You're getting called up again. ITN submitted press papers for you to cover Camp David in September. Looks like it's a go for you. I just wanted to give you a heads-up."

"Jack, you didn't have to call. I mean . . . thanks. It's great news, but I assume you are busy with so many things."

"Well, yes, I'm busy, but this is also part of my job."

"So this is a *professional* call?" Diane questioned.

"Well, yes. If I don't see you beforehand, I'll see you at Camp David." As Jack hung up the phone, he looked across his desk to Jody, who was listening in on the call too. He gave two thumbs-up and left the room.

After Diane hung up the phone, she rubbed her eyes and began singing Bob Dylan's lyrics:

And it's a hard, it's a hard, it's a hard, and it's a hard . . .
It's a hard rain's a-gonna fall.

Chapter 19

The summer passed quickly for Diane, who remained busy, researching and preparing for the peace summit, what many in Washington had dubbed the Camp David Peace Accord.

After Labor Day, Diane and Bart were given press credentials, just like Jack had promised. Mike, the quiet soundman, was not given permission. He failed a security clearance due to a misdemeanor he received that July after a bar fight with an off-duty policeman; that landed him in jail for three days, but Bart bailed him out.

ITN sent along a fresh, out-of-college upstart named Frank. As Bart, Diane and Frank drove from Washington DC to Camp David, Frank kept saying, "Like, wow! This is unreal." He talked about disco and The Bee Gees and without prompting confessed he really wanted to play music for a living. "At least I'm making money with sound," he said from the back of the news van, but it was as if he was talking to himself.

Bart was more talkative with Frank, allowing whatever feelings for Diane to exist in the frequent, uncomfortable pauses between work-related conversations and questions. Diane allowed these moments to hang in the air like damp clothes on a line, waiting for a warm breeze.

"You both realize the significance of this event," Diane said. She looked over her shoulder at Frank.

Bart kept his eyes on the road.

"Well, I'm not Jewish, but I know this is a big deal," Frank said. He had dark hair and acted cool like John Travolta but was more meek and goofy like Arnold Horshack.

"It's not about being Jewish," Diane said coldly. "It's about the Middle East. It's about finding peace."

"We've seen the Middle East. We have seen war and unrest, Frank," Bart said like he was talking to a younger brother. "I am more of a skeptic, but if Carter pulls this off, he could do down as one of the greats."

Diane nearly cut Bart off, adding, "Ever since the 1967 Six-Day War, Israel has occupied the Gaza Strip and the Sinai Peninsula, both former Egyptian territories," Diane said. She was repeating the information she'd written about as a way of staying on topic. "Back in 1971, President Sadat worked to reclaim the Sinai and drive out Israel. It was due to that failure of those repeated negotiations that Egypt and Syria launched an attack on Yom Kippur, and that was no mistake. It was a battle—a bloody one at that—and Egyptian forces were pushed back over the Suez Canal. It is so hard to believe Sadat and Begin are actually close to an agreement. It was not long ago they both had blood on their hands," Diane said.

The one thing the three shared in common was that no one had ever been to Camp David, its civilian name. *Officially the Naval Support Facility Thurmont,* Diane noted. Americans know it as the President's country residence in Catoctin Mountain Park in Frederick County, Maryland, located roughly sixty miles northeast of Washington DC.

As they drove closer, Diane recalled how many historic events took place in the main lodge. President Roosevelt hosted Winston Churchill in 1943. Eisenhower held his first cabinet meeting there. President Ford rode snowmobiles on the grounds, while Bess Truman found the place to be rather dull. Now Diane would be a fly on the wall for what certainly could be the most historic of events. She found it fitting that Jack would be there too.

It was September 5, 1978 when they pulled up to the highly secured entrance to Camp David. The leaders would spend twelve days together. Upon reaching the gates, their paperwork was scrutinized; the vehicle and all equipment were inspected and re-inspected. While Diane was among a select group of journalists who were granted onsite clearance, droves of others reporters were outside the camp's gates, hoping to get a look, a picture or a sound bite.

"There's been a change in plans," said a military police officer, tall, erect and showing no emotion.

"How so?" Bart said and shot Diane a look.

"The media will be allowed onsite for the introductions this morning. You will be segmented at a distance," he said.

"Segmented?" Diane said.

"Yes, ma'am. You will be able to set up your cameras and equipment at a distance. The President will greet his guests in roughly one hour, at which point you can take footage. After that, the camp will be closed to all media except for those with approved special clearance. You are not part of that group."

"And we can't come back?" Diane said, her voice was uneven.

"Approved media may be allowed back on September 18, which marks the last day of the event."

Diane could tell the young officer had relayed this same information countless times, and he wasn't interested in a conversation or negotiations on the matter.

Soon they were back in the car, driving through the winding driveway that led through beautiful lush trees and expertly manicured gardens. Diane thought it was, as President Roosevelt originally named it, Shangri-La. The pool, the tennis courts and golfing area were inviting. There was a sense of peace surrounding the grounds. For the first time in a long while, Bart and Diane shared a smile as they slowly drove. There was military personal everywhere. They were directed to a parking area for the media, within a stone's throw of Aspen Lodge, where Sadat and Begin would be greeted by President Carter.

Diane slid on wide-rimmed sunglasses and stepped out of the car. Her gray slacks were offset by a light white V-neck sweater that was highlighted by a silk blue scarf that she fashioned into an ascot. She took a deep breath and acknowledged some colleagues who were also milling about. Sam Donaldson gave her a wave and thumbs-up. He was friendlier than most people gave him credit for, and when he smiled, his dark arched eyebrows pointed downward, toward the bridge of his nose. He mouthed, "Welcome back," and Diane smiled and waved. She was definitely back. She looked across the lawn at the various administration officials but couldn't spot Jack. Diane did see Jody and National Security Advisor Zbigniew Brzezinski, who stepped out for a cigarette.

The leaders were to arrive by nine thirty a.m. Bart and Frank had set up and were taking B roll.

Diane scribbled in her notepad. "Bart, can we do this in sequence?" she asked.

"What do you mean?" Bart asked as he checked film.

"I want you to roll when they arrive, and I'll report in real time instead of a voiceover back in the studio," Diane said assertively.

"Well, you haven't done this in a while. If it was last year, I would say yes."

"So you are refusing?" Diane questioned.

"No. I'm just saying it makes me nervous."

"Don't be nervous," Frank interjected. He bopped as he talked, as if music were playing.

Bart shot him a look. "Stick with the sound, kid."

"Bart, trust me on this," Diane said. "I can do it." The warm September sun bounced off her shades.

The late summer day was picture perfect. The murmurs from other reporters and camera operators were sporadic, and no one knew what to expect. There was no sign of President Carter, which upset Bart, but Rosalyn Carter was spotted carrying flowers into the lodge. Three minutes earlier than the time they were set to arrive, two limousines pulled up to the driveway.

"Here we go," Bart said. He signaled Frank and gave a thumbs-up to Diane.

A hush fell over the crowd. Secret Service were perched like owls, turning their heads every few seconds. President Carter walked out the front door of the lodge, toward the vehicles. His wide, toothy smile beamed in the sunlight. He wore a dark blue, casual, button-down shirt and gray slacks. *He looks thin,* Diane thought, but his usual affable self comfortably waved at the reporters, or more so, the cameras.

Moments later, President Sadat appeared, surrounded by a few men. His skin was dark, and he wore an infectious smile. Dressed in a white casual jacket and dark slacks, he was balding, and his face bore a mustache. He shook Carter's hand for an extended period, eventually doubling his hand on Carter's. They broke their embrace as Prime Minister Begin began his slow approach. He was dressed in a dark sports jacket, tie and slacks. The most formal of the three was also balding, with wisps of gray at his temples. He wore thick, tinted glasses. Carter embraced his hand for an equally long time, allowing for pictures. Next, Sadat and Begin shook hands. *If peace came as easy as their smiles, this would be a short summit,* Diane thought.

Still photographers bobbed and weaved around the three men, whose smiles served as the only dialog for those watching from a distance. The dark wood of the lodge blended with the gravel, green grass and trees that surrounded the compound.

Diane positioned herself, and Bart gave her the five-finger countdown. She began, "On this September 5, 1978, Anwar Al-Sadat, Menachem Begin and Jimmy Carter meet at Camp David to discuss a possible peace treaty."

The ITN microphone looked natural in her hands, and Bart nodded with approval.

"These two bordering nations have been at war for hundreds of years, we cannot expect this to be solved in a day, but if handshakes and goodwill show promise for historic happenings here at Camp David, that could be the first step to peace in the Middle East. This is Diane Babel, reporting for ITN News from Camp David."

As the men were invited into the house by Carter, Diane glimpsed Jack, who was following behind. He wore khaki pants and a short-sleeved polo shirt. He turned around before entering the lodge, caught Diane's eye and offered a polite wave.

"Good old Jack, huh?" Bart said as he packed his camera gear.

"He's a good guy," Diane said and smiled, not breaking her stare.

"Well, we have to hit the road. We got the footage, and now we have to do some studio magic," Bart said. "You did good, Frank."

"Cool, man," Frank said as he wound cables. "My first real gig." His bellbottom pants dragged against the gravel.

"I haven't been this excited about a story in a long time," Diane said as she sat in the car.

"Me neither," Bart said. "Me neither."

*   *   *

Later that evening, Jody and Jack were outside the lodge, talking.

"I swear these things are gonna kill me one day," Jack said, looking at his cigarette and coughing.

"That's the least of your worries," Jody returned.

"How so?"

"Well, I want you to put on your reporter hat, Jack."

"What do you mean?"

"Since Jimmy isn't going to bring the press back and feels it will detract, we're going to need you to take notes as events transpire. You're not the only one who will be doing it, but Jimmy asked for your inclusion specifically. We have you set up in one of the cabins. We're actually bunking together."

"Are we going to do daily press releases?" Jack questioned.

"Internally, yes. Maybe not daily for the press, but certainly some. Jimmy also wants this for his files, maybe source material for a book down the road," Jody said.

He yawned. "You got it. I'll just write what I see."

"Maybe you should call Babel for some advice," Jody said with a chuckle and patted Jack on the back.

*   *   *

Later that day inside in the living room, Jack watched from afar as Begin played chess with Brzezinski, who wore a striped blue and white shirt and sat like *The Thinker*. Both men were intent and watched each other closely, as if they were carrying a gun and could pull it out at any moment. A small crowd sat around the table and watched them play. Jack noticed Carter and Sadat in the distance, in the midst of conversation and pointing at the game.

The lodge could have been located next to a ski slope. Despite the warm weather, a fire crackled in the hearth that was surrounded by expertly placed field stones. Large, comfortable leather couches and chairs filled the room, and beautiful, ornate rugs offset the hardwood floors.

Carter watched the two men play chess, a battle of wills. He studied their faces, their hands and their movements. Jack wasn't the only other person in the room, as there were guards and Secret Service, but after years of being in and around the White House, those figures became as common as curtains or paintings to Jack; they simply blended in.

After an hour, with nearly no board movement, Carter walked toward the chess players. "All right, gentlemen, I think that might be enough chess for now."

Begin nodded and stood up. "Leave the pieces as they are, and we will continue this," he said.

Brzezinski stood and extended his hand. "So far, a good match."

Begin smiled and shook the offered hand. "Indeed."

The next day, Jack watched as Carter walked alone with Sadat in the woods. The tall trees, still green and lush, provided protection from the strong sun. When Sadat spoke, his hands moved like he was conducting a symphony. Hours later by the pool, Carter spoke with Begin, who shook his head for most of the conversation and paced back and forth. At a distance, Jack thought it similar to pantomime. Sadat approached the table next. Like Begin, he was dressed in a suit. Carter was still in casual dress and looked, Jack thought, like a well-placed ombudsman. Jack noted that when not exchanging pleasantries, the men leaned toward each other when talking, almost always in hushed tones.

A few days later, the men found their respective strides. Whereas they were polite initially, they began speaking more freely and doing so more and more in front of Jack and the others. It was as if Jack was also becoming a part of the décor, a wallflower.

"I want all of your men out of Sinai. That is our land," Sadat said plainly to Begin.

Carter was seated at a leather couch. A coffee table was in front of him. On either side of the table, in plush chairs, the two leaders talked across from each other. Most of the time, Carter looked back and forth, as if he were watching a tennis match.

"How do you expect me to give you complete control of that coast and all its oil?" Begin said.

"Because it is Egypt's land!" Sadat said, his voice raising.

"This is over," Begin said, standing up.

"Now wait. Please take a seat," Carter begged of the men. He fanned his arms like an air traffic control operator.

"I'll take a seat when I get the respect I deserve," Begin said with a spiked tongue.

"How can I respect a man who stole my people's land?" Sadat offered, speaking directly to Carter.

"Let's settle on this. Minister Begin, Israel will have the West Bank, as long as you remove your people from the Sinai Peninsula," Carter said.

Jack watched as Carter cleared his throat. It was the first time he'd ever seen Carter nervous. Sadat and Begin could hardly look each other in the eye.

"We are here for a specific purpose, gentlemen—to come to terms and to secure peace." Carter's voice was stern.

"Does he promise to keep *his* army way from *my* border?" Sadat said.

Begin stood up and walked a few feet away. He stared out the window, and Jack couldn't see his eyes. Jimmy walked over to him and whispered in his ear. Jack watched as Begin shook his head. Carter again whispered. Sadat looked on but didn't leave his seat.

Jimmy whispered one final time, and Begin turned toward Sadat and began to walk over to him. Sadat turned to Begin and smiled. Begin eventually returned a slight smile.

"Do we have terms? Please, this will be good for our people as long as we stop the root of Islamic radicalisms that are growing in the Persian Gulf area. As you know, we have been fighting these extremists in the mountains of Oman and Yemen with our good friend the Shah of Iran," Sadat said. "This is becoming bigger than our initial and longstanding conflict."

"I agree it will be good for all the Middle East," Begin said. "There are new challenges ahead."

Jimmy was again seated between them. He leaned forward like a coach. "Let's not talk about the Shah and the Islamic radicalism in the Persian Gulf. Let's have a drink and some food and celebrate this treaty. Thank God," Carter said, extending his hands to both men.

Together, in unison, they shook.

"But I do believe we need to discuss this radicalism," Sadat said.

"Yes, but one step at a time. We don't want to confuse people with too many issues. Peace is enough for now," Carter said. "Please take some time, and we will meet back here in one hour for dinner," Carter added with a smile.

With that, Sadat and Begin, accompanied by their staff, left the great room.

Carter walked across the room to where Jack and Jody sat, smiling and not knowing exactly what was said. "Get the press conference going and make sure the message stays away from Islamic extremists or the Shah and his fight against Islamic extremists in the region. This is my moment. This could spell reelection!" Just shy of fifty, the thirty-ninth President of the United States, James Earle Carter Jr., shook his fists in the air and softly cooed.

With all the goodwill and positivity surrounding the accord, Jack felt isolated as he looked at Jody and Carter, who were now whispering in each other's ears. Jack was not privy to all information, as was always the case. Although he was "a fellow peach," he had fallen further from the tree than Jody. Just like the hard-fought days in Georgia, Carter knew his political life came down to votes, regardless of what might have hung in the balance—the Shah, Islamic extremists and all.

Chapter 20

A day before the end of the year, secured in a dark, windowless room, all the major players of the Carter administration sat around a table in the Situation Room. Carter, Mondale, Huyser, Brzezinski, Jody and Jack looked sternly back and forth at each other.

Harold Brown, Secretary of Defense, sat pensive, with his arms folded, as if there was no cause for celebration. Jack had only met Brown once before and thought he looked too scholarly to be the secretary. His wide-rimmed glasses spoke to his background as a scientist, but Carter tapped him because he was Lyndon Johnson's Director of Defense Research and Engineering and Secretary of the Air Force.

"I'm just not sure it's the right timing," Carter said, pointing to a map of Iran.

"It's now or never, Mr. President," Zbigniew said in no uncertain terms.

"I have to agree," said General Huyser.

Carter circled the table, tapping his index finger on his upper lip. "We're heading off to the Guadeloupe summit meeting tomorrow, and we need to figure our stance on Iran."

"What's the real problem?" Jack questioned. As the words left his mouth, he realized a little too late that he'd spoken out of turn.

"It's the Shah. We need to get him out of power," Huyser interjected. He moved forward in his chair slightly and looked to the map.

"He's done a lot of good for his nation, but it's what we don't know that troubles me," Carter said, now seated at the head of the table. His blue and gray tie was loose around his neck. The whites of his eyes were red and offset the blue.

"It's simple. He has become too powerful for us to control, and it's time to get him out," Zbigniew said. His forehead was beginning to moisten. "He plays to the media, to the Diane Babels and Barbara Walters of the world, but there is a bigger game at play. It's about power, and sources have it that the Shah has gotten *intimate* with Walters . . . and who knows about Babel?"

Jack stiffened in his seat and looked at Jody, who didn't break his stare from the map.

"This is how he is controlling the media," Zbigniew added.

"These dalliances are but conjecture. It's not all about power. It's about human rights. That's our position," Carter said with authority.

"Whatever reasoning you need, Mr. President. Some know it's about oil contracts. I just know that if we don't act fast, we will lose our place in the Middle East," Zbigniew said.

"How quickly can we get this done?" Carter said.

"I have men in place to carry out the orders any day," General Huyser said, his voice soft but certain. "Just give me the word. We have Khomeini set to return and take over Iran seamlessly. The tides have turned, Mr. President."

*   *   *

Days later, January 4, 1979, on the island of Guadeloupe, Jack and Jody watched as French President Giscard d'Estaing, German Chancellor Schmidt, English Prime Minister James Callaghan and Chancellor Helmut Schmidt of the Federal Republic of Germany greeted each other on a pristine green lawn, surrounded by media and palm trees. The men were dressed in casual suits and all had varying wisps of gray hair, askew from the wind.

Jack studied the leaders, who smiled and shook hands. To Jack, their handshakes weren't like dove wings coming together; rather, they were more akin to shoulders locking in a rugby scrum, the ball a slippery cannon ball.

As the men were led to an outdoor conference room, the media was held at a distance. Jack looked for Diane; to his surprise, he only saw Bart directing a male young reporter. As Jody pushed Jack along toward the conference room, he looked around once more, but he still didn't see Diane.

As the doors to the room closed, Jody and Jack flanked the walls, along with Secret Service and members of the other leaders' administrations.

The room fell quiet after pleasantries were exchanged and drinks were served.

"Gentlemen, the answer to our main question is in a name. I will say his name once," Giscard said. His hairline had receded so that his face was a near-perfect oval. His blue suit and white tie fell perfectly on his slender frame and a light blue handkerchief fell from his breast pocket. "Ayatollah Khomeini."

"With all due respect, we find the man to be far from sane and more so dangerous," Callaghan quickly retorted. His gray, stringy hair was nearly gone, but he managed to pull it across his head. He was big boned, and his dark-rimmed glasses offset his pale, English complexion.

Jack was back to taking notes and shot an equally puzzled look to Jody, who didn't break his stare from Carter, who sat still observing.

"No, we have been in talks with him and his people. He is a deeply spiritual man. He's promised to go back to the holy city of Qum to preach Islam and stay out of politics," Giscard countered.

"You actually believe him, Mr. President?" Schmidt said. His voice boomed from his saddlebag cheeks and bounced off the walls.

"We have no choice. He's indicated that he'll support the current government once the Shah leaves the country," Giscard countered.

"With all due respect, Mr. President, I do not trust this man and his ideology. As we all know, he has a personal vengeance against the Shah. He has Islamic extremist followers all across the Middle East and even in Egypt, and he would cause more problems for all of us. I don't like this plan," Schmidt said and called over a member of his administration. Schmidt whispered in the man's ear, and the man quickly fell back from the table. "We also need to discuss issues with China and the Soviet Union."

"Let's stay on topic, if we may. What if he is not the right person for Iran? In exile, Khomeini spoke of the creation of a revolutionary Islamic republic, which would be anti-Western, socialist and with total power in the hands of an Ayatollah," said Callaghan.

Carter smiled widely and raised his hands, and the table yielded. "It's not about being the right guy for Iran. It's about being the right person, the right man to lead Iran. Ayatollah will give us the right amount of access that we need to stabilize the area. So we also agree with his endorsement?"

*   *   *

The following day, the four men appeared again before the press. Each gave a statement, words that circled the globe with great speed. Jack was still shocked that when he looked out at the media, Diane was missing. He made eye contact with Bart briefly and offered a half-wave, but Bart didn't respond.

Carter approached the podium that had been set up on the lawn. The sun was bright. The air was warm, and tall palm trees danced.

"This is going to change things," Jody whispered to Jack.

"I know. We wrote it," Jack whispered back to Jody.

"One of the dearest and most valuable assets of the American people, and perhaps even most of the world, is the close harmony, the easy communication and the common purpose of those peoples who are represented here by myself, by Chancellor Helmut Schmidt, by President Giscard d'Estaing and by Prime Minister Callaghan," Carter said, motioning to the men who were seated behind him. "Most of our discussions were about regional problems and global issues, because the differences that exist among us bilaterally are very minor and of little consequence. We have been determined to strengthen even further the valuable ties of friendship and cooperation militarily—for common defense and for peace—politically, culturally, and economically," Carter continued. "We discussed the potential trouble spots of the world, and we tried to capitalize upon the unique opportunity that one or several of us have to alleviate tension, to let the people of those regions find for themselves, with our assistance on occasion, an avenue toward peace, so that stability and development of a better quality of life and enhanced human rights might continue throughout those regions where our influence might be felt." Carter smiled, nodded and took his seat.

Schmidt next approached the podium. The paper he held in his hand blew in the steady wind. He steadied the microphone and cleared his thoughts. His accent was thick, and he spoke slowly, "Now I would like—in dealing with the cordiality, the directness and the cooperative friendship in which our discussions have been led—I would like to concede that we made one mistake. We should have invited the press for at least one session, in order to let it be witnessed by yourselves how friendly the atmosphere really was."

The media and those in attendance laughed. Despite the gravity of the decision that was made, between the lines of diplomacy, the tropical setting lightened the mood like a vacation for distant cousins.

"We talked about other matters in the field of arms control, which was a chance for me to express my desire to bring about progress also in the field of mutual balanced force reductions. And in this context, of course, we also dealt with the French proposal for a European conference on arms limitation. I think one could sum up this part of our deliberations in telling you that we did agree on the global necessity to stabilize the equilibrium of the world and to carry on detente with the Soviet Union, of course, especially so, including limitation of armaments."

Chapter 21

While it took nearly six months, the unthinkable happened on March 26, 1979, when the Egyptian-Israeli Peace Treaty was signed in Washington, DC.

Diane was nominated for an Emmy award for the two twelve-minute shorts she did leading up to the event. She didn't win but was pleased all the same; it was the first time she and ITN had been recognized. She had even received a congratulating letter from Jack:

> *If it weren't for television, I might just forget how you look. A feather in your cap, to be sure.*
>
> *All the best,*
Jack
>
> *P.S. I thought you would have been in Guadeloupe.*

Diane never responded but placed the note in a box of mementos that included similar votes of confidence and encouragement from her parents.

These many months later, Diane found herself reporting from the South Lawn. Almost in amazement, she watched as President Carter, President Sadat and Minster Begin sat at a table with the treaty in their hands. Behind them was the American flag, the Egyptian flag and the Israeli flag. They were dressed in varying colors of suits and ties. The spring sun was forgiving, and a light breeze bounced across the lawn.

Carter addressed the crowd and preened for the news media. "The main feature of this historic treaty is the mutual recognition of each country by the other, the cessation of the state of war that had existed since the 1948 Arab-Israeli War and," Carter said, clearing his throat, "the complete withdrawal by Israel of its armed forces and civilians from the rest of the Sinai Peninsula which, as you know, Israel had captured during the 1967 Six-Day War."

Begin and Sadat smiled but otherwise did not react to the President's words.

Carter continued, "The agreement provides for the free passage of Israeli ships through the Suez Canal and recognition of the Strait of Tiran and the Gulf of Aqaba as international waterways. That said, it's time to sign this treaty."

Sadat was the first to sign, followed by Begin. As the mediator, Carter was the last to sign the document. The three men stood and, with great pomp and circumstance, joined their hands together as if they were teammates celebrating a World Cup victory. Six hands stacked high, holding all the hope and promise of peace in a region of the world desperate to have it.

"It's difficult to predict how this treaty will go over in the Middle East. If anything, this is simply a sign that peace might one day be possible for all the nations in that land. This is Diane Babel, reporting live from the South Lawn."

Bart continued to roll film as the three leaders posed together for pictures like unlikely rock stars on a promotional tour.

Diane spotted Jack and rolled her eyes in a surprised motion. She gave him a thumbs-up, and he smiled and did the same. She couldn't stick around, though, as she'd received a message from Richard earlier in the day to meet her after the signing of the treaty. She nodded at Bart as she walked by. "Good job, old friend. Gotta run."

*   *   *

She walked to a park a few blocks away, where she found Richard waiting on a bench. He had a brown bag and was feeding pigeons, throwing the crumbs as if he were seeding a field.

"So maybe this Carter administration isn't as incompetent as we thought," Diane said with a smile.

"I told you not to count him out," Richard said, his voice hoarse. His legs were crossed, and he held a cup of coffee in the other hand.

"A peace treaty in the Middle East. Who would have ever imagined that?" Diane said, transfixed on the birds that were pecking around his feet.

"Don't get ahead of yourself. My sources have revealed that it may do more bad than good."

"How so?" Diane questioned as she sat down next to him.

"Sadat is a great man, and bringing a Jewish and Muslim nation together is a major step forward to peace. But not everyone in that region wants peace. He's created a huge target on his chest," Richard said.

"You think someone is going to try and kill him?"

"Our intelligence is warning us that ever since he visited Israel, a group of Muslim extremists has been planning his assassination. We have a pretty good idea who they are, and as soon as I get confirmation, we'll have to warn Sadat."

"What exactly are you saying, Richard? Did my report contribute to this? God, I hope not."

"All I can tell you right now is that the Shah, Sadat and Begin are not the most popular figureheads in the Middle East, despite the fact that they are fighting Islamic terrorism and trying to preserve peace in the region. They have more than one enemy."

Covertly, from across the street, Jack watched as the two conversed. He waited for Richard to leave before he deftly approached.

"Jack! What's up?" Diane said, her voice shaky. "What are you doing here? Did you follow me?"

"It took years, but I finally figured you out." Jack's blue eyes were steely.

"You did?"

"Professor Stanley got you this job and somehow is getting you access to everyone and everything. We know all about Richard and ITN," Jack said and pointed in the direction Richard had walked.

"I already told you, Jack, that I didn't finish top in the class."

"Don't lie to me, Diane. I just saw you talking with him! I saw his picture in the professor's office, the two of them together when they were young and in the service. He's got you on the inside. We could use that info for something better then advancing your career, which you nearly ruined. If not for this treaty and all it included, you might not be back in the spotlight," Jack stated matter-of-factly, his tone terse and derogatory.

"I'm not admitting anything here, but what I do is give the people knowledge rather than withholding it like the White House does."

"But *we* have power. If you know something bad is about to happen, we can stop it. I know you've been aware of things over these last few years—things we should have known first."

Two joggers ran by, and Diane hushed her voice. "Listen, Jack, you could stop things too. You know things as well. I think your heart is in the right place, but your brain isn't."

Diane couldn't help thinking about the fate of the Shah, Sadat and Begin. Part of her wanted to tell Jack to protect Sadat. She wanted to tell him like she wanted to tell about the headless men in Yemen years ago, but she simply couldn't.

"Tell me the truth," Jack blurted.

"I did. I was not top in the class."

"What? I don't believe you," Jack said.

"Jack, *you* were top of class," Diane said, shaking her head. "And thanks for the note," she shouted over her shoulder as she walked away.

Jack kicked the ground and watched her leave. He was torn between feelings of love lost and frustration, realizing their power of difference. He headed back to his office, where he found Jody waiting for him; it was January 10, 1979.

"Did you see *ABC News World Report* last night?" Jody said.

"No, I missed it, but I heard something about the American support for the Shah's ousting."

"So the word is out," Jody said, pushing play on a tape machine and drumming up the voice of ABC's Frank Reynolds, reporting.

"Good evening. Now we know the United States has passed the word to the Shah of Iran that it's time for him to leave his country. This isn't being said publically, but officials in Washington are confirming it privately," Reynolds said.

"Who supplied this information?" Jack questioned.

"I did," Jody said, lighting a cigarette. He offered one to Jack.

"But why the Shah?"

"General Huyser did all he could. It was decided, and it's important that you embrace it. This is administration policy now."

*   *   *

The following month, Diane was reading the paper. The headline read, "Iran Ousts Shah: Months of protests and violence culminated in the overthrowing of the Shah on February 11." The article included a picture of the Shah, and Diane ran her fingers over his face. He looked older and wearier than the last time she'd seen him. She reflected on his accent and how he pronounced "Babel." She'd never heard her name spoken that way before, in a distant, effortless tongue.

As she reflected, it was hard for her to believe that a short time ago, she'd been with the Shah, in his palace, with a belief that a new world order was to come. This was now Khomeini's country, and Diane wondered how it could have all come to be. The article noted, "This massively popular movement replaced a Western monarchy with a theocracy-based on guardianship of the Islamic jurists. Its outcome—an Islamic Republic under the guidance of an extraordinary religious scholar from Qom, was clearly an occurrence that had to be explained."

Diane felt thousands of miles away when the phone rang. She picked it up and heard Richard's voice on the other end. He said three words, "Iwo Jima three," and then hung up. Diane looked at the clock and saw that it was five minutes past noon.

Diane was never as close to the monument as she was that day. The gray clouds were heavy, creating a ceiling in the sky. The sculptor had expertly captured the soldiers' emotions and need to raise the American flag amidst grave conflict. It was as if they were only moments away from victory but still had to push just a little more, a little harder. With the Shah defeated and her career stumbling, that was how Diane felt. Her flag was but half-raised, and she felt less and less like she had soldiers backing her up.

She spotted Richard walking on the north side of the monument and walked quickly toward him. "This is bullshit, and you know it," Diane said, short of breath.

"Listen, I put the Shah in power in the first place. I know how much bull it is."

"And Khomeini, of all people? The man was exiled from Iran for denouncing his country and ours!"

"It's an easy solution. Iranians love him, and his transition to power will be swift and popular," Richard said, looking around, paranoid as always, and lighting a cigar.

"The Shah had so much potential," Diane reasoned.

"That's exactly why they're stopping him."

"The people of Iran can't all believe this. There is material on those Shah interview tapes that we didn't air," Diane reminded him, and even she recognized a pleading in her voice.

"There are some people in high places behind all of this. As I told you, they could be dangerous to upset."

"I *want* to upset them. What do I have to lose at this point?"

"There is logic to your reason, and as it turns out, you're right. We made the call to send you back to Iran anyway. So pack your gear, call Bart and get ready to cover the event."

Not less than seventy-two hours later, Jack was seated in Jody's office. The television was tuned to PBS/ITN. As Jack watched the prerecorded news piece, he saw Iran, the land he had once visited, now full of new color and excitement as fireworks filled the sky. As he watched the camera pan, he thought about Diane and the fireworks they had watched together before graduation. He knew it was the same person, but she was most definitely not the same girl.

"In the weeks following Mohammed Reza Pahlavi's, the Shah of Iran, ousting, a full revolution has been realized under the leadership of Ayatollah Khomeini. Because the Carter administration did not support the Shah, Islamic extremists are now in power in the Middle East," Diane said on camera, amidst the yells and screams of Iranians.

She wasn't a girl anymore; she had become a woman. Jack saw it not only in the shape of her face, which was more angular, but in the poised way she held herself.

The Iranian celebration, this revolt, was different than the protests and civil rights marches of the 1960s. In the distant eyes of those rebellious youths, Jack saw condemnation of the West and a religious entitlement, the very things Carter thought to ignore.

Jody, smoking a cigarette, walked over to the television and shut it off.

"She can't say that, can she?" Jack questioned.

"First Amendment—that fucking First Amendment," Jody muttered.

"But do you think she's right?" Jack offered.

Jody walked over to the door and shut it. He looked at his watch; it was nearing seven p.m. "The Shah was an old, stubborn man. Unless you think he believed in democracy, it was a different brand than we know or than his people were ready for. This revolution could be the best thing to happen to Iran."

"But what if it's not? Are we sure about the outcome? It looks to me like we're starting a political earthquake in that region, especially if Islamic radicalism takes over the Persian Gulf region. Did you see the look in those kids' eyes?"

"We'll deal with problems as they arise. We're in the business of putting out fires, Jack, not starting them."

Jack shook his head and walked toward the window. A Ficus plant sat nearly lifeless on the sill. Jack lowered his voice. "I just think Jimmy should have thought more about this. All the leaders should have. Maybe there is something I'm missing here?"

"So you're still not at ease? You think you have the answers here, huh?" Jody said. He looked at his watch again and grimaced. "You know, Jack, you've been loyal. You've shown promise, and you have a bright career. I know about your connection with Babel. You are both idealistic. I respect that, but it doesn't have place in this house."

"I just want to know I'm working for the right team," Jack said. "I told you a little about my brother, but . . . there is more," Jack said.

"Jack, I have a dinner meeting with Secretary Brown."

"This will just take a minute," Jack said, motioning Jody to sit. "He was idealistic too. He believed all the crap Nixon had to offer and opted—signed up—for a tour of Vietnam when everyone else in the world knew the war was a lost cause. That was around 1971. He was a smart kid, bright and full of promise, just like you say about me. Now he walks the halls of Walter Reid, not knowing where he is. The worst of it is that he was injured by *friendly* fire."

"Hey, Jack, I'm sorry. I lost an uncle in World War II, so I understand sacrifice and loss," Jody said in a warm tone.

"That was a war worth fighting though," Jack said. "Now there is a new enemy out there, and we can't seem to pinpoint them because it is a religious movement, not one based on borders. I lie awake at night wondering if I'm working for the right cause. And sure, Diane is idealistic, but sometimes I think she has more information."

"We have the right answers," Jody said and walked over and patted him on the back.

Jack rubbed the deadened leaves of the Ficus plant between his thumb and forefinger.

Down the hall, Zbigniew was sequestered in his office. Compared to Jody and Jack, his office was organized. Books lined the shelves, and papers were neatly stacked at his desk. He lit a cigarette and picked up the phone. He twisted off the receiver, ran his finger through the oval shape and blew into it. Dust kicked up; he looked closely at it, shrugged and twisted the receiver back on. He dialed a number and sat back in his dimpled leather chair.

"It's been a while, Richard," Zbigniew said.

"It has. Listen, we kept her off the air for many months. What else could we do?" Richard said without missing a beat. It was a call he had been waiting for.

"I make a call, and the FCC is investigating ITN, shutting it down if need be. This is a matter of national security, and we can't have her running her mouth. Let her report. That's fine, but she can't speak her mind. If she tries it, edit her! These latest reports from Iran might be her last," he said, raising his voice an octave with every word.

"You haven't held up your end of the deal, and you know it. The Shah is out, and that wasn't the plan," Richard said. "Carter is headed in the wrong direction, and I'm prepared to stop it."

"Plans change, old friend. Careful how you tread. At this level, actions have the highest consequences," Zbigniew warned.

"Are you threatening me?" Richard scoffed. He listened for a response but only heard the line go dead.

Chapter 22

Nearly a week passed, and Diane was back in Washington. She caught flack in *The Washington Post* op-ed section for "editorializing" her reporting. The anonymous author wrote that ITN was a shill for the Republican Party, which was in the early stages of mounting arms against the Democrats.

She was surprised that Ronald Reagan had won the Iowa Ames Straw nomination, even though George H.W. Bush had won the poll. Diane couldn't help but laugh when she read a quote from the former actor, Democrat, and Republican California governor who said upon winning: "Politics is supposed to be the second-oldest profession. I have come to realize that it bears a very close resemblance to the first."

Diane received word from Richard that a meeting was to take place. With Republicans gaining momentum, there was a palpable sense that Washington and the White House could be headed for transition. Diane wondered what would become of Jack, although she couldn't recall what he smelled like or the way his skin felt to the touch. It was those thoughts she held secret late at night, alone.

As she headed to the meeting spot on the Washington Mall, Diane found herself increasingly more paranoid. Days earlier, she'd overheard people talking about her at a coffee shop. They whispered that she was a "non-American" and a "pinko" who didn't support the President.

Diane came across Richard, who seemed disheveled and sleep deprived. "Richard," she said, her tone almost motherly.

"Don't worry, I'm fine. I haven't been sleeping well and ran out of razors. Don't you worry," he said. He looked around. The Mall was teeming with tourists and onlookers taking in the sites. Every movement, even the wind, seemed to put Richard on edge. "I just want to stress the importance of your next assignment. It comes back to the beginning of all this," Richard said.

"Where am I heading?"

"You're already there."

"Washington? We need to get coverage of the Iranian revolution. We need to show Americans how much we screwed up. That's the story," Diane said.

Richard grabbed her by the arm and pulled her close to him. His hands were large and moved Diane with little effort. "Diane, the network is being told to lay off Iran and the revolution. I don't know if you've noticed what is happening here. Because of the protesting that pushed the Shah out of control, the Iranian oil sector has been shattered. Ayatollah has not been able to resume the oil exports consistently. Prices are up, and panic is imminent. We need to show the other side of it."

"Prices are all people are talking about—well, that and that I am a pinko," Diane said.

"Pinko?"

"The comment I made about the Carter administration's handling of the Shah is causing trouble," Diane said. "People are talking."

"You don't think I know that? You don't think I'm not getting calls? We're in a pressure cooker now and can't afford any further reprimands. Stay the course. Let the stew cook until the pot blows," Richard said.

"Is the gas price issue the I-told-you-so to the American public?" Diane questioned.

"That's not what our knowledge is about. We don't want to hold it above people. We want to bring it to them."

"So what can I report on here?"

"Show Americans what is happening and tell them the truth. Isn't that what you've always wanted to do?"

*   *   *

Bart rang Diane early the next morning. "I'm downstairs with Mike, donuts and coffee. We have a location scouted in Falls Church. C'mon down."

Diane wasn't running late. She had been up since five a.m. Like Richard, she wasn't sleeping well. The outside judgments that once fueled her passion for finding the truth had found a way to weigh on her shoulders. She could carry the weight, but it changed the way she moved, her trajectory. Her once long, thick hair was now cropped short, just above the collar. She took to wearing pantsuits and wore makeup, red lipstick and blush, only when reporting.

It had been months since she'd been involved with anyone, romantically or otherwise. She thought about getting a cat but thought her responsibility level closer to owning a fish, and even that decision was one she couldn't make without prejudice. Her apartment was cold literally and figuratively—not unlike a library after hours, full of potential knowledge but baron and soulless.

She climbed into the van and gave Bart and Mike a warm hello. Bart had taken better care of his health during the previous year and had lost almost thirty pounds. He was clean shaven. Like Diane, his face was cultured from love and sin.

Nearly thirty minutes later, Diane looked up from her notebook and began to see cars lined up. She craned her head backward, realizing the line of vehicles was miles long. People were honking, standing outside of their cars and shaking their heads.

"This is bullshit!" one man yelled. He drove a red 1960s Mustang that had seen better days.

Bart pulled the news van over across the street from a Shell station. The yellow seashell logo was faded, and a handwritten sign read, "Limit five gallons. Estimated wait: two hours."

Diane positioned herself, Bart rolled film, and Mike rolled sound as she began, "In the past few months, the price of crude oil has risen from $15.85 to $39.50 a barrel. Motorists are waiting in endless lines to fill their tanks in exchange for empty wallets. Looking for someone to blame? Those rallying against the Carter administration say it is because of their American-supported coup in Iran that left one of the highest oil exporting countries ravished. Adding insult to injury, since the Shah was ousted and replaced with an enemy, the oil is now literally being held hostage by Ayatollah Khomeini," Diane said. Fearing her detractors but resolute with Richard's support, she signed off, "Good luck at the pump."

* * *

At the White House, Jack quietly watched the broadcast as he was flanked by Jimmy, Jody and Brzezinski.

"That Diane Babel is completely out of line. She and that network must be stopped," said Brzezinski.

"A busy-mouthed reporter is the least of my problems. I've been delivering these speeches on energy conservation, and nobody is listening. What's it going to take to get through to these Americans?"

"We're stubborn, aren't we?" Jody said.

"And scared," Jack said softly.

Jody and Jimmy looked over to Jack.

"Sorry. Excuse me," Jack said.

"No, go on, Jack. What were you saying?" Jimmy coaxed, walking closer to him.

Though Jack had been in Jimmy Carter's presence numerous times and had come to feel comfortable, the man still carried the power and influence that the office of President dictates. He looked up and answered, "Since I've been alive, I've see a beloved President assassinated, a terrible war fought and another President impeached due to scandal. Things haven't been good for a long time. This gas shortage is just another in a long row of crises we've been through."

"I appreciate your candor, Jack. Maybe there's simply just a national malaise that needs to be addressed. Jody, how about a pep rally? Think I can get this economy back on track?" Jimmy's smile widened, but in his eyes Jack could see that optimism was no stranger to idealism.

"It's worth a shot," Jody said.

"Great, then let's set up a speech, primetime. I'm feeling good about this," Jimmy said as he left the room, flanked by Brzezinski, who rolled his eyes.

Brzezinski stopped and walked back to Jody and Jack. "It won't be done with speeches. The American people know too much. The media is giving them reasons to complain."

*   *   *

The following Tuesday at eight p.m. Eastern Time, President Jimmy Carter addressed the nation from the Oval Office. Pristine flags were expertly placed behind the desk, and behind them were long, flowing brown and gold drapes. Dressed in a dark blue suit and tan tie, he looked squarely into the camera like a doctor delivering sobering news to a patient.

"I want to talk to you right now about a fundamental threat to American democracy. I do not refer to the outward strength of America, a nation that is at peace tonight everywhere in the world, with unmatched economic power and military might. The threat is nearly invisible in ordinary ways. It is a crisis of confidence. It is a crisis that strikes at the very heart and soul and spirit of our national will." He continued, "We can see this crisis in the growing doubt about the meaning of our own lives and in the loss of a unity of purpose for our nation. In a nation that was proud of hard work, strong families, close-knit communities and our faith in God, too many of us now tend to worship self-indulgence and consumption."

Across town, Diane was seated on her couch. Numerous yellow legal pads surrounded her, decorated with writings, doodles and scribbles. She sipped on a cup of Earl Grey and watched with interest as Carter, a man she still had yet to officially meet, addressed the nation.

"Human identity is no longer defined by what one does, but by what one owns. But we've discovered that owning things and consuming things does not satisfy our longing for meaning. I'm asking you, for your good and for your nation's security, to take no unnecessary trips, to use carpools or public transportation whenever you can, to park your car one extra day per week, to obey the speed limit, and to set your thermostats to save fuel. I have seen the strength of America in the inexhaustible resources of our people. In the days to come, let us renew that strength in the struggle for an energy-secure nation."

As the speech concluded, Diane stood up, turned off the television and picked up the Bible. She had been reading it with interest, especially the Old Testament. She opened to Job 7:20, a passage she'd earmarked:

> *If I sin, what do I do to you, you watcher of humanity?*
> *Why have you made me your target?*
> *Why have I become a burden to you?*

Chapter 23

The next morning, as instructed, Diane met Richard at the familiar café across the street from the university. The waitress Diane had scoffed at was no longer there, but another fresh-faced girl was in her place.

Diane was a few minutes late and found Richard sitting alone at the corner booth, reading the paper. "Still haven't managed to buy a razor?" Diane said.

"What's the point? There is no need," Richard said, his voice dry.

"Some speech last night, huh?" Diane said with a hint of sarcasm.

"This is all a shell game," Richard said. "Three-card monty."

"Americans hate when their money is impacted, so maybe they will wake up as they wait in those long lines," Diane said. She looked at the menu and signaled to the waitress for coffee.

One of the reasons Diane liked the café was their choice of music. It was always the perfect song at the perfect volume; music, more than anything or anyone else, had become her trusted friend. She tapped her feet slightly under the table as Bob Marley's "War" played:

That until that day,
the dream of lasting peace, world citizenship,
rule of international morality
will remain in but a fleeting illusion

"Diane, by now you know I'm a glass-all-empty kind of guy," Richard said.

He never seems to notice music, Diane thought.

"We're not going to let those people be free for long. We'll invade them soon enough and kick the supposed communists out, all in the name of democracy and oil," Richard said, looking out the window at a carefree, shaggy, chocolate-brown dog with golden almond eyes who relieved himself on a blue federal post box.

"America can't continue to support corrupt regimes," Diane said.

"Oh, Diane, part of what I like about you and always have is your optimism. But the fact is, they can and will support those, and now ITN wants us to focus on the next victim."

"Next victim?" Diane asked, her voiced hushed.

"You're next assignment is to interview the president of Iraq, Saddam Hussein. The CIA is making him the new policeman of the Persian Gulf area, since the Shah is gone and in case Khomeini turns his back on us, which he will."

"Another questionable policy," Diane said, shaking her head as she snapped a sugar packet in her hand.

"Right," Richard said with a slight nod of his head. "They think an Arab will have more support in the area."

"Is he a good guy, this Hussein?"

"Not sure, but that's what I want you to find out. You will be supplied questions, but do your due diligence. This will be a tough interview, and they'll likely call the shots. If he feels disrespected in the slightest, it'll be game over."

In preparation for her trip to Iraq, Diane read as much as she could find on Saddam. After spending three years studying law, he dropped out and joined the Ba'ath party in 1958, the same year army officers, led by General Abd al-Karim Qasim, overthrew Faisal II of Iraq. Not only did Saddam and the Ba'athists oppose the new government, but in 1959, Saddam was involved in an unsuccessful United States-backed plot to assassinate Qasim.

During that time, Saddam was out of the country and supported himself as a secondary school teacher. In 1963, army officers tied to the Ba'ath Party overthrew Qasim in a coup. Later, Ba'athist leaders were appointed to the cabinet, and Abdul Salam Arif became president. To settle an old score, Arif later called for the arrest of Ba'athist leaders. When Saddam returned to Iraq in 1964 as Assistant Secretary of the Regional Command, he was imprisoned and spent three years in jail before escaping. He rose through the ranks and in 1968 participated in a velvet revolution led by Ahmed Hassan al-Bakr, a movement that overthrew Abdul Rahman Arif. Al-Bakr was named president, and Saddam was named his Deputy Chairman of the Ba'athist Revolutionary Command Council.

In the years that followed, Iraq was considered a strategic buffer state for the United States against the Soviet Union. America viewed Saddam as an anti-Soviet leader, and while Diane couldn't confirm that, Richard had told her that President John F. Kennedy's administration supported the Ba'ath party's takeover.

"The roots run deep," she wrote in her legal pad and underscored it several times.

When Diane and Bart landed in Baghdad, they were again without Mike. This time he wasn't in trouble; it was simply that ITN couldn't afford to send him. Tariq Aziz, the Iraqi deputy prime minister, met them at the airport, flanked by four highly decorated guards. The adornments of foreigner military uniforms had once intrigued Diane, but now she saw it as fashion.

Aziz was rotund, with a shock of white hair and dark-rimmed glasses. He was polite and friendly. "We have followed your career with great interest, Ms. Babel, and we are pleased to welcome you to Iraq," he said in effortless English. He looked to Bart and shook his hand. "Please, please, come so you can get settled," Aziz said.

Onlookers in the airport watched as Bart and Diane, along with their equipment and luggage, were guided toward the entrance, where limousines awaited.

"This isn't half-bad," Bart whispered to Diane. "Better welcome than the Shah."

Diane smiled at Aziz as they were guided into the limousine. She whispered to Bart, "The Shah gave us a plane."

As the driver pulled out from the airport, Aziz explained they would be traveling roughly sixty miles south of Baghdad to Hillah, where the Al-Hillah Presidential Palace was located. "This is among Saddam's favorite palaces," Aziz said as the car entered a highway interchange. "It is close to Babylon. He felt it was an appropriate place to hold the interview, which is scheduled for tomorrow evening," Aziz said.

"I thought we were to begin a ten a.m.," Bart said, and Diane nodded in agreement.

"Yes, well, there has been a change of plans, and you will need time to prepare to meet Saddam," Aziz said softly. He motioned to Diane. "And as far as your questions, we will have to review them first."

Diane reached into her bag and pulled out a folder marked "SADDAM." She handed it to Aziz.

"Thank you," he said. As night began to fall, he switched on an overhead light and began to read.

"Do you mind?" Bart said, motioning to a cantor of whiskey.

"By all means."

Moments later, the car stopped, and Aziz, the driver and two guards exited.

"Salah," Aziz said with a smile.

Diane looked to the side of the road as the men knelt and prayed westward as the final light of day was leaving the sky. They chanted, and in a kneeling position lifted their torsos to the sky, waving their hands toward their faces. Minutes later, the car was again in motion. While each man had a colorful prayer rug, Diane noticed that Aziz's knees were dusty and soiled. He continued reading the questions.

"Any problems?" Diane said.

"We will continue to review these and return to you in the morning with comments," Aziz said with a smile.

They arrived at the palace as the night sky took hold. The palace was wide and formidable. It was lit up from every angle and appeared like a mirage in the otherwise rugged, unpopulated terrain. Aziz motioned for them to walk toward a heavily guarded entrance. Bart hesitated, pointing to the second car that contained his equipment, but Aziz waved him off.

"Please come with me."

As they approached the massive golden doors, carved and molded to perfection, Diane realized the opulence possessed a different energy than the Shah's palace.

"As per our custom, you will be staying in separate quarters on either side of the palace this evening," Aziz said softly.

The marble floors gave the cavernous hall a chill. A life-sized portrait of Saddam hung on the far wall. A water fountain decorated the middle of the floor, and the water gurgled and splashed. A guard stood at every hall entrance; Diane counted seven of them.

"You will be cleaned and inspected before meeting Saddam tomorrow, Ms. Babel," Aziz said. He snapped his fingers, and from the far left hallway, two women in black burqas approached Diane. Only their faces were visible, and their olive skin was only shades darker than Diane's. They didn't speak English but motioned for her to walk with them.

Diane turned to Bart and raised her eyes. "Well, goodnight."

Bart waved and was taken in the opposite direction by Aziz.

When Diane arrived at her room, she could hear the footsteps of guards in distant hallways. The walls and floors were all marble, and random art such as sculpted gold horses and portraits of Saddam captured her view.

The women led her into a room that was three times the size of her apartment in Washington DC. Tulips, in every color of the rainbow, adorned a table that was directly across from the largest bed she had ever seen. Gold satin sheets were soft and sleek to the touch and juxtaposed the women's black burqas. Diane was left alone moments later after she received a quick tour. She sat on the end of the bed and stared at a portrait of Saddam that was hanging on the far right wall. He looked affable but strong. Between his mustache and brow, she looked into the eyes of the man, trying to find his truth. When she grew tired of looking for answers, she crawled under the sheets, not bothering to turn the lights off.

The following morning she was awakened by the same two women, and they led her to a bathing room. Everything was in Arabic, and Diane could make out very little other than a sign that read "sanitation." She was stripped of her clothing and washed by the two women. It was the first time in months that anybody had touched Diane's body. She had lost weight but held on to her curves. She wondered what the women looked like under their burqas, which were now wet.

Later, Diane's nails were cut and polished to perfection. She was sprayed with perfume and taken back to her room, where her bags had been placed. A folder containing the itinerary and approved questions was placed next to the flowers on the table. Twelve out of the twenty questions had been omitted, and the interview would commence in one hour.

Thirty minutes later, Diane heard a knock on her door. She opened the door to find Aziz, flanked by two guards. "Ms. Babel, you look splendid. I see you have everything in order, yes? Ready to proceed?"

Diane nodded. She knew better than to question the omissions. She was jetlagged and had been pampered to the point of coma. "Yes, of course. The interview waits."

"You and Mr. Bart have cleared security. He has been assigned the necessary crew and is awaiting your arrival," Aziz said. "Have you been briefed by your organization on how you are to greet Saddam?"

"Yes," Diane said, "but it is not common to me."

Moments later, Diane entered a room in the palace that weighed heavy in gold and jewels. It wasn't that it sparkled; more so, *everything* sparkled. Diane was reminded of *I Dream of Jeannie*. An even larger painting of

Saddam hung on the far wall. Two gold couches faced each other, and there was a chair that looked like a throne carved from dark wood, decorated with a silk, pillow-back lining. In spite of its opulence and immaculate appearance, the room somehow still felt cold.

"You look and smell wonderful, Diane," Bart said, leaning toward Diane with a smile. He had also been pampered and had the sheen of a younger man.

"Zip it."

"Don't forget to kiss his armpits," he again whispered in her ear. "I mean it."

"Yes, I know."

Diane remained seated with the camera trained on her. She held up a white piece of paper to give Bart a blocking shot. She wore a lapel microphone, and two other microphones were positioned near Saddam's chair. Everyone was ready, but an undeniable nervous energy filled the room of roughly fifteen, half of whom carried weapons.

Aziz stood near the entrance of the door with his arms crossed, smiling. He had the air of any press secretary in any country, Diane thought. She offered a generic smile of her own.

Moments later, three guards opened the door to the room. In unison and with authority, they stepped inside. Saddam Hussein entered, accompanied by a translator. Diane found him to be younger and more regal than the portraits captured. He wore a tailored suit, crisp white shirt and brown tie.

Diane looked to Bart, who had one eye in the camera lens. She felt a nervous energy come over her, as if it was her first interview. Saddam stopped in the middle of the room and signaled to Diane with his fingers, as if summoning a servant to fetch him tea.

Diane approached the leader greeted him with an awkward but traditional armpit kiss on each side of his arms. He oozed arrogance and smelled like musk and spices.

"Please keep at least ten inches away from him, Ms. Babel," Aziz said.

"Of course."

Diane took her seat, and Saddam waited until she was settled.

Aziz whispered in Saddam's ear like a pit boss in Las Vegas talking to a dealer. He looked to Bart and said, "Proceed."

Diane steadied her notes, took one last look and set them aside outside of frame.

"Thank you, Ms. Babel. I appreciate your cooperation. It seems as if we know people who know each other. Those people thought we should talk," Saddam said through his translator, causing nearly a minute of lag between responses.

"Yes, the American public wants to meet the new police force of the Arab world," said Diane.

"I appreciate your country's support. Yes, I'm now in charge of this region," Saddam said sitting straight and proud. He only looked at her when she spoke.

"Why do you think you've received it? This support?" Diane questioned, angling her body toward Saddam.

"The Shah was weak. He spread himself thin and could not focus on keeping nations in line. Under his watch, Israel has become—to some—a recognized state," Saddam said, "too influential."

"You don't believe the Jewish people deserve a place in the Middle East?"

Bart and Aziz looked at the questions, realizing they were already off topic.

Saddam smiled and turned his head to Aziz. "Pardon my frankness, Ms. Babel, but I don't believe the Jewish people deserve to live. They are a filthy race."

Diane's face became slightly red, but she remained composed. "Why do you have such hatred toward people who are different than you? Especially since America is an ally of Israel, and the goal is peace?"

"Because Allah has chosen to love my fellow Arabs and me, and the Jews are useless. This is a Middle East concern, not an American one. They have entrusted me to know the difference, to keep order."

"That kind of talk will not help in getting the American people to support your cause."

"I already have all the Americans I need on my side. Do you know of Donald Rumsfeld?"

"I do."

"Mr. Rumsfeld is a member of your CIA and has been most gracious in getting me all the weapons and protection I need. I don't care what the rest of your people think of me. My nation supports my actions, as they are just. If your President Carter were against me, I wouldn't be speaking with you."

"What do you think about America's support? Let's say, their habit of supporting the wrong person in the Middle East?"

"How do you mean?"

"I mean, we don't seem to think things through when it comes to Middle East policy because it is confusing, especially to the average American. We look at the easiest, most obvious solution and go with that course of action."

"Am I obvious?" Saddam's eyes peered at Diane.

Bart's eyes grew wide, and he looked deeply at Diane, as if to warn her she was veering off in the wrong direction.

"I invited you here, Ms. Babel, because your reputation qualifies you as a professional. Now you attack me?" Saddam said. He smacked his fist on the arm of the chair.

The guards sprang to attention like watch dogs, but Bart held his hand up, gesturing for peace.

"With all due respect, I'm not attacking you. I'm just discouraged, as are other Americans. We are looking for answers."

"I am not the preferred answer?" Saddam said.

"That is the purpose of this interview, to find out—to better understand you."

Saddam rose up from his seat. "You are a disgrace. This interview is over."

Diane stood up as Bart was instructed to stop filming by Aziz. He walked into the frame of the camera, but Saddam waved him off and turned his focus back to Diane.

Saddam motioned to the camera, then back to Diane, who said, "Tell the American people, the world, that you are going to be a decent leader, that you're going to respect human rights and that you're going to honor your neighbors. I want to know that America is supporting the right police force for once."

Saddam looked to his translator, who tried to keep up. He turned his back to her, scoffed and walked off.

Two of Saddam's guards grabbed Diane by the arms and took her away by force.

Bart followed behind with his camera. "Hey! Watch it!" Bart yelled.

Outside the palace, Aziz stood, shaking his head. "This was not the arrangement. You crossed a line," Aziz said. "You will be taken to Baghdad at once. I'm sorry. There will be no more information or interviews at this time."

As they were driven away, Bart, flummoxed, turned to Diane. "And what the fuck was that? You were off script. Well, this is a good way to go back to the bench, Diane. Shit! I can't believe they let me leave with the tapes. Whether or not they—or we—make it back to the States is another story. You are calling ITN when we get to the hotel. This is not my deal."

"Bart, I'm sorry. I took my chance," Diane said and looked out the window.

They were dropped in the AdhaMiya district near the Tigress River. They found a hotel and managed to walk in with all their bags. Bart cared for the camera and footage like they were his own children. He approached the desk clerk, while Diane walked toward a pay phone.

With noticeable red bruising on her upper arms, she leaned against the wall of the dirty phone booth and asked the operator for an international line.

Moments later, Richard was on the phone. He had already received word of the debacle.

"It just went off course. I was trying to get at the truth. I know, and I apologize. It was not my best diplomacy. It's just . . . well, I'm feeling a bit disenfranchised here," Diane said. She listened and tapped her fingers against the phone. "I know, I know. Right now? Okay, I will. Yes, of course."

Diane, with a drawn face, hung up the phone and exited the booth.

"Well, do we still have jobs?" Bart said.

"For now, yes. They're not happy at all and want to review the tapes. Not only that, but we're going to Iran."

"What? Right now?"

"Next flight. Cancel the rooms if you got them."

"What's up?"

"The Shah is dying and in need of medical care."

*   *   *

Half the world away, Jack paced the halls outside Jody's office; two Secret Service men flanked the entrance. Jimmy Carter was on the other side of the door and had been for more than twenty minutes. The Shah needed medical care; he was dying from advanced cancer. He had sought exile in a number of countries, including France and Germany, and was now seeking refuge and medical care in America, in New York City, to be precise.

The door opened, and out walked Carter. The hallway was busy with the business of the day and this issue, while considerable, was but one of many decisions Carter would make.

"Jack," Carter said as he walked by.

"Mr. President," Jack returned and walked toward Jody's door.

"Close it," Jody said as he entered.

"What's the call? Are we taking the Shah in?" Jack said earnestly.

"Jack, the current leadership in Iran already thinks we sided with the Shah. Do you know what they'll do if we take him in for cancer treatment?" Jody said. He was seated at his desk reading over papers. He looked up every third or fourth minute.

"He was—*is*—one of the world's most important leaders. If we can help him, are we really just going to let him die?" Jack said.

"It's up to Carter," Jody returned.

"Carter or Brzezinski?" Jack said as he walked toward the door.

"Hey, Jack, don't forget about our little conversation about idealism," Jody said and buried his head in papers.

Chapter 24

Diane and Bart safely landed in Tehran the next day. It was Diane's first time back since attending the Shah's New Year's celebration. Richard made plans in advance for a hotel. As they drove in a taxi from the airport, they noticed an uneasiness, general unrest and commotion.

"Driver," Bart said, leaning from the back seat, "has there been much trouble?"

Diane looked at the man. He was a few years older than she was. He had dark hair and a beard that came to a point past his chin. His dark skin was offset by a white robe and tunic. He looked in the rearview mirror, catching Diane's eyes.

"I take you to hotel. To the hotel we go," he said.

Bart sat back in the seat and leaned toward Diane. "You have a strange feeling?"

Diane nodded and rubbed her bruised arms.

As they pulled up to the hotel entrance, a young porter greeted them. "Diane Babel?" he said softly as the driver began unpacking their bags from the trunk.

Bart stood close to Diane but kept an eye on his equipment.

"Yes?"

"With respect, you and your colleague have been requested at the Embassy."

"The Embassy?"

"Yes, yes—the American Embassy," he said, motioning to the driver to put the bags back in the trunk. "Right away."

"What's going on here?" Bart said to Diane as they sat back in the taxi.

"I really don't know."

Twenty minutes later, the taxi pulled up to the gates of the American Embassy. Large brick pillars, twelve feet high, were positioned between wrought-iron fencing and gates that surrounded the massive compound. Diane noticed scores of young people, seemingly angry, milling about in the streets. Some carried signs, while others had pictures of the Ayatollah Khomeini pinned to their shirts. His long white beard was juxtaposed against his black tunic. His eyebrows were dark, and his eyes screamed condemnation. The protestors, most in their late teens and early twenties, chanted in Farsi, but neither Diane nor Bart understood. As the car pulled toward the gate, someone spat on the windshield.

An America guard greeted the car. A corn-fed Midwestern man, he had blue eyes and buzzed blond hair. He really was strapping, standing over six feet tall. The driver turned down his window, and the guard stuck his head in to peer in the back.

"Passports," he said to Diane and Bart.

"Yes, we are Americans. We were directed here. Someone mentioned the name Claire Barnes."

The officer quickly looked over the passports and told the driver, "Stay put." He watched as more teenagers gathered, then signaled for another guard. "Grab your belongings and follow me," he said to Bart and Diane.

They exited the car as more students moved down the street in their direction. Banners were fastened to the Embassy walls. Diane looked up and down the street and remembered the stories her parents had told her about marching with Martin Luther King and the quality the air took on when revolution was imminent. Her mom had said it was like "low-hanging fog that the oppressed used as coverage." She had never realized what her mother meant by that until now; this rainy, dreary day had this *fog*.

"What do the signs say? What are they chanting?" Diane asked the guard.

He pointed to one sign, "America is the great Satan."

After being rushed through the gates and up a flight of stairs leading to the entrance, Bart and Diane were met by Claire Barnes. She had cropped, silky, brown, straight hair that fell to her shoulder line. Her green eyes were placid. She was pale-faced and slender and talked with the ease of a Southern Californian. "Glad you could make it. Claire Barnes. I'm in charge of all communications for the Embassy, and there has been a bunch as of late." She extended her hand to shake both of theirs. "Enjoy your work, Ms. Babel."

"Oh thanks. So, what exactly is going on here?" Diane said.

"Well, things have been a bit . . . well, uneasy, since the Shah was . . ." She looked around and whispered, "Since he was ousted." Claire motioned them to walk with her.

As they walked, Diane noticed that many Iranians worked in the Embassy. The place was as busy as any midtown Manhattan office, but Diane sensed fear in the eyes of those who hurried down halls.

"The Shah has been sick with cancer and is being treated out of country," Claire said, "but there have been riots for months. Still, they're mostly peaceful, and they usually pass."

"He is quite an interesting man," Diane said, "the Shah."

"I watched with interest your interview with him a while back. I saw Walters too," Claire said. "That was before I was sent here, so it was a real education."

"For us too," Diane said and motioned to Bart. "He produced that segment."

"Great!" Claire said to Bart. "Congratulations on that. It was a job well done."

"Thanks. So, we are here to get a story on the aftermath of all this, uh . . . what is happening in the streets," Bart said.

"Well, I applaud your willingness, but while you were in flight, it seems the Carter administration did an about-face and decided to allow the Shah into America to receive cancer treatments. As you can imagine, this is not sitting well with Ayatollah Khomeini."

"What do you mean?" Bart said.

"In deference to us, the Iranian government suggested that all media and government workers stay at the Embassy until this all settles down. Again, there are always protests in Tehran, but this seems different. We just want to be cautious," Claire said. "I'm sure you two have been in tight spots before."

"Yes, but honestly, I'm surprised by this. I didn't think they would bend to the Shah," Diane said.

"Well, word has it that there was a lot of pressure from Mr. Kissinger and Mr. Rockefeller. They thought it was the right thing to do, to let the Shah into the States. And again, as you can imagine, Ayatollah is not too happy about it. I'm afraid if Americans are seen outside of here, in any capacity, they will not be received positively. We can only pray that things don't get too bad," Claire said. She looked out the window to the streets, where more people were gathering, some carrying the Iranian flag.

"So I guess we'll be staying here for the night?" Bart said.

"As a safety precaution, yes. We have bunks for you downstairs, though you'll have to share the room, because space is tight. We'll get you out of the country safely tomorrow morning," Claire assured them. "There is a plane being arranged for diplomats, and we'll make sure to save you a seat. We're hoping to leave by late afternoon tomorrow. Get settled as best you can. If you need me, I'll be around—just super busy."

"Thanks."

"No problem. The room is in the basement, third on the left. There's a bathroom down the hall."

As the sun rose on November 4, 1979, the crowd outside the Embassy had grown to more than 300. Iranian students and protestors with pictures of the Ayatollah pinned to their shirts scattered the streets; hatred and rage filled their eyes, and clubs and protest signs were in their hands. The *fog* was now thick, and they chanted and screamed. They outnumbered Embassy guards, who stood strong but were at a clear disadvantage.

Diane awoke to the sounds of chanting. She looked across the small room that had two sets of bunk beds, military style. Bart was in the other bunk, on the bottom, snoring—a sound she recalled. "Bart," Diane whispered. Still half-asleep, she looked around. There were no windows in the room. "Bart!"

"What is it?" Bart said, turning over. It was the closest they had come to sharing a bed in a long while.

"Listen!"

The noises and chants grew louder.

Bart sat up in bed. His hair was askew. "What is that?"

"Maybe a riot?" Diane said.

Bart took a sip of water from a cup that was beside the bed. He rubbed his eyes and watched as Diane flipped on an overhead light. She put on a light gray sweater and pulled her hair back into a short, tight ponytail.

"Let's go upstairs and try and find Claire," Diane said, motioning toward the door.

"What about our things?" Bart asked, pointing to the bags.

"Just leave them. I'm sure they'll be fine."

As they ascended two flights of stairs, officers and workers were busy running around. "Stay away from the windows," one cautioned. There was clearly a sense of urgency. Bart and Diane cautiously looked out the first window they came across. Dozens of young Iranians were climbing the walls. Nearly thirty men were already standing on the brick pillars; one group was waving a burning American flag. Diane shuttered as the stars and stripes melted, disappearing into a black toxic smoke that drifted upward, toward the Iranian sky.

Guards were busy adding extra barriers to reinforce the gates, but the protestors were growing in numbers and pushing their way forward. The entrance where Diane and Bart first arrived was now a mob scene that stretched up and down the street.

"Jesus," Bart said, looking at Diane.

"You might be safer to say 'Allah,'" Diane said.

Moments later, a glass bottle careened toward them and smashed next to the window they were peering out of; it didn't break the glass, but it certainly startled them.

Diane cocked her head and watched a girl, nearly twenty, approach the gate with bolt-cutters. With help from chanting men, she pried at the gate. The cheers and sneers grew louder and louder. American guards had their guns drawn but were ordered not to fire by a commanding officer Diane noticed in the far right corner of her view.

"Hold your fire!" he yelled.

In what looked like one fluid motion, the main gates broke free from the force of the protestors. Like an army of ants, they pushed forward, even trampling some of their own. The men burning the flag cheered and danced. The guards didn't fire and were now faced with rioters who had guns, some of whom fired shots in the air, further confusing the situation.

Bart and Diane looked on in disbelief. Only minutes earlier they'd been asleep, and now they watched as the rioters stormed the entrance. Only wooden doors stood between. The pounding echoed through the halls. Claire was nowhere in sight, and those who rushed by Bart and Diane paid them no attention. Diane overhead frantic phone calls; a military officer walked into the hall dragging the phone and looked out the window. "Stand down, sir?" he questioned.

"Bart," Diane said, her voice troubled. "This is different. Something's not right here."

The banging on the doors grew louder. Rocks began to shatter windows. The crowd began to chant in broken English. Diane could make out the word "spies" and "Who is your CIA?"

A rock crashed through the window, sending shards of glass in all directions. "Stay close to me," Bart said, reaching for Diane.

They huddled and peered out the window and watched as American guards were blindfolded and stripped of their rifles and weapons. Protestors had draped the entrances and gates with banners and signs; while they couldn't read them, they knew it was anti-American.

"What the fuck?" Bart said. "Back to the room! C'mon!"

He grabbed Diane by the hand, and they hurried down the stairs to the basement, where they found themselves alone. They slammed the door behind them, but since there was no lock, Bart pushed one of the bunk beds against the door. There was no phone. Bart and Diane rifled through their bags looking for something, for anything that might help, but all they had were their personal belongings. Their gear, which included the footage of Saddam, was held in another room.

Minutes pass slowly. The noises echoed and grew louder. Screams and shouts were heard floors above while Diane and Bart huddled in the corner of the room on the bottom bunk.

Diane heard a woman scream and plead, "Don't hurt me! Please! I have a family at home."

"We'll be okay," Bart consoled, looking around nervously. "We'll be okay."

In a rare moment of concession, Diane allowed herself to be coddled. "I hope," she said quietly.

The noises drew closer and closer, until the two Americans heard pounding and yelling on the other side of the door. Bart covered Diane's mouth with his hand. Slowly they watched as the bunk bed slid from the door. The metal posts scraped against the concrete floor, producing a sound worse than nails on a chalkboard. The men yelled in Arabic and Farsi, which neither Bart nor Diane understood.

In a final push, the bunk bed toppled over, and in rushed four Iranian men. They were out of breath and sweaty but energized, waving clubs in the air. They were dressed in Western clothes—just jeans and t-shirts. *They sure don't look like rebels,* Diane thought, just before the world went black. Diane and Bart had dark sacks cinched around their necks. Their hands were tied, and they were led from the room.

*   *   *

Back in Washington hours later, Jody Powell stepped to the podium in the White House press briefing room. He was pale. Jack, for the first time, saw Jody as vulnerable; the man had answers, but they weren't the right ones. He cleared his thoughts and looked down at a statement that Jack had helped him craft: "This morning, the American Embassy in Tehran, Iran was overtaken by Iranian militants. We estimate that seventy Americans are being held captive. President Carter and his cabinet are working at handling this issue peacefully and diplomatically. As of now, there have been no reports of injuries or casualties, and we are awaiting information from the rioters responsible for this action. I'll answer a few questions." Then Jody looked around the room. "Yes, Helen? Helen Thomas."

"So no demands have been given? Are these terrorists?"

"They have some specific demands, including the return of the Shah for execution. They also want us to issue a formal apology for our interference in their internal affairs, and they've requested that we unfreeze their assets."

The press core erupted with questions. Camera flashes clicked off each second.

Jody pointed to the second row. "Sara."

"So there have been no casualties or injures, even during the takeover of the Embassy?" said Sara, sounding skeptical.

"There have been no reports of death and only minor injuries. Right now we can only pray that those reports stay the same," Jody said. He waved his hands as more questions were yelled. "We will be back to brief you when we have more information." Jody then grabbed his papers from the podium, along with his glass of water, and walked toward the door. He signaled Jack to follow as more questions were yelled.

"When will the hostages be released?" was the last question Jack and Jody heard before the door closed.

"Walk with me . . . and move quickly," Jody said to Jack.

As they traversed the busy halls, Jody was handed papers which he quickly scanned. He passed some to Jack. A wire report stopped Jack in his tracks: "Among the hostages are ITN journalist Diane Babel and crewmembers."

Jody pulled Jack into his office and closed the door, and Jack handed him the paper slowly. "You didn't know she was there?" Jody asked.

Jack shook his head.

"I'm sorry, Jack."

"I didn't realize . . . the consequences of being too close to the story. Shit. Do you think she'll be okay? I mean, all of them . . . will they be okay?" Jack asked, biting the nail of his middle finger.

"Like I said in the press conference—"

"Right, we can only pray, but I'm not the press. Tell me, Jody. Is this going to end badly?"

"Listen, I'm meeting with Jimmy on this now. You want me to be honest? I don't feel too good about it. I'm sorry to say that, but I just have a bad feeling. Keep your spirits up though. This is just the beginning."

Chapter 25

Diane awoke and found herself under a table in an office. The sack had been removed from her head, and she'd somehow fashioned it into a pillow, despite her hands being tied. The rope had caused a rash, and she tried to rub her wrists on any surface that provided the right angle. Disoriented, she looked across the room that was roughly the size of a school bus and whispered, "Bart?" She noticed two other hostages sleeping, but Bart didn't respond. "Bart!" Diane said in a loud whisper.

"No talk!" a student yelled. He had been positioned in the corner of the room, a blind spot to Diane. He had a pistol and was not afraid to show his faith in the cause. He was no more than eighteen. A patchy beard sprinkled his otherwise smooth face. There was hatred in his voice that was not a result of nurturing.

Diane motioned to Bart. "He is a friend. I just—"

"NO!" He walked over and pushed Diane to the ground and covered her face with the sack. He pulled it tight around her neck, till it felt like a snake constricting.

Diane sat still, frozen, in a darkening fear. She heard the door open and other students enter. There were three or four voices, none of which she could understand. In a violent rush, she was lifted by her arms and dragged toward the door, then down the hallway. Her legs were limp, and she tried to walk, but her feet dragged. She hadn't eaten in over twelve hours.

The men stopped, and Diane nearly collapsed. She heard another door open, followed by voices crying out words she understood: "Please! We are thirsty and hungry!"

She was dragged into the room and dropped, and her sack was removed. Bleary-eyed, she looked around the room, noticing other hostages, some of whom wore white blindfolds. The room reeked of body odor and urine.

"No talk!" the student yelled at Diane. "No talk!"

As the hours passed, Diane noticed that the students were also growing tired, some nodding off and others reading or periodically checking the windows.

Of the roughly ten hostages in the room, half were still blindfolded, some sleeping and others softly crying, whimpering like lost children. The only other person who wasn't blindfolded was a man in his late forties. Together they watched as the student grew tired and exited the room to talk with other students in the hall. The man signaled for Diane to come closer to him. She slowly dragged herself across the floor and shimmied close to him.

"I'm David," he whispered. His gray, button-down shirt was open, revealing a white undershirt that was stained from sweat and dirt. He was rugged and looked like he had seen the world, a Marlboro man. A quiet confidence surrounded him. His salt-and-pepper hair was full and thick like his mustache.

"Diane."

"I know who you are," he said in a hushed whisper. They waited seconds before responses so as not to draw attention. "They are going to . . . expect things from you."

"And who are you?" Diane whispered, watching the door.

"I'm a contractor, a former FBI agent, but I don't think they know that."

"My producer is in the other room. They took me from him," Diane said.

"Likely on purpose."

"How many days has it been?"

"This is the second, on my count," David said.

"Feels like the third," Diane said. "How many hostages?"

"Most others are in the library, best I can tell. That was where they first took me when we got here," he said. "Barry Rosen, the press attaché for the Embassy, was able to negotiate the release of some Iranian workers. Some of them have guns. They put one to Barry's head at one point."

"They have guns there?" Diane's voice rose with panic.

A new guard burst through the door. "No talking! SILENCE!" Then he walked back into the hallway, chanting a common phrase.

"What are they saying?" Diane asked David.

He whispered, "Death to America."

Diane leaned her head against the wall and felt a tear run down her cheek. She looked to David, who offered a warm, empathic smile.

"It shouldn't be long before we're home," David said. "How long can they really keep us?"

*   *   *

After nearly two weeks of limited food and bathing, Diane hadn't seen Bart, but she and David had learned that Ayatollah Khomeini's front, the students, ordered the release of thirteen female and black hostages in response to an oil embargo the United States had placed on Iran.

"Are you upset?" David said to Diane later that evening.

He had grown a beard and was starting to look gaunt. They, along with a handful of others, had been in the same room for the duration. When they were taken outside for brief exercise and fresh air, they were always blindfolded. They were given meals to eat, but they were often in short supply and never on time. Diane was allowed to bathe every third day; others waited longer, and some outright refused, waging their own protest with their bodily stench.

"I don't know what to think," Diane said. "The reporter in me wants to see this through, but I have no medium on which to report." Her head felt heavy, as if it took more energy just to keep it up.

*   *   *

Snow was now falling in Washington DC. President Carter had the full support of the American people, and his decision not to use military force was generally considered the right course of action. Economic sanctions, such as the oil embargo, had already produced results with the release of some hostages. Carter placed Secretary of State Cyrus Vance as the lead diplomat on the effort, and one of the Carter "mafia" members from his days in Georgia politics, Hamilton Jordan, spent countless hours working secret channels. One pundit said of Jordan, "He is the dog that chases the car and catches it."

Carter's words on the crisis were direct: "It's vital to the United States and every other nation that the lives of diplomatic personnel and other citizens abroad be protected, and we refuse to commit to the act of terrorism and the seizure and holding of hostages to impose political demands."

Among the demands put forth by the students, the mouthpiece of the Ayatollah, was that the Shah be returned from the New York hospital where he was being treated. The students surmised that the U.S. was treating his illness so he could be placed back in power. *Newsweek* ran a lead story on the topic, and the cover depicted blindfolded hostages. The headline read: "Blackmailing the U.S.: 'America is the great Satan' - Ayatollah Khomeini"

The same magazine sat on Jody Powell's desk. He and Jack were looking out the window as snow fell on a cold December day. Christmas decorations blinked in the distance.

"We can't fully celebrate the holidays while our hostages are over there," Jody said.

"How long can this last? Why don't we send some forces over there?"

"It's almost a suicide mission, and it's exactly what Ayatollah wants us to do. Show how ruthless we are. Kill a bunch of those students. We'll be hated even more," Jody said, shaking his head and lighting a cigarette.

"I just can't imagine how bad it must be to be locked up for so long, especially during Christmas," Jack said, looking out the window.

*   *   *

Weeks after the release of the thirteen hostages, the students began to ease up on restrictions, allowing hostages to write letters to their family; however, they were forbidden to engage the media, and if they did, it was all propaganda.

Diane found herself with pen and paper in hand for the first time in a long while. Her first thought was to try and get a message to Bart. Instead, she began writing to Richard but soon stopped that notion too. It was Jack she decided to write to.

Dear Jack,

You may be as surprised to receive this as I am to write it, but given the option of whom to write, with my parents being gone, I thought of you. Conditions are . . . well, rough. I have no idea what you have read or heard, but we are being given only the basic necessities. My spirits are questionable, as every day, every hour can be different. All the other women were released except me. I fear my profession has labeled me genderless.

It's Christmas Eve. Every gesture they make to prove kindness is just a further reminder to me how awful they are. I'm supposed to cherish these little pieces of freedom—this pen and paper—when it's their fault I'm in captivity.

You can write if you wish. I'd like that, but no one has received mail, and we are unsure if our letters are even being mailed. We've been on the wrong foot for too long, Jack.

Yours,

Diane

While the letter was clearly opened and inspected, it did arrive at Jack's apartment on New Year's Eve. Having just returned from visiting his brother and dropping off a gift at Walter Reid, he read it more than five times before the first tear fell.

Free as bird, Jack felt caged by his feelings for Diane. They were always there, he knew, but the letter surged them with a great force from within. The feelings were never dormant, but they'd been suppressed for years, almost purposely forgotten. In reading the note, he realized their love might have an effortless purpose not yet fully realized. Jack poured some whiskey and turned the television on. Dick Clark, braving the chilly winds of New York's Times Square, was counting down to the New Year, the dawn of a new decade.

"In just one minute, we will say goodbye to 1979 and welcome 1980," Clark said in his signature smooth voice. "Millions of people around the world are watching this ball drop this very minute. Our thoughts and prayers are with the hostages and their families."

As Jack watched the ball drop and the 1980 numbers light up, he raised his glass and said aloud, "Happy New Year, Diane. I love you."

While he didn't know it, hours earlier at the American Embassy in Tehran, Diane, along with two other hostages, David and Barry Rosen, was sitting against the wall. Their hands were all bound, and two students approached them.

"So this night marks the end of your year?" the shorter, portly one asked.

"Yes," Diane said, and the others nodded.

"Do you celebrate?" the other student asked. He had a gun sticking out of his belt and was chewing on a toothpick.

"We do—a new beginning," Diane said, trying to manage a smile. Her cheeks were indented slightly, and her hair was unkempt. She tried not to raise her arms because of her own odor.

The two students looked at each other and began speaking in Farsi, then departed. Moments later, they returned with three cans of fruit cocktail. They handed one to Diane, Barry and David.

"Happy New Year." the portly student said, but he didn't smile.

Diane examined the can. Her wrists were loosely bound and she managed to slowly peel the lid back. She held the can up. "To the 1980s. They can't possibly be worse than this," Diane said.

David and Barry smiled and raised their own fruit cups with Diane for a cheer.

"To the eighties!" David said with a wide smile.

The following morning, Diane awoke to boots in her face. She looked up and noticed a student she had seen from afar, the leader of the movement.

"Do you know who I am?" the man asked, bending down. He was around twenty-four, and from what Diane had heard, he was an engineering student. He had a tight black beard and wore a green, button-down shirt and khaki pants.

"Do you know who I am?" Diane countered.

He made a hand gesture, and two other students lifted Diane by her arms and escorted her out of the room into the hallway. Diane looked back to David and Barry, who offered a warm but concerned smile.

"Stay strong," Barry mouthed.

Down the hall in a disheveled office, Diane was instructed to sit. A guard unbound her arms, and she instinctively twisted and stretched her wrists in circular motions. Her arms and legs were noticeably thinner.

"Yes, Ms. Babel, I do know who you are."

"You're in charge, right?" Diane questioned.

"I am Ebrahim Ashgarzadeh, one of the leaders of the militants who helped plan this seizure. To be clear, we have been fair to you and your people. You have no right to complain, because you took our whole country hostage in 1953. I want you to interview me. I want the American people to know why we did this. I want them to hear the truth from someone they know," he said, talking *at* her rather than *to* her.

"Some say you are from Palestine, with the PLO," Diane said.

"All you need to know is that we are supported by the Ayatollah. The problem you Americans have is that you see things through—how can I say—selfish glasses. We are embracing a greater philosophy that is lost on your privileged minds."

Ebrahim handed Diane a notepad and pen. She looked at the pad like it was some kind of foreign object. The last words she'd written were to Jack. Biased journalism, she quickly realized, would be her currency.

"Do you know why our government would bother to be so accommodating to you, the Great Satan?"

"Accommodating? What are you saying?" Diane said. She was weak, but adrenaline kept her focused. "I know nothing of recent news."

"The whole operation was planned in advance by the revolutionary guard as a favor to your President Carter in return for Carter having helped depose the Shah, and this was being done to ensure Carter's reelection. Carter helped us, and now we help him. Then, we discovered secret documents that proved that your General Huyser formed the military coup against our Imam Khomeini and our Islamic revolution," he said, pacing the room. He looked out on the large crowd of protestors that rallied each day in front of the Embassy. Whenever they caught a glimpse of him from the window, they cheered.

"Well, that's not news to me. Brzezinski and Huyser had it out for the Shah and your Imam for a while now," Diane said in a whisper. She knew this would curry favor.

"I'm talking about controlling us again! The U.S. wanted to overthrow our Islamic government through a military codetta and take our oil. They are working with the British government and its British Petroleum. Huyser had a shoot-to-kill order from your Brzezinski. It would have started a massacre of our people. Ayatollah was the only man who would stand up for us against the U.S. We are now a powerful force in the Middle East region and have strong ties with our PLO friends." His voice was loud and direct, and he spoke so anyone in earshot could hear.

"But you've shunned one of the only people trying to bring peace to this land, the Shah," Diane countered.

"So have you. You have let the Shah, the evil man, into your country."

"But he's ill and has cancer. He's only there for a medical treatment."

"Nonsense! He's a liar, and your precious America is his friend."

"When are you going to let us go?"

"Right now."

"Now?"

"We have already let women and people of color go because they have suffered enough in your country. I waited to speak to you so you can deliver my message, but you have also suffered enough."

"Why not everyone?" Diane said, pointing down the hall. "Haven't they all suffered?"

"Not enough. I trust that you will print my words, my message, as I dictated. Otherwise, your friends, your colleagues, may be here for a long time."

He made another gesture, and two guards took Diane down a hall she didn't recognize.

The following day, a bewildered Diane, flanked by two contracted Canadian diplomats, felt estranged and lost as she was led with a coat over head from a side entrance to the Embassy. "You're safe now," one man said to her. He could have been any man, but he was the one who shielded Diane from protestors who spat at her saying, "Death to America!" as she left the gates.

After a quick stop at a hotel for a shower, they headed to the airport to catch a chartered flight to Zurich, Switzerland, then to New York. There were six other men onboard, all about her age. She recognized two of the men from the Embassy. Diane learned they were diplomats who'd escaped in a joint effort between the Canadian government and the CIA. One of the men that saved Diane proudly called it the "Canadian caper," a ruse the intelligence agencies concocted about a science fiction movie called "Argo" that was to be filmed in Iran.

Diane mustered a smile but didn't speak to them. All the freed hostages possessed a hollow look of despair, mixed with joy. Diane began rereading the notes she had taken one day earlier. It seemed both distant and near. She began transcribing her interview notes into article form. She wondered how Bart was and if David and Barry would survive. "Will death come to the American hostages?" she wrote and underlined it several times as the plane took flight. She sat on the plane wide-eyed and clasped her knees together in an attempt not to tremble.

Chapter 26

The following day, Jody knocked on Jack's office door. "Good news, Quaid. Babel was freed last night. She is in the air with other freed diplomats, and all are headed home. Finally, some good news."

"Really? That's great news. Is that story really true, the *Argo* science fiction movie farce, the bait and switch?" Jack questioned.

"Sure is. We fooled the Iranians into believing they were movie executives looking for location shoots and the like. I couldn't believe it either," Jody said with a relieved smile.

"What about the other hostages? Any movement?" Jack asked.

Jody shook his head and walked off.

Jack picked up the phone and called Diane's number just to hear it ring. Next, he picked up a pen and paper.

> *Diane,*
>
> *What can words express? I just received news of your release, and I'm . . . well, overjoyed. When you are ready, please get in touch. I want to see you. Your letter touched me.*
>
> *All my best,*
> *Jack*

It wasn't until March that Diane reached out to Jack. In the time that passed, she was the subject of numerous interviews, including one with Barbara Walters. Initially, she turned the interview down, but Richard and ITN executives thought it would be good for ratings, so she finally agreed. The interview which was pre-taped in Washington and was scheduled to air on March 18, the same day the students released a tape of Barry Rosen. Diane couldn't stand to watch either alone and invited Jack over.

When the knock came at her door, Diane flinched—a reaction she had to any sudden noise. A psychiatrist had prescribed valium, but she had yet to take one pill. She opened the door to find Jack holding a bottle of red wine and tulips. The last time she'd seen those flowers, they were in Saddam's palace. Jack, with his hands filled, shrugged awkwardly. His hair fell past his ears and collar, though only slightly. Diane couldn't resist looking into his blue eyes.

She took the flowers from him and motioned for him to come inside. The apartment was like a time capsule; not much had changed since Jack was there years earlier. He couldn't believe she hadn't moved. There were more books and papers than he remembered, as well as photographs and awards from her travels and work.

"I'm at a loss for words, to be honest," Jack said. The bottle of wine weighed heavily in his hand. "I've accused you of many things, some of which you know and other things you don't. It all made sense to do so before the hostage crisis, but . . . well, I don't know. After that, with you over there, I just . . ."

Diane took the bottle of wine from his hands and placed in on the kitchen table. "Shh," she said, putting her index finger to her lips. Still thin, she moved closer to Jack and gently rested her head on his chest. Her eyes were closed, but tears welled. Jack couldn't see her eyes or the salty tears, but he did feel her warmth. His hands were outstretched in a confused fashion. He slowly brought his arms down and embraced Diane. They swayed in front of the kitchen sink for minutes, and no words were spoken. Finally, Diane pulled away, and tears streamed down her cheeks.

Jack put his hands on her face gently and with his thumbs wiped them away. "Diane, I—" Jack's words stumbled from his mouth.

Diane put her finger to her lips again. "Let's just sit, Jack," Diane said. She handed Jack the bottle opener. "Do you remember where the glasses are?"

Jack nodded.

Diane walked over and turned the television on to NBC.

Jack joined her, offering a glass of deep red wine, the color of love. "I thought you wanted to watch the Walters interview on ABC?" Jack said.

"I'd rather see Barry," Diane said. "There is nothing of real value from that interview, and off camera, all she talked about was the Shah. There is *something* to their relationship. She visited him in New York, at the hospital."

"Really?" Jack said. "So, Barry Rosen, huh? What a shame. I met him a few years back. He was at that New Year's party. Did you know that?" Jack said. He sat with room to spare on the couch.

"Barry was there?" Diane quickly said. "I didn't know that, but maybe he was. We shared a nice moment this past New Year's Eve. People looked up to him there," Diane said.

"I toasted you," Jack said.

"You did?" Diane said with a breaking smile.

"I did."

"Oh, here it comes now," Diane said pointing to the television. She gasped at the sight of Barry. He sat at a table, visibly worn. He was far skinner than Diane recalled, and his face was without spark or emotion. His plaid shirt hung off him as if it were three sizes too large. "Oh my God," Diane exclaimed, then grabbed Jack's hand.

The report featured a phone interview with Barry's mother. She called in from Brooklyn, where he was raised. As pictures of Rosen were shown, his mother spoke. "I didn't recognize my son. His arms are like sticks. He can barely pick them up. Something happened to his eyes, his face. He's so . . . worn out. He looks so tortured, so thin," she said, sobbing. "President Carter, this is my plea to you as a mother to a father. My husband is gone. I want my son back. Barry is fading away. Please help me."

Jack, now holding Diane's hand, looked at her. "We are doing everything we can." His voice took on a respectful almost business-like tone.

"Everything," Diane questioned. She took her hand from Jack's and put her wine glass down. "Is there any word on Bart?"

"He is only listed as one of the fifty-three hostages, I'm afraid. I'm sure he is doing as well as possible," Jack said.

"When I was over there, I wrote you, Jack. No one else. Do you know why?"

"I'm really not sure actually," Jack said.

"I was writing to the Jack I *knew,* not the Jack I know," Diane said.

"I'm the same Jack," he said.

"You have only convinced yourself of that. I'm sorry you came all this way, but I'm just not up to much more than this now and would like to be alone," Diane said coldly.

"Sure, of course. I just want you to know I'm here for you," Jack said.

They stood from the couch. There was an awkward silence that hung in the air, as if it was without gravity. They walked over to the door, and

Jack leaned in to hug Diane; this time he meant it, and it was Diane who stood limp. As Jack pulled away, he leaned in to kiss Diane.

She pulled away quickly. "Please just go."

*   *   *

In the weeks that followed, Jack tried to call Diane several times but was unable to reach her. Time was passing, and pressure continued to mount. It was April 23, 1980, and nearly seven months had transpired since the hostages had been taken. Jimmy Carter was behind the eight ball, a President without support of his country. He had increasing pressure to rescue the remaining hostages.

While President Carter initially called the hostages "victims of terrorism and anarchy," adding, the "United States will not yield to blackmail," too much time had passed without results. Carter's diplomacy and business dealings showed glimmers of promise. Negotiations led the United States to agree to release several billion of dollars in Iranian gold and bank assets, which had been frozen in American banks just after the Embassy was seized.

Iran was now in a war with Iraq and desperately needed those funds. Saddam's positioning as America's watchdog for the Middle East was paying dividends. Carter felt this reality would end up freeing the hostages, but as days turned into weeks and weeks into months, an agreement wasn't reached.

A contributing factor was that the Iranians wouldn't speak directly to Carter or any other American official; they would only speak with Algerians. By the time Carter's words were translated into Persian, the message was often lost.

"Seven months! I'm just sick every day over this," Carter said as he sat around the Oval Office with Brezensiki, Brown, Jody and Jack. His tie was loose, and his sleeves rolled to his elbows.

"Mr. President, if we don't save these men, we may not be able to win a reelection," said Brezensiki.

"Being President can last, at most, eight years. These men have the rest of their lives to live," Carter countered.

"Do we have a plan?" Jody said.

Carter looked at Secretary Brown. "Tomorrow afternoon, Operation Eagle Claw will send eight helicopters that will deliver a task force one mile outside of the Embassy. The soldiers will then blow a hole in the wall and attack the students."

"Sounds risky," Jody said.

"It's all we've got, Jody. These are the best soldiers we have. It's our only chance to save our people. Negotiations have stalled. They won't speak to us directly. What other choice do we have? What choice do I have?" Carter said. "If we can't save them, this will be the end of this administration. Depending on the outcome of this, history will look at us as heroes or fools."

The following evening, from the Oval Office, Carter addressed the nation. His tone was somber but hopeful. "Late yesterday, I canceled a carefully planned operation that was underway in Iran to position our rescue team for later withdrawal of American hostages, who have been held captive there since November 4. Equipment failure in the rescue helicopters made it necessary to end the mission. The helicopters are being refueled. As our team was withdrawing, after my order to do so, two of our American aircraft collided on the ground, following a refueling operation in a remote desert location in Iran." Carter paused only briefly, then went on, "There was no fighting. There was no combat. But to my deep regret, eight of the crewmen of the two aircraft that collided were killed, and several other Americans were hurt in the accident. As President, I know our entire nation feels the deep gratitude I have for the brave men who were prepared to rescue their fellow Americans from captivity. And as President, I also know that the nation shares not only my disappointment that the rescue effort could not be mounted, because of mechanical difficulties, but also my determination to persevere and to bring all of our hostages home to freedom.

"We have been disappointed before. We will not give up in our efforts. Throughout this extraordinarily difficult period, we have pursued and will continue to pursue every possible avenue to secure the release of the hostages. In these efforts, the support of the American people and of our friends throughout the world has been a most crucial element. That support of other nations is even more important now. We will seek to continue, along with other nations and with the officials of Iran, a prompt resolution of the crisis without any loss of life and through peaceful and diplomatic means."

The speech didn't impress Diane, who watched from her apartment. She had just returned from the Caribbean for what Richard called "much needed R&R," but not before a three-day debriefing by federal officials. It was the third such integration since returning from Tehran.

She wrote an op-ed, more like a journal entry, detailing her experiences for *The Washington Post*. It was well received, but her explanations of the students' position did little to sway or dampen the American hatred for their actions. Americans had taken to protesting in the streets, often castigating anyone from the Middle East as the enemy. "Go home, camel jockeys!" were among signs Diane had seen.

She had written Bart numerous times but couldn't be sure her letters were received, as she never got a letter in return. ITN had also inquired but only was told that he was healthy—the description they used for every hostage.

With pressure mounting on the students and the Iranian government, the hostages were separated and moved from the Embassy to various locations, such as prisons, to avoid intelligence gathering and another possible rescue mission endeavor. The *Argo* caper didn't help matters for the remaining hostages, and Carter's military attempt was considered a massive failure.

ITN continued to have money issues, and the hostage crisis did little to help matters as foreign investors became torn over the editorial mission of the news service. As a result, Diane was called in only for domestic stories, including the heated presidential race; by summer, Carter was in a dead heat with Ronald Reagan, who had beat out George Bush, the former Director of the CIA, in a tough-fought primary battle.

In late October, Richard called Diane. Their last meeting had been just after the death of the Shah; after years of poor and declining health, he'd ultimately passed away in July while a guest of Sadat. He was given a state funeral in Cairo, Egypt. The streets were filled with thousands of mourners. His casket rested on a wooden wagon, draped in the Iranian flag and drawn by horses.

At the conclusion of the miles-long procession, President Nixon stood at attention with Sadat, who was dressed in his military garb. The Shah was interred at the Al-Rifa'i Mosque in Cairo, which marked the resting place of Egyptian Khedive Isma'il Pasha, his mother Khushyar Hanim and numerous other members of the royal family of Egypt and Sudan. To many outside Iran, he was a hero.

Diane and Richard met at the same café, what had become a familiar eating spot for Diane, who was asked by Professor Stanley to give guest lectures at the university. The cloak-and-dagger aspect of their meetings had become dated or were no longer necessary, which Diane secretly questioned.

"Months ago, Jack Quaid came to my apartment. He was genuine in his concern but had no word on Bart. Do you? I haven't received a word back on this," Diane said. Her hair was noticeably longer, and her thirtieth birthday was only months away.

"ITN has done its best to secure his release, to make sure he is safe. We know he was moved to a prison. He and the others will be released, but not until Reagan is in office," Richard said, his face drawn.

"So Carter has no chance of winning again?"

"If the hostages are not released alive or before November, Carter can't win."

"So Reagan will be seen as a hero?"

"The country needs a hero, and who better than a movie star riding in on a horse? I want you to cover the debate this evening."

"The presidential debate?"

"We need to lie low until the heat blows off of you. My contacts have revealed that there are very high-up people who are worried about the intelligence you may have gathered in Iran," Richard said, signaling the waitress for coffee.

"I have been deposed three times by the Feds, wrote about it in the paper, and talked about in classes," Diane said, pointing across the street toward the college. "What else can I know?"

Richard waved his hand to silence her. "Some things are too powerful for anyone to know, and it is these things they think you know but have yet to tell. Your perspective is unique, Diane."

"Richard, I know some things that I haven't told anyone," she whispered and took a small bound diary from her bag. "It's all in here. This is what you really want to know; what they want to know—my private conversations with the Shah, Saddam, the student leaders. It's all there." She slid the book across the table, a book titled *The Leadership Crisis.* "It's the only copy," Diane said.

Richard looked down at it. "And you think I should read this?"

"I couldn't have written it without you," Diane said. "The administration can't be trusted. They're funding Saddam now with this war, and we know what they did to the Shah, but still, the hostages are not free."

Richard nodded his head. In a stealthy move, he placed the book on the booth seat to his left. "Diane, there'll be many more chances to rock the boat. For now, you must just ride the current. Meet me tonight after the debate. I may have more information for you."

As the waitress came over to the table with coffee, Diane leaned across the table and whispered, "Okay." She stood up, excused herself and walked away.

Richard waited five minutes before opening the book and reading. He flipped through the pages with astonishment. He stood up and walked over to a pay phone, then dialed and took a deep breath.

"Hello?"

"Our deal is off, Brzezinski," Richard said.

"It's not that easy, Richard. There are consequences to everything."

"It is over for me. I'm out. I know what you did—how you *really* got the Shah ousted—and soon the American people will know too." Richard hung up before Brzezinski could offer a response. He looked back to the table. His coffee cup was steaming, filled to the brim.

Chapter 27

The presidential debate, which took place on October 28, 1980, was one week before Election Day. Four eventful and tumultuous years had made a big difference, as the Carter camp was fearful of a loss. While Carter was bashed by both sides of the aisle for his handling of the hostage crisis, that was but one hot-button issue among many that could result in his undoing. Earlier in the year, dark clouds followed him for his handling of the Three Mile Island nuclear disaster, when more than 65,000 people marched in opposition to his support for nuclear energy, while others bemoaned the President due to climbing gas prices and the jobless rate.

On July 15, two days before the Shah passed away, he addressed the nation with candor, painting the state of affairs as they were: dire. A sobering delivery of words left his lips in the Oval Office and traveled through millions of homes coast to coast. "As I was preparing to speak, I began to ask myself the same question that I now know has been troubling many of you. Why have we not been able to get together as a nation to resolve our serious energy problem?" Carter said.

Carter embraced his born-again Southern roots and delivered the speech more like a sermon. While he praised the nation's "hard work, strong families, close-knit communities, and faith in God," he chastised Americans who were "self indulgent" when it came to energy consumption.

The speech, dubbed "The Malaise Speech," was written by Chris Matthews and officially titled "Crisis of Confidence." Originally an officer who served with the United States Capitol Police, Matthews was previously on the staff of Democratic Senators Frank Moss and Edmund Muskie. No stranger to the political machine, Mathews mounted an unsuccessful campaign in 1974 for Pennsylvania's fourth congressional district seat in the U.S. House of Representatives.

Positive and exuberant, Mathews wore his emotions on his sleeve like a magician giving away his tricks. It was his ability to tap into the American psyche that impressed both Carter and Jody Powell, who ultimately green-lit his position. Jack thought Mathews was "spontaneous and bright," or at least those were the adjectives he'd offered Jody upon review. Secretly, Jack wanted more of a hand in speech writing. He wanted to hone the message but knew Mathews bested him in that pursuit.

Days after the speech, Carter shook things up and surprised the media and Washington insiders when he asked for the resignations of his entire cabinet. He eventually accepted five, including Energy Secretary James Schlesinger and Joseph Califano, the Secretary of Health, Education and Welfare. It was seen as a "strong" move on Carter's part. In the weeks that followed, his poll numbers rose.

Still, aside from a failed economy and the poor handling of the hostage crisis, Carter made what most considered a controversial decision when he opted out of the 1980 Summer Olympics held in Moscow. This was in response to the Soviet invasion of Afghanistan and marked the only time America had ever boycotted the Olympic Games. He not only had rivals from the Republican Party and its candidate, Ronald Reagan, but from his own party with Ted Kennedy, who sought the highest office by critiquing Carter's handling of the hostage crisis, the economy and his questionable healthcare plan. Carter refused to debate Kennedy in the Democratic primaries. What hurt Carter most, noted Diane, was that liberal college students did not support him because he reinstated the draft.

Diane recounted these events that had taken place over the last six months and was surprised that only a week before the election, the Associated Press said the race was "too close to call." With her laminated red and yellow ITN press badge around her neck, Diane reported at the debate sans a crew. She always had an eye out for Jack but wasn't ready to see him. She wondered what Richard would think of what she wrote in her journal.

She watched from the wings of the stage as Jimmy Carter and Republican presidential candidate Ronald Reagan exchanged terse words, jabs and innuendo. The unbiased journalist that lived within her saw Reagan as more confident and in control.

Reagan said, "Are you better off now than you were four years ago? Is it easier for you to go and buy things in the stores than it was four years ago? Is there more or less unemployment in the country than there was four years ago? Is America as respected throughout the world as it was? Do you feel our security is as safe, that we're as strong as we were four years ago? And if you answer all of those questions 'yes,' why then, I think your choice is very obvious as to whom you will vote for. If you don't agree, if you don't think this course we've been on for the last four years is what you would like to see us follow for the next four, then I could suggest another choice."

Diane was busy scribbling notes when she felt a tap on her shoulder.

"A word with you, Ms. Babel." It was Brzezinski. He was dressed in a perfectly pressed suit and tie and spoke calmly form the wings of the auditorium.

Diane, bothered by the intrusion, brushed him off. "I'm working."

"As am I."

Diane walked farther backstage and whispered. "What do you want?"

Secret Service walked toward them, but Brzezinski waved them off. "I—we—want to know what you know. There is a war on in Iran, and it directly impacts our country . . . and those hostages."

"You already know. You made the orders."

"What orders?"

Diane leaned in and whispered, "You supported Khomeini and his efforts to violently overthrow the government of Iran, and now we have total chaos in the Middle East."

"That's a lie—just anti-American bullshit." His voice grew cold.

"You and Carter gave rise to one of the worst rights' violators in history, the Ayatollah Khomeini, even though you knew he hated the Shah—and not because he was an oppressive dictator. They hated him because he was a secular, pro-Western leader who, in addition to other initiatives, was expanding the rights and roles of women in Iranian society." Diane walked farther backstage and continued, her voice low, but loud enough to be heard over the applauding crowd. "Then, when Carter took office, the Shah was a staunch American ally, a bulwark in our standoff with the Soviet Union, thwarting the dream held since the time of the czars of pushing south toward the warm waters of the appropriately named Persian Gulf," Diane said. She felt her face redden. "We then forced him into exile, like a man with no country, and we supported the same group of Islamic extremists who introduced the idea of suicide bombers to the Palestine Liberation Organization and paid $35,000 to PLO families who would offer up their children as human bombs to kill as many Israelis as possible." The words erupted from Diane.

"Ms. Babel your interpretation of events—and it is merely your interpretation—" When he paused to scoff, she cut him off.

"He is the same guy whom you guys thought was a religious man and man of God, who would live in the holy city of Qom like an Iranian pope and act only as an advisor to the secular, popular revolutionary government. Khomeini's regime has executed more people in its first year in power than the Shah's Savak had allegedly killed in the previous twenty-five years," Diane said. "I don't trust you, and I'm going to make sure the public doesn't either."

"You don't know what you're talking about," he said. He removed a handkerchief from his pocket and dabbed his forehead.

"The Shah, President Sadat and Prime Minister Begin were trying to fight these Islamic extremists to protect U.S. and Israeli interests and preserve peace in the Middle East. There are warning signs about President Sadat, as head of Israeli government assassinations already knew. And now look what's happening. Khomeini's followers are preparing for jihad and a holy war against us, and pretty soon a nuclear war with Israel and the West. I'm writing a book, and it's all in there," Diane said defiantly. "Harper Collins is publishing it."

"You will do no such thing."

"You can't stop me. I'm one step ahead of you."

"Not when your information source dries up."

"It won't."

"It already has. I know people who have not been too happy about General George Grady feeding you all the news for these many years."

"General George Grady?"

"Of course you know him as Richard Harden. He listed as both with the CIA."

"What? You wouldn't—"

"Of course I wouldn't do anything. I'm a member of the Carter administration. However, there are others who might have a different agenda," Brzezinski said. He lit a cigarette and walked toward the stage, where Carter's back was in sight.

Diane felt a lump drop from her throat to her stomach. She ran through the backstage area, passing Secret Service and security guards who tried to grab her. She burst through a group of doors and ran for her car.

She sped through the streets, looking at the time. The café was closed that time of night. She was to meet Richard in the park adjacent to the cemetery, where his wife and daughter were buried. It was nearing the anniversary of their death, and he wanted to bring flowers, she recalled him saying earlier.

Minutes later, she screeched to a halt, parked the car and ran toward Richard. He sat on a bench, flowers in hand. She could see smoke rising from his cigar. She was roughly a hundred yards away when she saw him wave the flowers. He stood up, and a single shot rang out in the night. Richard collapsed to the ground, and the flowers fell to his side. A second shot fired, and his body convulsed.

"Richard!" Diane screamed, but the park was empty. She looked in the darkness as she ran franticly. She moved in a zigzag fashion. As she got closer, his body seemed motionless. She crawled over and noticed the blood dripping from his mouth. His breathing was irregular.

"Diane, get out of here! They'll shoot you too!" He could barely speak.

She took her blue scarf off and wiped the blood from his face, then placed it under his head like a pillow. Diane looked around, but it was too dark to see. She heard rustling in the trees and bushes. "Your real name is . . . you're General George Grady?" She smoothed his hair back from his forehead.

"I-I'm sorry," he said, motioning to the inside of his coat. Diane's journal was in the pocket with Richard's blood on it. "Take it. Go, Diane. Just go."

"But I can't just leave—"

A third shot was heard; it seemed to be a warning.

Richard screamed out in pain. "GO!"

Diane scrambled down the nearest hill, in the opposite direction of her car, passing through the graveyard. She tumbled and fell several times.

Out of breath, she hailed a taxi. Her clothes were soiled, and she had some of Richard's blood on her hands. She tried to wipe them off on her blouse, but the blood had already dried and flaked. She told the driver to pull over at the first phone booth.

"There's been a shooting," Diane said into the receiver.

When she returned home, she closed the curtains, locked all the windows and door and ran the shower. She took of all her clothes, put them in a plastic garbage bag and tied it tight. She stood naked in her apartment, wishing she could rest her head on Jack's chest. She slowly walked into the shower, slid to the floor and cried.

The following morning, Diane retrieved *The Washington Post* from the hallway. She looked up and down the hallway suspiciously. Below the fold, the headline read: "Former General Found Dead in Park." The article suggested that he'd suffered a hidden drug addiction after the death of his wife and daughter, and his shooting was likely drug related, though an investigation would continue.

She ordered in enough Chinese food to last a few days. Diane spent the next three days in her apartment, peering through the blinds. She feared leaving. She looked at her journal, bloodstains and all. She read her reflections with the Shah. He spoke of the relationship between George Bush, Brzezinski, Donald Rumsfeld and their support of Saddam. "He will want the power," the Shah said of Saddam, "and there is no reason to fight me so I will be ousted or worse."

Diane thought to call Jack but knew that, as a member of the administration, he would be of no help. She didn't want to believe Brzezinski capable of where her darkest thoughts led her. She became increasingly paranoid. She hid her journal and all the writing for her book under the kitchen sink in an old plastic bag filled with outdated magazines.

*   *   *

The funeral service was scheduled for November 6, the day after the election and the anointing of a new President-elect. Diane couldn't believe that an entire year had passed since she was taken hostage and that the others, including Bart, were still being held captive. Reports surfaced that students had all the prisoners stripped down to their underwear at gunpoint, only to be told it was a joke. Others were tortured, solitarily confined, while one prisoner tried to commit suicide.

Diane finally called Jack and asked him if he would attend the funeral; he agreed. While still paranoid, he was the only person she trusted. She had stopped at the bank and placed all her notes and writings in her safety deposit box. It was a rainy Wednesday afternoon. A small group gathered around General George Grady's grave. Professor Stanley was the only person they recognized. He looked considerably older and walked at a slower pace, almost oblivious to his surroundings. As he passed, Diane stepped closer to him.

"Professor Stanley," Diane said.

"Oh, Diane, so nice of you to come. What a tragic, sudden loss." He looked up as rain fell.

"Is that you, Jack?"

Jack took a few steps closer. "Yes, Professor."

"Forgive my eyes," he said. "There is a lesson in death, but it is for each of us to figure out," Professor Stanley said. He raised his cane and walked closer toward the grave.

A Catholic priest read from the Bible, while a trio of soldiers stood at attention.

> *Better is childlessness with virtue;*
> *for immortal is the memory of virtue,*
> *acknowledged both by God and human beings.*
> *When it is present people imitate it,*
> *and they long for it when it is gone;*
> *Forever it marches crowned in triumph,*
> *victorious in unsullied deeds of valor.*
> *But the numerous progeny of the wicked shall be of no avail;*
> *their spurious offshoots shall not strike deep root*
> *nor take firm hold.*

Diane stood off in the background. The words the priest read were dampened by the rain, and tears slowly streamed down her cheeks. She wiped each tear as quickly as it came. Jack was beside her with an umbrella, dressed in a black suit and tie.

"He was an excellent man," Diane said, appropriately dressed in a black dress and shawl.

"I know you two were close," Jack whispered.

"Too close apparently."

"What do you mean?"

"Nothing you can ever know."

"I want to know everything. I want to be on your side," Jack whispered and put his arm around Diane.

As the priest blessed the casket, the soldiers assumed position and fired shots into the sky.

"I'm retiring," Diane said as she slowly backpedaled. The site of a grave was a harsh reminder that her parents had never received a proper burial.

"From reporting?" Jack said.

"I'm writing a book to set the record straight on all of this," Diane said. She signaled that they should walk away from the ceremony as the casket was being lowered. "I can't watch them throw dirt on Richard."

"What will you do now with Carter's loss?" Diane said, tying to change the subject, fighting away tears. She moved her hand from underneath the umbrella. "It stopped raining."

Jack looked to the sky and closed the umbrella. "I honestly don't know."

Chapter 28

President-elect Ronald Reagan beat Carter by 10 percentage points, a huge margin, with some pollsters having Reagan behind Carter by as much as 5 points before Election Day. While Carter's team continually tried to negotiate the release of the hostages, it was clear that it wouldn't happen on his watch.

Jack tendered his resignation before Christmas. He wanted to start 1981 fresh, anew. Jody understood, and Carter personally thanked him, calling Jack "an honorary member of the Georgia mafia." Carter's smile, his trademark, became thin and forced in his last days in office. He was a man beaten by circumstance and fate, Jack thought. Like many U.S. Presidents before him, Carter believed in his plight to a fault.

As Jack packed up his office, he was flooded with cards and well-wishes. The Carter administration was an extended family; the election fractured it like a pending divorce.

Jody walked into Jack's now empty office with a cupcake and single candle. "Make a wish, kid," Jody said.

Almost thirty, Jack wished he wouldn't be seen as the *kid* any longer. "Thanks, Jody," Jack said, placing the cupcake on his empty desk. A box of belongings sat in the middle of the floor.

"Are you going to miss it here?" Jody asked. "You were pretty wet behind the ears four years ago, and now you have it all in front of you."

"I'll miss the days when I felt really important, when I felt like I was a part of something bigger than me." Jack paused. "When I thought we were making a real difference in the world."

"Listen, every administration could have been better. The point is, when it comes to most of the issues, I think we did the best with what was given to us."

Jack whispered, "Maybe we could have gotten more things right."

"Those thoughts and regrets will keep you up at night. If you want to sleep well, think of the future, my friend—not the past."

"But the Shah, Iran—we could have done that differently."

Jody leaned closer. "Are you still that fucking naïve, Jack? You think everyone was just going to give him back the contracts and all that oil? C'mon! He can't just make a speech in '73 demanding this and think there's a snowball's chance in hell it would happen, let alone in six years," Jody said.

Jack shook his head at Jody. "And you sleep well at night?"

*   *   *

Despite his best attempts to see her, Jack couldn't persuade Diane to spend any time with him. Before Christmas, she left for the Caribbean to work on her book. "I'm no good to anyone until I get this all out," Jack recalled her saying the last time they spoke.

Jack spent Christmas and New Years at Walter Reid with his brother, James, whose condition had gone from bad to worse. He had early onset Alzheimer's and couldn't remember Jack's name, but on some days, he recalled he was once a soldier. Jack promised him that if he ever had a son, he would name him after his brother.

Without a job or much else to do, Jack took to reading the newspapers and watching the final days of the Carter administration from the sidelines. They all had worked so hard to pull an October surprise and have the hostages released before the election, and now they hoped to have them released before his term ended on January 20, 1981. In a last valiant effort, Carter approved *ABC News* to cover every minute of his last night as President in the Oval Office. He negotiated to the last minute, ultimately accepting failure.

Jacked watched the inauguration of President Ronald Reagan from his apartment. It was a news field day, as once he was officially sworn in; the deal was made for the release of the hostages. Reagan was seen as the hero, riding in on the great white horse and saving the day. *Maybe this is exactly what the country needs,* Jack thought.

*   *   *

Diane watched the news from her hotel room in the Caribbean. She shook her head, scribbling notes on a yellow legal pad. She watched as news reports came in from Iran. The hostages had boarded a plane. They were finally free, like Diane, but also like her, she knew they would never be the same—forever altered by failed policies over which they had no control.

The following day, Diane watched as a young female reporter, whom she didn't know, covered the story. She saw more and more female reporters, some of color, which made her smile. This woman was a few years younger than Diane and was of Mexican descent.

"At the moment newly elected President Ronald Reagan completed his twenty-minute inaugural address. The 52 American hostages were released by Iran into U.S. custody, having spent 444 days in captivity. The hostages were flown to Algeria as a symbolic gesture for the help of that government in resolving the crisis . . ."

Diane's eyes widened as the news footage showed images of David, Barry and Bart ascending the steps to the plane. They waved and smiled.

The reporter continued, "The flight continued to Rhein-Main Air Base in West Germany and then on to Wiesbaden USAF Hospital, where former President Carter, acting as emissary, received them, a nod of partisanship from President Reagan. After medical checkups and debriefings, the hostages were directed to a second flight to Stewart Air National Guard Base in Newburgh, New York, with a refueling stop in Shannon, Ireland, where they were greeted by a large crowd. From Newburgh, they will travel by bus to the United States Military Academy at West Point where they will stay for three days at the Thayer Hotel."

Diane learned there was going to be tickertape parade on January 30 in Manhattan's Canyon of Heroes. Since Richard's death, she was no longer affiliated with nor contacted by ITN which had grown as a news organization. She remained the only former employee to be nominated for an Emmy award.

When Diane arrived home days later, she had received a formal invitation to participate in the parade due to her "bravery and sacrifice on behalf of her country." Jack had left three phones messages too. She thought to call him back but decided to take an Amtrak to Manhattan later that evening. Her parents' apartment was sublet to a Columbia professor and his family. This provided Diane with income, as the apartment was paid off. She took a room at the Chelsea Hotel. She had longed to stay there, as one of her favorite songs by Leonard Cohen was of the same title:

I remember you well in the Chelsea Hotel
You were famous. Your heart was a legend.
You told me again you preferred handsome men,
but for me you would make an exception.

The only person Diane wanted to see was Bart. On the day of the parade, the skies were overcast. The weather was seasonable and cold. She headed downtown toward the Financial District. Thousands of people filled the streets, cheering. Random people would burst into the national anthem. On occasion, Diane was recognized by passersby. Red, white and blue flags and streamers were strewn about. The procession started uptown and wound its way down Broadway. Streamers floated from buildings, where workers stopped, watched and cheered the freed hostages. Some held signs that read, "Deport all Iranians Now!"

Diane looked down to see the smiling face of a Middle Eastern boy who held the hand of his father. He waved a small American flag. "USA!" his little voice chirped but was swallowed by the roar of the crowd.

Convertibles carrying the hostages drove at a snail's pace. The bewildered men looked gaunt and perplexed but happy. They waved, as if only to stay in the moment and forget about what they had endured.

Diane looked at every car until she saw Barry and David, who rode together. She yelled their names: "Barry, David!" but her voice was swallowed up like that of the little boy.

Moments later, she spotted Bart. He was gaunt; a full red beard highlighted his pale, freckled face. His smile hadn't changed. "Bart! Bart!" Diane yelled. She waved her arms. "Bart!"

He looked over, almost bewildered, and they made eye contact.

Diane pushed her way through the crowd to the barrier, but police officers held her back.

Bart jumped from the car and ran over to her. "She's okay. She was a hostage too. Let her in!" Bart pleaded.

The officers smiled and parted the gate. The crowd cheered, and Diane was led by Bart's hand to the car.

An onlooker yelled, "Hey! That's Diane Babel."

Bart and Diane hopped into the back of the red convertible Mustang. They sat propped up in the back of the car and took to waving. Diane didn't notice it, but Jack was in the crowd, taking pictures of her. The tickertape looked like a blizzard. The sounds of cheers were deafening.

Diane leaned into Bart, who was half-hugging her, smiling ear to ear. "It's been 444 days. How did you do it?" Diane said into his ear.

"I lost count," he said, still smiling and waving. "They beat us, you know—tortured us," Bart said. He had a look her father used to refer to as a "fifty-yard stare."

"Oh, Bart! Did you get my letters?" Diane said.

"Just one, but I read it every day, and those from my family too."

"I sent many," Diane said into his ear.

"What?" Bart said, trying to hear over the cheering crowd.

"I sent many letters!" Diane screamed.

Diane had prepared another letter that included her contact information and where she could be reached in the hopes that she would see Bart. "Here," Diane said. She tucked the envelope into Bart's jacket pocket. "Call me when you are ready. I'm so happy you are home!" She hugged him tight.

Bart looked Diane in the eyes for a moment and mouthed, "Thank you."

Diane jumped out of the car. People cheered as she made her way back to the crowd. On the other side of the barricade, she was again part of the collective. She walked east toward the Staten Island ferry. She recited the opening paragraph of her book, which she'd committed to memory: "We didn't go to the moon. We didn't win a war. We were simply casualties of diplomacy—old, wrecked cars on the side of the road to freedom. I certainty wasn't a hero."

As she broke from the parade route and crowd, Diane walked faster. Chilly winds blew. She didn't notice that Jack was following her three blocks behind, trying to catch up.

"Diane! Wait!" Jack yelled, but his voice was engulfed by the parade.

Moments later, Diane was at the ferry gate. She entered the turnstile and made her way through a crowd of smiling tourists snapping pictures, some waving American flags. Despite the cold winds, she positioned herself against the rail, lower Manhattan serving as her backdrop. She took a deep breath, a sigh of relief to have connected with Bart.

As the ferry jolted and launched from the dock, Diane felt a tap on her shoulder.

"Not a parade fan?" Jack said with a smile. He wore dark jeans, a pea coat and a gray wool scarf. His face was scruffy, and his blue eyes were as comforting as ever to Diane. He was at ease; the pomp of his White House circumstance was gone though Diane surmised that like her experiences, his, too, were buried deep within.

"Jack? What the hell?" Diane said. The winds from the Atlantic blew in, messing Diane's hair, and she fought to keep it off her face. "Well, not parades I'm a part of. Listen, I'm sorry I—"

"There is no need to explain. I just missed you," Jack said. He leaned closer. "But wasn't that what you always wanted, a parade in your honor, people cheering your name, making a difference?"

Diane's body language softened. "Maybe it was about that at first, but it became so much more."

"I know . . . for all of us," Jack said. The wind was loud and constant. An American flag whipped from the ship's mast.

"What?" Diane said. She smiled into the wind. Her brown leather coat, cinched at her waist, kept her warm.

"Don't worry about it," Jack said, raising his voice.

"So, what are you up to now, today? Why are you here?" Diane said close to his ear.

Jack leaned in. With their bodies close together, the wind was slightly thwarted. "I came looking for you."

The winter sun was setting on the city skyline; thousands of glass windows reflected a seemingly warm glow. Diane smiled and invited Jack closer. She interlocked her fingers with his. He was soft to the touch, a needed life force. Diane looked into his blue eyes, those blue eyes. He appeared to be morphing back into the Jack she *knew*.

Jack put his arm around Diane and pulled her close. She silently pointed toward the World Trade Center.

"Those two massive towers stand at attention like soldiers guarding the city," Jack said.

"Yes, but somehow, I still don't feel safe," Diane said, squeezing his hand tighter and turning into the unrelenting wind.

The Leadership Crisis Volume II coming soon.
To learn more about the trilogy, please visit

www.theleadershipcrisis-book.com

About the Authors

A. Patrick is a successful businessman and a student of Middle Eastern history. While a teenager in the late 1970s, he, along with his family, was forced to flee Iran after the Shah was ousted from power. Proud of his Persian heritage, Patrick celebrates his ancestry while engaging in the promise of the American dream.

W.B. King is an award-winning journalist, collaborator and author who teaches writing courses at New York University.

CPSIA information can be obtained
at www.ICGtesting.com
Printed in the USA
LVOW10*0355161216

517543LV00001B/1/P

9 781475 973334